T2-FHQ-288

HYÆNAS

Sandy Dengler

Wichita, Kansas

PUBLISHED BY ST KITTS PRESS
A division of S-K Publications
PO Box 8173
Wichita, KS 67208
1-888-705-4887 (toll-free)
685-3201 (local)
316-685-6650 (fax)
stkitts@skpub.com
www.skpub.com/stkitts/

British spelling has been maintained throughout this work.

Edited by Elizabeth Whiteker
Cover design by Diana Tillison; rendering of hyænas by
Christi Robert

ISBN 0-9661879-1-1
Library of Congress Catalog Card Number: 98-85605

Printed in the United States of America

First Edition 1998

Table of Contents

	Preface	ix
1.	He Lost His Head	13
2.	She Lost Her Mate	25
3.	They're Inviting Their Ruin	41
4.	His Spirits Failed the Job	47
5.	She Was Pummelled by Fate	59
6.	He Was Such a Fool	75
7.	She Says She Didn't Do It	79
8.	He Trades People	91
9.	He Up and Disappeared	101
10.	He Took Death Well	109
11.	No One Listens to Him	115
12.	He Should Have Known Better	127
13.	He Doesn't Know What's Happening	139
14.	He Prefers to Throw His Spear	149
15.	He Makes Foolish Decisions	159
16.	She Is Definitely a Hyæna	169
17.	Hyænas Are Out There	177
18.	The Hideous Child Should Be a Beaver	187
19.	The Snake Ate the Moon	197
20.	So Gar and That Woman Are Together Again	205
21.	The World Is on Fire	213
22.	Terror Changed Her Mind	223
23.	The Spirits Are on *Her* Side	227
24.	He Relishes Being a Protector	231
25.	These Pictures Are Obscene	237
26.	You Have No Private Life	247
27.	You Can't Trust Hairies Worth Spit	259
28.	They Really Don't Want Him	267

29. The Shaman Hates Everybody 275
30. Bad Odds Aren't Good 283
31. They Finally Worked in Concert 293
32. She Doesn't Deserve to Live 303
33. She Wants to Live After All 311
34. Now He Has to Cooperate with Eel 319
35. They Are All One Together 327
36. His Spirit Calls to *Her* 337
37. Here Is Kelp's Killer 341

Preface

The protagonist of *Hyænas*, Gar the shaman, holds in his memory the collective lore of 50,000 years, from a time when Real People flourished unchallenged and ice had not covered their ancestral lands. Now they are a remnant, struggling to survive in a shrunken world that increasingly favours Hairies.

Today, we call the Real People Neanderthals. And the Water People, the Hairies? Those were the other folk, the historically recent interlopers with a penchant for travel, strangers with beards and long hair, who didn't mind getting wet. Western Europeans claim them in their ancestry and refer to them as the Cro-Magnons.

I used the latest research, parallels in similar cultures today, and the best of archeological discoveries to fashion a picture of what Neanderthals might have been like. And that goofy old stereotype of the caveman clubbing his lady on the head and dragging her by the hair to his cave just isn't it.

I've also adopted the speculation of the presence of a bicameral mind in primitive human beings, with Head and Heart essentially working independently.

This is an adventure into our most distant yesterdays. The world of Pleistocene France may have been much different 37,000 years ago during the Würm glaciation, with its oddly different animals and uncertain climate, but Love and Death have been with us always.

Sandy Dengler

1

He Lost His Head

Gar generally did not count himself among those men who paid undue attention to women, but this one was pretty hard to ignore. For one thing, she was quite comely, with golden orange-brown skin and the squared-off form—broad hips, broad shoulders—of a classic beauty. For another, she hovered over the lax body of a decapitated man, a bloodied skinning blade in one hand and a flint bone-chopping adze in the other.

As Gar stepped out into the clearing by this creek, she snapped erect and stared at him a moment, her anthracite eyes crackling. Before he could speak or even assay her mood, she wheeled and bounded down the boulders of the streamside hard beside her. With an admirable leap she sprang out across the open water and managed to alight firmly enough on a rock at the other side that another strong stride carried her safely clear of the stream and up the far bank.

He expected her to race across the open meadow

beyond and lose herself in the larch grove on its far side. Instead, she turned downstream abruptly and crashed into the willow thicket on the bank. Pity. Picture a woman that pretty, her pendant breasts gracefully accentuating her movement as she fled out across the meadow, through the grass all a-spangle with summer flowers. It would have been a lovely view to call back later, when winter winds howled.

He listened, expecting to follow by ear as she crunched her way through the willows. Silence. Either she was cowering in the thicket right close by, or she was a far better woodsman than he, able to make way through dense cover without a sound.

Heart cried, *Follow her! There is adventure here!*

Head counselled, *Investigate! Were you a headless victim, you wouldn't want to be ignored, would you?*

This time at least, he heeded Head. No need to rush, though. He had plenty of sunlight left in the day, for only half of it was spent. With nose, eyes, and ears he savoured summer's magic on his land. The low bushes that studded this swale and the broadleaf trees on the rolling hills beyond had leafed out fully now. They splashed their shades of light green, each unique to itself, against the heavy darkness of the firs clumped here and there. And the flowers! There would be nothing but flowers and more flowers from now until frost. Would that summer with her extravagance might never end.

Gar squatted beside the trail here, where the wooded copse behind him opened out into this streamside clearing. Neither malevolent spirits nor benign spoke to his heart.

The sun slipped behind a fir top and, betimes, emerged from the other side. Apparently no lions or bears had smelt the free-flowing blood and were coming to claim a meal. Good. Gar didn't like disputing with carnivores bigger than he. Now and then his protective magic worked well; occasionally it didn't. Why tempt fate?

The body sprawled on its back, shoulders downhill on the sloping shore, the severed neck only inches from the water. It almost appeared as if it had been stretched thus to bleed out properly. Very little blood trickled now, and that nearly black. Gar could see the blood's route as the body had drained; it coated the short grass and moss between the luckless fellow and the stream, and disappeared among the rocks. *Fortunate,* Head mused, *that the women draw our drinking water from upstream.* The victim's head had rolled a couple feet and lodged down in the boulders at water's edge. Gar couldn't see its face.

The fellow's dark pubic hair curled in an unusual wave. The palms of his hands, a paler brown by far than most of his skin, looked soft and smooth. And what was this? Gar frowned.

He stood erect, listening, watching for one more moment, and stepped over to the body. He lifted the fellow's stiffening hand for a closer look. Where fingernails met skin ran thin lines of colour. Blue. Yellow. When Gar butchered meat, blood dried in the same places on his hands. This obviously wasn't blood.

The willow thicket rustled. So she indeed lurked near. Was she at all curious? Gar might do better luring than chasing just now.

Casually, he stretched out his arm and, grasping the head by its topknot, pulled it to himself. Its weight surprised him. He cupped it in both hands to study the face. The jaw fell open, so he propped it shut with a thumb. Not of his moiety, not of his clan, not even of his tribe. A stranger, an interloper. But then, so was the woman. He didn't recognise her either.

From his shaman's pouch, he took a pinch of dried blood and marked the fellow's brow. He began the cant for the dying and dead, keening it softly so as to avoid attracting any of these strangers' relatives who might be passing near.

This was the first time he'd ever sung the cant to a bodiless head before. Usually, most parts were still attached, save the rare occasion when the victim fell to hyænas. He laid a hand on the shoulder as well, to make certain the complete fellow was accounted for. He wouldn't want the head being ushered into the Beyond without the rest going along.

His own Head praised him. *Exactly what you would want done, were you the unfortunate.*

Don't forget about the woman, Heart reminded him. *Fine figure of a woman.*

From the thicket, rustling told him she was moving. He followed by ear, hastening the cant a bit toward the end. He laid the head down at almost its normal position on the neck, shimming it with stones to make it stay put. Then he stood up and looked around to ascertain the woman's location.

She perched on the far creek bank, watching him intently. She was a mother. For beside her, gripping her hand, huddled the ugliest, scrawniest, most pitiful-looking little boy that Gar had ever seen. Only a mother could have anything to do with that one.

The child must have been gravely ill recently, for his colour top to bottom was waxen. Yellowish. His hair, longer by far than any normal person's and not dressed in any way, tangled in back, as wispies blew around his cheeks. Strange cheeks they were, puffing out to either side of the ridiculously short nose. The forehead bulged high as well, throwing his whole face off balance.

She pronounced her words so oddly that Gar had trouble understanding her. "Death song." She waved her free hand toward her child. "I am small, like Hare here, the last time I hear the death song."

This is a trap! roared Head. *She's bait in a trap, good fellow! And you without a spear.*

Heart cooed, *You don't smell anyone else around, do you? Except No-Head there, of course. Look at her! Broad and solid as a bison, yet as light on her feet as a rabbit. Aren't you glad it's summer and that magnificent body isn't all wrapped up in furs?*

He gestured, *friend.* "Gar."

"Mouse." She nodded toward her spindly child. "Hare." No *friend* gesture.

He pointed to No-head. *That one.*

"Kelp."

Kelp. So. Named for marine plants, No-head would therefore be part of a seaside clan. The most powerful People lived farthest south, along the broad sand seashores and saltmarshes. The warmest, sunniest land with plenty of fine caves. Gar's clan was nowhere near powerful enough to be living in prime territory by the sea.

Then she confirmed it. "Tribe of Seashore. Elk Clan." Since Mouse knew Kelp's name and ancestry, she was probably a person with powerful connections as well.

So far, she wasn't running off. *Quit mooning and get the introductions out of the way so you can talk about other things,* chided Heart, *or she'll wander away out of sheer boredom.*

Gar ambled down to the water. "Mammoth clan, Dusk moiety." Dusk, his mother's half of the clan. When declaring bloodline, why did Real People always mention the half of the clan in which they lived, Dusk or Dawn? Everyone inside the clan already knew that, and no one outside the clan gave a hoot.

She didn't approach, but she didn't retreat, either. "Horse clan, Dusk moiety." She nodded toward that misbegotten child. "Mine, Horse. Baboon on father's."

"Baboon." Gar frowned.

She dropped to a squat, scratched her side as if her ribs itched, and made a hooting sound. Gar recognised that behaviour, and from the motions he remembered the word. His uncle had once made those same gestures, giving the animal the name *baboon.* Gar bobbed his head. "Baboons live far beyond the sea to the south. Eh?"

She stood erect and nodded. "Hare's father lives far away, too. Good."

Heart chortled, *She likes you, you lucky fellow! She just told you that no jealous mate is going to come roaring down on you.*

Gar eyed the distance across the stream, gauging the likelihood that he could leap it from a standing start without embarrassing himself by falling in. Not bloody likely. "Tribe of Scarp Country."

"Tribe of Cold Lakes."

No direct relation! This is getting better and better, good fellow! Now lure her to this side of the creek before you decide to jump it and make an ass of yourself.

"Welcome. Come, stay with us tonight, you and Hare. Tell us your story then."

She studied him a few moments as her spindly child pressed against her. Obviously, if it were the boy's choice, they'd be running away across the meadow now. Gar hoped she wasn't one of these foolish mothers who let the child make the choices.

"You ever see baboons?" Her speech bounced and bumped.

Gar wagged his head *no.* "My uncle travelled to the sea once, with Rat. Didn't see baboons; they're across the sea, he said; but he told us about them. Went south to see elephants. Didn't see them either."

She was thinking about something, he could tell, but there was no guessing what from the impassivity of her face. Suddenly she blurted an order in a strange language, stepped backward a few steps and took a running leap at the stream. Gar was there for her as she came flying to this side, his arm out and his legs braced. She grabbed his hand and allowed him to pull her up to good balance again. He let his grip linger; she broke it by withdrawing her hand, and he accepted that.

That ludicrous child simply plopped into the stream and swooshed his way across, wading waist deep with his elbows held high. He came trudging up the bank as the cold water cascaded off him.

Of course! *Why didn't you think of it immediately?* Head chided. Because Heart was distracting him, that was why. Gar saw clearly now. This child was half Water People. That explained the unnaturally long hair, the ashen skin colour, the misshapen face and limbs.

The strangely peripatetic Water People, the Hairies, were the ones who had usurped most of the south, the ones who would range near enough to the sea that their ancestral lines might include animals that did not even live on this side of the water.

And the thought made him half ill. In his mind's

eye he pictured one of those hairy-faced, pallid, long-legged people violating a Real Woman. This splendid woman. Gar knew it happened on rare occasion, but he'd never known a child to result from the encounter—not until now. Poor, benighted Mouse.

No need to push with questions. He'd find out all about her when she told her story beside the fire tonight.

The main trail would take them over the copse directly to Larch Cave, but it had to be threaded single file amid the trees. Instead, therefore, he led her out into the open bog where they could walk side by side, except when they had to skirt deep holes. Besides, out here away from trees, he could keep a good eye out for dangers, not the least of which might be, despite her possible connections, Water People.

She moved with the fluid grace of a sable. He enjoyed immensely watching her move. Her child had received that grace and to spare. Hare bounded from tussock to tussock without once slipping or wavering. He alternately ranged out and moved in close, investigating some little thing over there, then gambolled again at his mother's side. Where did he get all that energy? Gar realised belatedly that this Hare, half-grown though he might be, was protecting his mother. Laughable, in a way, and admirably noble.

By custom, of course, children were the foragers, and adults could claim two of any three food morsels the children brought in, simply by asking for them. Gar wondered about this child; either he was very good as a forager, being so active, or a terrible provider by not staying in any one spot long enough to find something.

His mother seemed fairly well kept, but that didn't mean much, since women forage also. She wasn't fat enough to be called pleasantly plump. Some men might hold out for a thicker woman. But she wasn't skinny at all, the way old women became. And look at her colour! Her skin glowed golden red-orange like a sunset, silky smooth, absolutely lustrous.

When they angled northeast back into trees, she had not yet said a thing about herself or even Hare. Gar felt somehow cheated. She dropped behind him to single file and he could not so much as look at her, however surreptitiously.

He stopped so suddenly, she almost ran into him. In the virtually still air he detected a vague smell from up ahead. It whispered to the dimmest, most distant caverns of his memories. What...? Rather, who...? For it was human smell, a gossamer shred of a woman's essence.

Behind him the half-grown half-breed's mother barked a few startled words. Even as Gar turned on his heel toward them, Mouse and Hare bolted back the way they had come. In moments, the silent firs and hemlocks blotted out their footfalls and their forms. They were gone.

He wheeled back to face the trail ahead.

"Gar." She didn't have to sign *friend*. Gar knew an old friend when he saw one. She stood in the bend of the forest track, dark and sleek as an otter, and laughing.

"Kohl." The puzzle of why the skittery Mouse woman should flee so precipitately dismissed itself. Gar sniffed and listened for a moment to assure himself Kohl was alone, then hastened to her.

She opened her arms, and he his, and as they embraced, clouds of fragrant memories swirled in close to make them the only two people in the world. For years as they were entering adulthood, Gar and Kohl had eagerly experimented, determined to develop the sophisticated sex techniques they heard about from others but never actually witnessed.

Had Gar not let the clan's elders talk him into entering training as a shaman, would he and Kohl have pledged? Many the time he dreamt so. Would the union have lasted until now? Of course! And why not? They took such pleasure in each other, once upon a time.

Can such pleasure be recaptured? An hour ago Gar would have said, "Probably not." Now, as soft embers flared to life and began to warm his depths, he could say, "Quite possibly."

He loosened and drew back enough to look at her smooth, dark face, those familiar dancing eyes. "A long, long time. We have been five winters here at the Larch Cave. We were still up in the Long Cave when you left. You've been gone six winters."

"I went off a-mating. You didn't hear?"

"I heard you found yourself a powerful warlord far away. But you know when a woman leaves her homeland, rumour always claims, 'She pledged to power.'"

"Who leaves to look for a dirt-grabber? The rumour is true. He is double power. Both shaman and warlord."

Absently on purpose, he massaged her back, her shoulders. She pressed in against him, an invitation. Arousal was fast making his secret hopes vividly obvious. Heart sang, *You lucky grouse! She knew delightful little tricks when she left here. Imagine what she must know now!*

Head sulked. *Are you certain you want to take this up again? You were done with her once, when she went away. What if the twice-powerful fellow who feeds her happens to be the jealous type? And worse, in the area here?*

He ran his hands down her back and pulled her in tightly against him. "Do I know him?"

"No. South. Down by the sea."

"Name."

"Kelp."

2

She Lost Her Mate

A breath of cool night air swirled in past Gar's ear and stirred the flames of the main fire in front of him. At the very back of the cave, it nudged the children's fire. The darkness and the chill of night at his back, the brightness of the dancing flames before—he savoured the magic in evenings like these, a magic extending far above and beyond the whispering spirits who hovered near.

Gar glanced up at the slanted ceiling, shadowy in the gloom but still discernible. He liked this Larch Cave pretty much the best of the four in his clan's territory, despite that it tended to be draughty when the wind blew in from the south. It was not so shallow as to afford scant protection and feeble defence, yet it yawned quite open, compared with some. Its water-streaked ceiling sloped from high overhead out here at the front down to soft, sandy floor a good twelve man-lengths back. It protected well without making one feel tightly enclosed. Gar particularly disliked caves with low ceilings and narrow necks, that tunnelled deeply into the Mother Earth. It was important to be embraced by Mother Earth at night, but too much was too much.

As always when the full clan gathered like this, the honoured elders sat closest to the front fire. Gar, the shaman for his Dusk moiety, enjoyed one of the three best seats. His back to the night, he hunkered at the right of the clan's warlord, a bulky fighter with the amphibiously innocuous name of Newt. Newt's unique hair, a thick shock of glistening white, reflected yellowish tonight. In full sun it glowed brighter than snow.

The clan's other shaman, Cloud, carefully adjusted his game leg as he settled onto his bearskin. He belonged at Newt's left, since he was Dawn moiety.

Hunters in a rather fluid hierarchy ringed the other side of the fire, and the least positioned gave their seats to the elder women. It was the custom. Gar appreciated the reassuring security of custom. So little in life was secure.

Newt stood up and spread his arms. His white hair glowed. "I yield to the honour of age and wisdom." Solemnly, the warlord swapped places with Cloud.

Cloud took a few moments getting his crippled leg repositioned. He had more than earned the best seat. At nearly forty—ten winters Gar's senior—he was the oldest person Gar had ever known. Curious, that Cloud's head hair, as well as a few scattered little old-man bristles on his chin, were not nearly so white as the warlord's, although he was fifteen winters older than Newt. Cloud wasn't even all that crippled up, for being so old. An arm broken in his youth hadn't healed quite straight, and he would never again have the full use of the leg a rhinoceros once stepped on, but then, shamans weren't expected to run down game. Not bad for forty winters, all in all.

Newt stretched an arm out behind Cloud, poked Gar and asked, "See Rat lately?"

Gar shook his head. "Blossomtime. Went north."

Newt grunted in that noncommittal way that made one wonder what he was thinking, if at all—in this particular case, about the tribe's once and only travelling barterer, Rat.

Who is this who watches everything from out there beyond the light? To get his attention, the spirits prickled the back of Gar's neck. Voices of the forest and the night tittered amongst themselves. *She wraps the night around her shoulders, a cape softer than the finest beaver, and renders herself invisible. She hides in clear view; her eyes miss nothing.*

Gar resisted the impulse to turn around and look out into the night beyond the cave. What would be the use? With his eyes burned by the bright fire, he'd see nothing whatever beyond the lip of the cave. But the spirits piqued his curiosity. Who—or what—lay observing him beyond the circle of light? It felt ominous and female. Distinctly female. But it could be a forest cat. A civet. A lion. Anything.

Then Gar's sister's mate's cousin stepped forward with her month-old baby and he dismissed the vague sensation. Gar and Cloud both marked the infant boy with powdered blood as she declared the baby's parentage. Fortunately, the father happened to be her current pledge. No woman dared lie about so grave a matter as paternity, lest her infant and perhaps herself as well eventually be denied entrance to the Beyond. Still, when a woman identified as the father someone other than the man feeding her, nasty little scenes tended to erupt. Gar recited off the baby's pedigree back ten generations, and she carried her child away to the rear of the cave.

Just the week before, Cloud's eldest grandchild had killed a bull elk virtually unaided and, within hours thereafter, experienced his first sexual union. Neither by itself would usher him into adulthood, but now, as he approached his thirteenth winter, he had completed both. Tonight, with the appropriate dance and voice and descriptive gesturing, his father announced the lad's manhood to the full clan.

See his pride! crowed Heart enviously. *Cloud's, too.* Gar wished fleetingly that he himself were a father. Something like that must taste delicious.

Gar had never pledged to a woman. It was not easy for a shaman to feed a woman when so often he provided no direct part in the taking of big game. In his thirty years, Gar had occasionally joined with one woman or another, Kohl being first and best—one might say his only real love. None had ever named him as a father.

His Head abruptly cut short his dream-wandering. *What's this? Newt mentioned nothing about this.*

Heart cooed, *Look at her!*

For Kohl, sturdy, supple, handsome Kohl, had stepped forward onto the bare floor beside the front fire. She was, Gar realised, about to tell her story. *What a lovely figure! Always was, always will be. Not a bone shows.* Heart was practically salivating.

Like just about everyone else's, of course, Kohl's body hair and shoulder-brushing head hair were wavy black, and as did most People, she pulled her head hair up into a convenient topknot, pinning it down with loon wing bones. Somehow, though, on her, this common hair arrangement looked uncommonly attractive. And her skin! She was the darkest Gar had ever noted in People, a rich, deep brown the colour of chestnuts. Glorious!

Respectfully she turned her back to the honoured three and presented her bottom to the eldest, Cloud. Cloud dipped his head and gestured *union*, a ceremonial acknowledgement of her strictly ceremonial obeisance.

She stood erect and turned a full circle, indicating that this story was for all to hear, and commenced her tale. "I had eighteen summers when I left this clan." She combined voice, dance, and hand signs as eloquently as Gar had ever seen it done, but then he was just a skittling prejudiced toward her. "I wished adventure, and a good mate."

Don't we all, murmured Heart.

"I wandered alone, drifting south. By and by, I came to unbroken forest and then the sea. Water People everywhere. Hunters. I hid from four different groups in a month, two months. Then I found Real People hard by the sea. Less than a day from the sea. Powerful People. Elk clan, tribe of Seashore."

Seashore. Cold Lakes was Mouse's tribe. And Mouse's sleek sunset-orange colour whisked across Gar's memories, then settled in to bind his thoughts. His mind compared the two, Kohl's sophisticated presence against Mouse's nervous caution; Kohl's beckoning smile against Mouse's withdrawn silence. Somehow Mouse emerged as the more appealing, and that thought startled Gar.

Every woman and man developed a specialty that would be useful to the clan. Warlord, shaman, flintworker, tracker, singer. What was Mouse's? What did she give back to the clan that nourished and protected her? Besides that grotesque, woebegone child of hers, that is.

Somewhere to the southwest, a hyæna filled the cool night air with its mounting wail. Another answered from the west. Hunting pack on the prowl, probably half a mile distant. Where was Mouse now? Gar would assume she was safe, since she'd obviously made it through life this far.

"First they allowed me as an outsider," Kohl continued. "Then they accepted me as a member, because the clan is shrinking. All are shrinking, they say, even powerful clans. Losing men, losing children, losing women.

"The woman of their shaman and warlord died. That one, he chose me next. Pledged me, fed me.

"He came north with some of his People. I came too, a guide. I know these places, been here and there. Now he's dead." With a few precise gestures, she provided a graphic portrayal of the head rolling. She expressed sadness. "I am alone again."

From less than a quarter mile away, a hyæna broke into that maniacal laugh that told the world the pack just cornered something luckless and tasty. Soundlessly, four men picked up their spears and moved off to the lip of the cave. They hesitated a few moments for their eyes to adjust, then dissolved into the gloom to go see what the hyænas had found and whether it was worth wresting away from them.

Kohl expressed her mourning with the appropriate dance. Afterward, she danced a thank you for the welcome she received here among her kin. That broad, dark body swayed, her breasts swinging belatedly, half a beat behind. With sign and gesture, she declared herself fully adult, which everyone knew anyway, and available, which everyone more or less assumed.

Gar glanced about. The only persons in the cave not absolutely rapt over her undulations were the small children who had fallen asleep and the glaring women, especially the younger ones. Gar smiled to himself. Nothing infuriated a woman quicker or more thoroughly than the introduction of a rival. He was surprised that the women of the Elk clan would allow Kohl's adoption into their circle, dwindling numbers or not. Were these Mammoth women here tonight not bound by blood ties to accept her, Kohl would find herself out on the tundra with the hyænas.

Almost too eagerly, Newt handed her a strip of jerked reindeer venison, thereby placing her under his ægis. Looking contemptuous and not the least bit thrilled, Newt's woman, Crow, gave Kohl a bird skin stuffed with crushed, larded berries, the other token of acceptance. Gar recited Kohl's genealogy ten generations and it was over. Whether the nubile women liked it or not, Kohl was back in the clan.

The ceremonial business pretty much taken care of, moiety mixed with moiety, cousin with cousin. They got some games going, the younger men and also some of the older ones. Gar disliked games of strength and speed. They bored him. So much effort expended on nothing, to prove what? That men love to make losers out of their kin.

The chattering and laughter built until the noise echoed off the ceiling, multiplying itself to the point that Gar could barely hear Newt's voice as the warlord settled in beside him.

"That dead one, Kelp." Newt wrinkled his nose as if he'd just chewed a week-old clam. "Good thing he's dead, eh."

"Why?" Gar frowned at him. "You knew him?"

"Heard about him. Rat knew him."

"Rat knows everybody." And it seemed very close to true. Rat the Trader was the only person Gar ever heard of who circulated freely among more than one clan of Real People and also maintained a cautious congress with Water People, the lanky, pale-skinned Hairies who roamed so widely.

Kelp. Dual leader, being both shaman and warlord. Pledged to Kohl. Known to Mouse; possibly even killed by Mouse. Interesting. Heart and Head clamoured inside him, confusing him with myriad questions. Did Newt know any answers?

Gar asked, "What does Kohl say about her Kelp?"

"Didn't ask. We didn't talk much yet. Do that by and by."

Gar heard a chorus of hoots over at the southeast end and sighed. "What does Rat say?"

"Didn't see Rat. I hoped you did. You remember Goose went with Rat early, last starvation moon, to help him carry salt, so I asked Goose. Goose met Kelp. He says Kelp loved power. More like those Hairies than his own People that way. Goose says Kelp worked hard, did many things to gain power. He wanted to travel to new territory to test his power."

And failed the test, obviously, smirked Heart.

"And came to our country." Gar felt again the vague tingle of being watched. He dismissed it, more interested in the puzzle Newt had just raised. "Strange. Very strange. Left his own country, eh?"

Newt bobbed his head. "Leave because he wants to? Did they throw him out? I asked Goose that. He says he doesn't know. But sometimes Goose does not tell all."

Rarely did Rat tell all, either, or tell the truth, for that matter. Prevarication must be a habit People who travel develop. Too much time walking with nothing to think about, perhaps. Rat told only what Rat wanted others to think. That, plus Rat's propensity for walking all over from territory to territory, made him much more like Hairies than like the Real Person he was.

Real People stayed put in one place, come feast or famine, snow or sunshine. A Person was part of his world—his or hers—and it was part of him. To walk away was as unnatural as walking out of one's own skin.

Gar couldn't understand why Kohl went away for all those winters.

Uncharacteristically loquacious, Newt rolled on. "Dangerous one, a stranger who loves power. Thinks he's strong. He comes to a place and upsets everything."

Gar frowned and gestured, *What?*

Newt waved a hand, as if in that meaningless flap Gar would somehow see what he wanted to say. "You, a shaman, never say you want to be warlord. And Cloud? Too old."

"Cloud never wants to be warlord anyway."

Newt nodded vigourously; his white hair rose and dropped. "Eh! You see!"

Actually, Gar rarely saw what the stumble-tongued Newt thought he was saying. Newt plunged on, explaining himself. "Whole clan... Uh, whole clan... Uh, balanced. Eh, balanced! All's right. No trouble, no fight. Fit together. Shaman, warlord, each one in place." He beamed, apparently triumphant for once over the limitations of the spoken word. That too was uncharacteristic of the verbally artless Newt. "Get stranger come in here, power greedy, don't know what happens next. He messes the balance all up, eh."

"Eh." Gar had never thought about such a thing as balance in the clan before. Everyone had a gift and used it. He wouldn't have called that balance exactly, but he could see Newt's point, vague as it might be. Should this Kelp, athirst with power and so unlike a Real Person in his thinking, seek to expand his strength by exercising dominion over other clans, he could have posed an interesting problem for Newt. That sort of thing just wasn't done. But if it were, Newt's clan would be a good pick.

As Gar thought about it, it would be natural for Kelp to come here to Gar and Newt's Mammoth clan of the Scarp Country tribe, people totally unrelated to the southerner, even though far better territories lay to the south. Not hard to see. Northern clans lived closer to the worst winters exactly because they were weakest, and therefore easy pickings. A northern clan offered less, but it also cost less. Kelp was no fool.

Oh? Then why, Heart teased, *did he end up in two pieces?*

But Head was already tackling this newest puzzle. *Why would Kelp seek more power than what he already possessed? Real People just don't do that. Why try to wield dominion over someone who does not even live in your territory? You're not going to spend any time there. They aren't coming here.* Unthinkable.

In the western night, the hyænas voiced a noisy and frenzied objection to something or other—probably to men, because men's voices ululated just as noisily. Three young men from Dawn moiety leaped up and went running out into the darkness without waiting for their eyes to adjust. It would serve them right if they tripped over a log. Or a hyæna.

Newt studied the fire a moment. "Reindeer coming soon, looks like. Couple mammoths. Early for them. Aurochs. Maybe rhino, Beaver says. Saiga antelope over at the hill. Since the clans are both here, these young fools all eager to kill something, we'll get some parties together. Glory. Good time for glory. I need you on the hunt; Cloud's too crippled up, not much use. I'll send him out with the boys instead, teach them. Let his magic help them learn."

"Last time my magic failed, you said I'm no use hunting either."

"Maybe your magic's getting better. Sure hope so." Newt leaped to his feet. "At least you keep up."

Somewhere in the general hubbub, Gar's uncle's step-brother on his mother's side, Aster, howled a general challenge, something about prowess at lifting. Gar paid scant attention; the fellow boasted much and lifted little. For as big as the man was, and Aster was a hulking beast, he wasn't all that strong.

Heart: *That watcher out there in the darkness grows annoying.*

Head: *Nonsense. An animal. So what?*

But you do feel it, eh? It's not just me.

I feel it.

Just then Gar's uncle grabbed Gar by an arm and hauled him to standing. "You show him!"

"Show him what?" Gar should have taken less note of watching animals and paid better attention to what was happening here under the overhang. He hated these contests the men kept getting into.

"How to do it." His uncle dragged him out onto the floor beside the fire.

Grinning, Aster rumbled, "You think you can lift more, eh."

"More than what?" As shaman, Gar usually did not take a direct part in hunts. Sheer strength of arm was therefore about the only other route available for demonstrating his qualities as a man. Fortunately, for he did not work at perfecting feats of strength, he was naturally stronger than some.

Squirming, Aster hovered over a round river boulder of considerable size. Suddenly he picked it up, and with a mighty lurch, heaved it a man-length. It rolled another man-length and *whupped* against a bed of bearskins as a chorus of hoos applauded him. Aster stepped over beside the boulder. "You."

Gar walked over and stared down at the rock. He studied from whence it had come. "Man-length, at least."

"At least."

Gar nodded. He reached for the rock, a ploy. Instead, he snapped around, grabbed Aster by an arm and a leg, and straightened up. The big man roared as Gar swung him up overhead and heaved him across the beds. The fellow plopped onto a pile of bearskins—luckily, a fairly thick one—nearly two man-lengths distant.

Gar received a very gratifying chorus of hoos. He pointed at random to any nearby male, this time his cousin. "You."

He turned away then to avoid getting sucked deeper into this inanity. Everyone knew everyone else, and each person knew every other's strengths and weaknesses. Why...?

He wandered over to the pile of bones from the feast earlier, mostly because they were on the other side of the cave from the site of Aster's contest. Idly, he pawed through the bones, but they were pretty well broken up and picked over. Tomorrow the women would drag them out of the cave and down to the river, lest the remains draw scavengers and vermin—not to mention lions and hyænas—here to where the small children played.

"Hungry?" Kohl had stepped in behind him too silently to be heard. She didn't smell, either.

He turned to her. "Took a bath, eh."

"Nice to do in summer sometimes. Water's warm." She extended her hand, and in it lay the birdskin of larded berries.

He scooped out a few polite fingers-full.

"You didn't change." She said it appreciatively. "Still strong."

"You either."

She glanced over towards a knot of gabbling women. "Not too easy for me to be here. My sister, cousins, nobody likes me now. Are they mad because I went away?"

"Because you have lots of fat; it bobs in all the best places when you dance. Ask the men if they like you."

She smirked. "I'm not blind."

Gar licked lard off his fingers and was pondering the chance of cajoling some more from her when the hunters returned, and exuberantly.

With a whoop, the lead fellow, Toad, flung the mangled haunch of a horse colt on the floor. Everyone shouted, despite that all were still sated from the feasting. Gar's second cousin tossed down the rest of the carcase. The only major piece missing seemed to be the other back haunch. Hyæna teeth had ripped out a few chunks and shredded the hide over the forequarters, but meat aplenty remained.

Gar had no part in this taking, but he stepped forward anyway and squatted down by the colt's head. He pointed to a narrow cord pulled so tight around the colt's throat just behind the ears that you could barely see it within the shaggy coat. "See! Clever hyænas. They learned how to snare prey."

Clever indeed. The cordage was the most tightly made that Gar had ever seen, some kind of long hair intricately twined amongst itself.

"Snare!" Toad stopped his clumsy hunter's dance in mid-hop—not all that hard for a man who can't jump more than a hand's breadth off the floor—and stooped to glare at the offending cord.

Vulture roared with delight. "Toad can catch a colt after the hyænas snare it for him!"

"Not hyænas. Him!" Toad stood erect, wheeled, and pointed. "He snared it!"

Gar had to twist and strain to see beyond the laughing, howling, derisive hunters.

Out on the edge of the night, not outside the cave but not quite in it, that gangling half-Hairy lad, Mouse's misbegotten child, cringed against his mother. Two Dawn moiety striplings flanked them closely.

Gar gestured to the striplings, *Bring her here.* They dragged mother and son forward, and the one fellow seemed loathe to handle the boy. Gar couldn't exactly blame him.

Mouse and Hare, two against the world, were instantly surrounded within the circle of hooting hunters. Mouse stood straight and tall, defiant, exhibiting none of the cautious reserve she had shown when Gar first saw her. Curious transformation. Her pitiful child presented himself just as boldly, his fists clenched. Whatever shortcomings he had, and they were many, he displayed a courage Real Children ought to envy.

Gar moved in until only the colt carcase lay between Mouse and him. "Toad. Story."

"We followed the hyæna noise. When we got to them, we saw this ugly child and his mother up in a tree. They had the colt dragged up into the tree with them. Hyænas were below them, snapping at them, all around the tree.

"I think, 'These two, they stole the colt from the hyænas. Maybe they surprised the hyænas, threw rocks, grabbed meat, climbed fast.'" Toad wagged his head. "Nobody saw the truth: 'Hyænas were trying to steal the colt from these two.' We attacked, speared some hyænas, the others ran off. We brought home these two and the colt, eh."

"Eh." Gar watched Mouse a few moments, assaying her mood. Did she recognise him? Yes. Did she trust him? No more than she trusted any of these, and that was not at all. What a strong, sturdy woman. Beautiful.

Her eyes flitted past him, settled on him again.

"Mouse, tribe of Cold Lakes, Horse clan, Dusk moiety." He nodded toward her child. "Water People, of Baboon. Mouse, you knew Kelp."

Newt grunted, surprised by the revelation. He didn't ask how Gar might know all this, but then shamans were supposed to know such things as lineages.

Gar held Mouse's eye. "Do you know Kohl?"

Newt's heavy brow rose. "Hm! Think so?" He waved an arm, "Kohl!" and motioned *come*. Instantly, half a dozen youths helped Kohl forward through the group, laying hands upon her as much as possible in that short walk across the floor. They thrust her into the centre of the bunch so eagerly that she almost tripped over the colt carcase.

Were the Mammoth women fuming that Kohl had been forced among them? That fury was nothing compared with the rage in Kohl's stormy eyes as she glared at Mouse.

Apparently these two women did indeed know each other. For as one, they spat in each other's face.

3

They're Inviting Their Ruin

She was a forest cat, graceful and strong. *She* was a slinky civet, pouring like water up the trunk of this tree. *She* was a prowling lion, dangerous and beautiful. *She* was a tree rat, virtually invisible as *she* bellied out along this limb.

Impatiently, *she* brushed *her* hair out of *her* eyes. *She* really ought to obtain a loon wing bone and pin *her* hair up. Beyond this tree and beyond another tree as well, lay the huge, yawning cave *she* wanted to observe. *She* hungered for *her* own kind; *she*'d been without People so long; still, they were no longer of *her*. *She* was not a Person anymore; *she* missed it and yet *she* did not, for now *she* was bolder and stronger than *she* had ever been, with the heart and strength of a hyæna.

A leafy branch obscured part of *her* view, so *she* moved up another limb. Now *she* could see the whole cave, every bit of it. Many People clustered around the two fires. A few women moved between them. This must be a gathering of both moieties.

These Mammoth People were a robust clan yet, not decimated like *hers*. See! Over a dozen children gambolled about, and half a dozen women held small babes. Strong, handsome men and plenty of them. Strong, fat women. A prosperous clan.

She assayed the three leaders. One shaman was too old and crippled to count. The warlord, that strangely white-haired one, seemed decent enough. Not bombastic and overbearing, like Kelp. Certainly not haughty. Brusque, but then what else would one expect from a man?

It was the other shaman, though, who seized *her* eye and heart. He was not of unusual size, but he was big enough to fight and hunt well. *She* liked his colour, a lustrous medium tan. As he moved, she read into his movement power and authority. And yet he seemed so gentle. He laughed well.

Perhaps this clan enjoyed such good health because of the cheerful fidelity with which they completed the rituals. They praised life and the spirits with hearty joy. Before eating, they identified those Persons who had put forth a noble effort of some sort recently, calling that Person forward and declaring the deed with a brief dance. *Her* clan had ceased doing that. Then they divided the honour pieces of what looked like three stallion quarters, well aged. Whatever the hunt that brought in the stallion, at least two horses must have been taken and perhaps even more, for they would have eaten the first within three days.

They certainly ate well. Well-aged horse was very

tasty. However—and this interested *her* greatly—they ate at a leisurely pace. They joked and told stories during the eating. They shared amongst themselves, passing chunks of meat and flint blades back and forth. No fighting for meat; no wolfing it down; no hunching over to protect a portion. Even the children seemed to lack greed and possessiveness.

She smelled the rich aroma and wished *she* had fire to roast meat with. Someday. *She* envied the nurturing warmth of that cave and that clan, two kinds of warmth, both necessary.

Perhaps here was another reason for the clan's strength. A woman brought her baby forward and both shamans marked it. Not just the woman's moiety's. Both. Double the blessing, double the power. No rivalry between the two halves, no jealousy.

Now a father danced his son's manhood. See how eagerly they all welcomed the lad in, and laughing. This father's son, a brand new man, enjoyed the support of the whole clan behind him.

Wait! Oh, no! What was this? The dark woman! Her! Now the dark woman was stepping into the circle beside the fire. She presented herself to the eldest and turned a full circle. She was dancing her story now. If they let her stay with this clan, the dark one would ruin it!

From behind *her* somewhere, hyænas in a pack called to each other. Only four hunters left the cave. Bold or foolish, for so few to go. *She*'d guess bold.

Maybe they would chase the dark woman off tomorrow. No, here came the warlord with the jerky and a woman with the birdskin. The clan was going to let her stay.

Fools!

Games began. Young men, laughing, jousted and sparred.

From down the valley, hyænas and men bayed out. Three more young men left. The moieties mixed so casually, so cheerfully. *She* envied that too.

The men seemed to enjoy their contests a great deal, as do most men. *She* expected hostility to break out, but no. The contestants remained good-natured. They laughed and heckled, though *she* could not make out words. *She* noticed a particularly burly fellow toss a huge river rock across the floor. Quite a feat. So the clan was strong physically as well as in other ways.

What was this? A fellow was dragging onto the floor that tan shaman, the younger one who had taken *her* eye. Agape, *she* watched the shaman pick up his challenger and with one magnificent swoop toss the fellow across the beds. *Her* heart soared. See how effortlessly he picked up a man half again his size, as if it were nothing, and how far he threw him! What a splendid man, this shaman.

Oh, but now look! He was wandering ever so casually over to the bone pile. And now the dark woman instantly got up from the group of men she was sitting with and crossed the width of the cave to the shaman. They engaged in conversation so quickly that it had to be a pre-arranged meeting of some sort. He was smiling. She was smirking. What was the dark woman planning with this shaman?

From very close beneath *her* tree came the seven hunters. Wait. Nine. No, the seven with... with...

Her! The orange woman and that ugly child! Oh, no, no, no. Now the clan was doomed for certain. They were not killing the grotesque child or the orange one. They were not driving her off.

They were allowing both these women to stay! Without doubt, they were guaranteeing their own downfall.

4

His Spirits Failed the Job

In that gentle, silent, final slice of late-night darkness, the one condemned to yield to first light, the spirits of the world held their breath. None spoke. None moved. They revealed no secrets, offered no warnings, conferred no protection or allegiance.

Without their ægis, Gar was on his own.

He paused a few moments on the brow of this rocky little knob, reading the world one more time. The night birds had ceased; the dawn birds weren't stirring yet. In the midst of shifting from westerly to southerly, the breeze had hesitated. Dead still, like the spirits.

The sky lightened perceptibly, blotting out the dim stars, threatening the middle stars. Directly to southward below this knob stretched a broad vale, wooded bottomland ringing nearly a mile of open bog. The land that rose in casual slopes to either side of the valley was virtually treeless, save for stunted hazel and clumps of firs. Beyond view to the east and west, it levelled off into open, soggy tundra, alive in daylight with summer birds.

The sky was awakening now, at last. When the bright stars faded, Newt, down in the trees a mile or so beyond, would set the glory in motion.

As air commenced to move, the spirits began again to breathe. Things not visible, things not audible, things not tangible, and yet they breathed. They teased. Gar could sense them flitting in close and darting off. Coy spirits, to tantalise, to promise help and then dance away.

Time floated on a vagrant breeze.

Soundless voices told him the hunters were starting to move. Gar closed his eyes and tipped his face up toward the sky. He raised his arms, letting the world speak to his mind's eye.

And now he could sense the prey as well as the hunters. Spirits of men and spirits of the land mingled their whispering. Out to the south at the far end of the bog, Newt was closing on a woolly rhinoceros. Interesting. What diverted him? The warlord had originally intended to go for aurochs in the forest beyond the bog.

The rhino wandered out in the open, moving this way across the mushy bottomland. The bog spirits magnified for Gar's inner ear the sloosh of those massive, stumpy feet slogging from tussock to tussock. They let him hear the ponderous head as it swung its great horn from side to side, ripping at the heath. Would the myriad spirits let him join the rhino enough to direct its thoughts? They did not always.

Gar raised his arms higher toward the lightening sky. He opened his heart and set his mind and spirit free out into the cool air.

I am that rhino.

A mature bull, probably of eight or nine winters. The massive horn weights the front end of my muzzle; when I swipe my head from side to side, that horn adds tremendous power to the swing. Tangles of long hair protect a rich, matted undercoat, allowing me, unlike paltry humans, to ignore rain and cold.

I stroll out across the bog, browsing in the predawn. Oblivious to fear. Stately in my bulky greatness. Cave lions might take a young of the year if the cow is not too near. Hyænas might fall upon a bachelor of one or two winters. But I am safe. No creature dares challenge my shaggy, brooding mass.

I hear sound behind me, as something or someone stepping through the bog mat into water. *It is nothing. I shall browse on, unconcerned. I shall ignore it.*

My squinty little eyes are next to useless but my ears and my nostrils tell me everything. They say, "Safety. You need not fear People. Take your ease. You are master of your world."

I feel the icy chill on my tongue as I rip out great, satisfying mouthfuls of wet plants. My huge, padded feet slip and slide a bit, for I am a creature of the solid tundra and the open grasslands. *No matter. Feeding is good here and I am invincible.*

The bright stars are fading out. Human smell pervades the bog now. *I pay no heed. People cannot hurt me. I browse on.*

Pay no heed to human smell.

Pay no heed to feather-soft footfalls.

Pay no heed.

The bog is alive with motion and aromas, but I will continue to disregard them. Let them come. They will pass by.

Humans shriek before me and behind me! Shouts to either side! Which way shall I turn? They are falling upon me! *They cannot hurt me; I need not strike back at them. I will try to escape this way.*

No! Instead I will escape the way I came.

I slip in the mire trying to pivot. Two men lunge at me from right and left, seeking glory. I throw my fearsome head about! Their spears pierce my flanks, ripping at my soul!

I fling my head, catching a hunter in mid-stride; I feel the fellow's great weight as I lift the luckless hunter high and send him flying. Glory!

I swing my head to the other side. Spears scuff along my ribs.

A man drives his spear into my shoulder and loses his balance in the cold mud; he's an arm's length from my horn, slipping and floundering in the water. Glory!

I lunge forward; *I must hesitate.* The white-haired one plunges at me head on, and roaring; his spear pierces my breast. For a moment we stand face to face, eye to eye. Glory!

My strength is ebbing. They've ripped my belly open. I flail my horn. Glory! My front legs buckle; the hind hold. The youngest of the men, shouting, falls forward against me, driving his spear between my ribs. I hurl my head toward him; I break his spear; I try but I cannot crush him; he presses against my flank. Glory!

My back legs collapse. I struggle. They all rush at me, to lay their hands upon me before I die, to partake of the glory.

My spirit is fading; I feel it depart. My dim eyes see the steam from my bowels rising off the soggy land, my smoking blood sinking into the soggy land. The bravest men grasp my horn as I try to swing my head. They laugh and sing to my spirit as it lifts away. I hear the goodbye shout as from a great distance.

Gar's head dropped forward, his chin on his chest. In the chill of dawn, as the first yellow brilliance came streaking out across the northeast horizon, he was sweating profusely. He let his arms fall to his sides.

Good magic, that!

He simply stood there awhile breathing deeply, too tired to wend his way down the knob to the bog. The rhino had been eviscerated before it fell; Gar was certain of that. He wondered which of the hunters managed that bit of glory, for the rhino had not seen the hunter and therefore neither had he. A coup indeed, to move in so closely with nothing but a blade, and to strike successfully. It took more than a few moments, not to mention a lot of muscle, to cut through a rhino's belly, even though the tough hair was sparsest there.

No doubt that hero would be hailed as the supreme honouree tomorrow, although Newt's face-on attack deserved nearly as much glory.

The sun perched as a full circle above the naked, rolling hills to the northeast. Gar sucked in a chest full of sweet morning. He picked up his spear and began working his way down through the rocks.

Curious, how much strength good magic sapped out. He could tell those occasions when his magic was inadequate; it didn't drain him like this. Why were the spirits so cooperative sometimes, when at other times they turned their collective backs? Newt claimed women were fickle. He should try communing with spirits awhile.

Gar froze and sniffed. Hairies nearby! Now why

would Hairies be prowling this area? They were supposed to be up north following the reindeer this time of year. They had a taste for young cattle. Maybe, like Newt, they entered this area seeking bison or aurochs and didn't find any yet.

No, the scent was not Hairies. Gar detected Real People, but oddly different People. Certainly not clan. His nearest clan were still nearly a mile away, beyond good shouting distance, and busying themselves with the fallen rhino. He gripped his spear and tucked it in tightly, pressed against his side with his arm.

In the clan lay his only real safety. He rock-hopped wildly downhill from boulder to boulder, from ridge to talus. His feet were as tough as they ever got in summer, and still the sharp stones poked painfully.

Forget the hurt, roared Heart. *You have worse things to worry about.*

With their characteristic capriciousness, the spirits refused to tell him where his enemy cowered or how many were they. He must get within hailing distance of the boys who accompanied the hunters. Newt, may his ears rot, couldn't pick up sound to save him, but the boys could hear a beetle breathing.

Somewhere off to his left, the alien People were moving downhill with him; Gar could detect that much even without the spirits' help. Who could it be, so far from their own country at this time of year?

Head was already hard at work on the problem. *They probably plan to cut you off from the clan before you can reach the willow patch ahead. Your best bet is the west cave. There you can stand against a whole tribe. There may even be some women there waiting to butcher the rhino. They can help.*

He swept down past the first of the trees at the base of the knob.

They would be expecting him to run for the bog, toward Newt. He lunged aside, cornering without pausing, and headed west toward the limestone scarp. He envied Hare's ability to leap and bound—Mouse's too, for that matter. The most agile of Real People do not leap much, and Gar's skills as a bounder left much to be desired.

He left the alder grove, skirted a hazel thicket too dense to push through quickly, and ran for the talus at the base of the scarp. He might not leap well, but over short distances, could he run!

Breaking their silence at last, spirits whispered, *Stay low and do not neglect behind. They are throwing rocks at you.*

The stony ground flashed brilliant white and slammed up against him.

Head babbled, confused and incoherent, mixing his thoughts with the equally confusing babble of distant voices surrounding him.

Heart suggested, *Perhaps you've entered Beyond.*

Head had nothing to offer.

He could not move his arms. His fingers tingled. The world returned by chunks and pieces, sounds first, then smells. His eyes were slow to regain their sight and for a brief moment his head feared blindness. Vision returned belatedly, dragging with it a pounding headache.

With rawhide, they had bound his arms and wrists, thrust straight out to each side, to his own spear. Its horizontal shaft cut into his back and shoulder blades as viciously as if it were the enemy's. These People summarily hauled him to standing by hoisting the spear. His knees buckled twice before he regained enough coordination to keep his feet.

Gar counted four and recognised none—three young men and a giant. They clustered around him. Up close, these Real People still smelled vaguely like Hairies.

The large Person, a *very* large, square-built Person, stood before him, smirking. The huge fellow gestured *you* and waved a hand to indicate the whole area. "Cold Lakes." His head hair, pulled into a topknot, showed a few grey streaks, but he looked otherwise youthful.

Gar almost shook his head, but the ringing headache warned him not to. "Not Cold Lakes. Scarp Country."

"Clan."

"Mammoth, Dusk." Gar paused. Custom dictated that the fellow respond with his own tribal affiliations. Apparently he did not feel bound by custom, so Gar prodded. "You."

Heart sniggered, *Why does the giant hesitate? Ashamed of his People?*

Head warned, *He's a crafty one. Calculating. You know he's Elk.*

Elk. Of course. Kohl and Mouse both said that Kelp, the murder victim, was Elk clan. These strangers would surely be Kelp's people.

Before the big Person could speak, Gar volunteered, "Elk clan." He kept his face relaxed, his expression amiable. "Tribe of Seashore."

The giant stared, gaping.

Gar let his voice purr, low and casual. "You seek your shaman and warlord, Kelp. He came into our Scarp Country hungry for power. He lost his head. I have questions. Why odd colours in his fingernails? And why did your Elk women accept Kohl into the clan? They should hate her, not invite her."

"Kohl..." The giant's brain was not what one might call swift. "Your spirits serve you well."

Gar smirked. "If my spirits served me at all, my fingers would not be purple now." He didn't mention how they were throbbing and turning very cold.

The giant was the only one who did not laugh. His beady eyes glanced around at his compatriots for guidance. They seemed to be enjoying the exchange and appeared in no mood to help him out.

From somewhere on the periphery a fifth Person approached. He looked nearly as old as Cloud. *Their other shaman,* spirits whispered. And indeed, Gar could feel his presence. Whatever spiritual gifts Kelp might have toyed with, this was the Person with the real strength.

The fellow stepped in beside the giant and addressed Gar. "Where is Mouse?"

"Near." Gar could not read the man at all.

"Who feeds her?"

"Her son. No one of ours."

"Who feeds Kohl?"

"All. She's Mammoth."

The answers seemed to satisfy the Wise One. He grunted. "Who killed Kelp?"

"No one knows. We don't care."

"We care. We want his murderer."

"You say murder. Many things kill. Lions. Hyænas."

"We found him."

"Ah." That still did not answer why they might be interested in learning who did it. It was generally considered improper to exact revenge on outsiders. Something out of the ordinary was afoot here.

"The colours," Gar prompted. "On his hands." He expressed *hands* by waving them. There was probably a spoken word for them, but Gar didn't recall it. Whenever he moved his hands, they hurt worse than his head. He would not talk about hands anymore.

"Magic," the shaman barked tersely. "He was killed in your Scarp Country. So you People in Scarp Country will bring us his killer."

"Why? No connection, Seashore and Scarp Country."

The giant entered the conversation. "Many connections. Rat. The women."

"Everyone has connections, if you count Rat." But not everyone had Kohl and Mouse.

"Hear me," the old shaman rumbled. "It must be the true murderer. The one whose very hand took Kelp's life. No other. And we will know if you brought us the killer. Our spirits will examine the one you name."

The giant stepped in closer. "You will bring that Person to us. You will come before the first starvation moon."

And the shaman completed the picture as only a shaman could. "Dawn, I watched you on the hill. I came with you. Your hunters, great glory! The white-haired one, face on. And gutting the rhino on its feet. Impressive hunters your clan has, and great glory."

Impressive? The fact that this old man could commune with Gar's spirits every bit as clearly as could Gar himself, and without Gar's knowledge—*that* was impressive. Here spoke real power, power the prudent would be unwise to offend.

The shaman continued, "Succeed and no harm comes. Fail and I will send spirits you cannot quench.

Your babies? Born blind, born sick. Your women? They will bleed from moon to moon. Your men? No heart. Why live if the glory departs?"

The old man turned then and walked away, back whence he had come. The spirit of his presence, so vivid while he stood here, faded as he moved off into the trees. Gar lost sight of him. The spirit stilled.

Gar's hands didn't hurt anymore. He couldn't feel them at all.

The giant turned his back. They were all departing after the old man, leaving him like a haunch on a roasting spit.

One of the younger fellows called to the giant, "Cut him loose?"

The giant twisted around and grinned, wagging his head *no*. "We don't need the rawhide."

"Maybe a lion finds him."

"He has his spear." Cackling, the giant followed his shaman off into the trees. With nary a backward glance, the three young men trailed after him.

Gar stood there, wondering if the blood that had trickled down his back from his scalp was going to draw carnivores before he could reach the safety of his clan. He wondered what Newt and Toad were going to say when he came stumbling in trussed up like this. He wondered if his hands would ever function again.

Up in the rustling alder leaves, and down behind the hillside boulders, and tucked in the sparse, whispering grass on the stony slope, the spirits cowered.

And giggled.

5

She Was Pummelled by Fate

Lightning all over. Its terrifying brilliance flashed in horizontal streaks across the dark cloudbank on the southwest horizon. With tiny, invisible stabs, lightning as vivid as that in the sky zinged up Gar's hands and wrists every time he moved his fingers. Three days since that embarrassing encounter with the Seashore Tribe, and still his swollen hands would not function well or comfortably.

Not that he needed his hands too much. He sat cross-legged on the outer lip of the Larch Cave floor as he had for most of the last three days, gazing out at the valley and hills beyond, waiting. He had not eaten. He had drunk only at dawn. And he wondered to himself why this wasn't working the way it should.

Usually, by now, a stringent fast would have invited the spirits into close companionship. By now he should have experienced some sort of vision or insight. So far he had heard no hint whatever as to who Kelp's murderer might be.

Half a mile along the ridge to the northwest at Alder Cave, the ancient Cloud also fasted. Perhaps Cloud would gain some inkling. He was very good at hearing spirits through fasting.

Although this scarp angled more or less northwest to southeast, Larch Cave itself faced almost directly due west. The cave's open, inviting shape aside, the view from its gaping front here pleased Gar even more. This broad valley with the ragged hills to either side stretched away from the cave for several miles before losing itself by angling south.

Sometimes through open fen and sometimes amid concealing trees wound the valley's glittering stream. Beavers had opened up most of the enclosing woodland along the valley floor, and their pond half a mile beyond the cave sparkled when the sun shone. Clumps of aspen and maple nestled within the dark green blanket of conifers to either side of the valley. Each autumn, in one last, splendid crash of beauty before the starvation moons began, those aspens and maples lit the valley with flaming colour.

The sun would set shortly. Were it not hidden by storm clouds, it would splay orange and gold across the sky. Today, dull grey. The spirits had precious little time left to reveal their secrets. Voices of the creek and valley must surely know who spilled blood. Why must it remain such a mystery?

Heart murmured, *You're being watched again.* Or was it a voice of the cave telling him?

He sensed it now. The intensity of the feeling grew,

as if he were being scrutinised by a carnivore. It made him uneasy. And then the ominous quality of the sensation faded. The feeling of being watched did not.

Head reminded him, *A shaman seeking wisdom is usually watched. Nothing remarkable.*

Heart murmured, *She's remarkable.*

Mouse. Gar sensed her behind him, and now that his heart revealed her, he could feel her. It must have been she whom he'd been sensing for some time now. He twisted around suddenly and looked right at her. She cringed back and hesitated a few long moments as Gar thought to her, *Come.*

She apparently heard the message, for here she came, tentatively. As she approached, he could smell mint on her fingers. She'd been out foraging.

Gently, he waved a tingling hand. "Sit."

"I must not bother you. Or speak to you."

"Sometimes a fast brings wisdom you need. Sometimes no. This time no. You break no visions."

She settled beside him just beyond arm's length, cross-legged like him. "What's Gar? I never heard of 'Gar.'"

"A big fish, as long as a man. Skin harder than flint. Fierce. Sharp teeth."

She stared. "I never saw such a fish, like so!"

"Not many of them anymore. Stories from the old times tell how fierce they are, and how big. Great glory for you if you catch a gar. You wait; by and by, they come to the top of the water, you snatch them. Spears don't work. The skin is too hard. Hooks don't work. The mouth is too hard. You have to grab it with your hands." He wished he hadn't said that. His fingers ached anew from saying *hand.*

"Hoo."

"And quick. If it bites your finger, no finger." He watched the lightning play a moment. "Too bad, there are not many gar anymore. None here, I know; I have never seen one."

She stared at him. "Too bad? Who wants a fierce fish like so in the water with you?"

Good question. Gar took a moment to collect an answer, but no matter how he thought to frame it, words did not seem to convey his full intent. "Here is half a life." He held up one swollen hand. "And this is a whole life." He held up the other and touched them together, then picked up a stick.

Her wonderful, deep-set eyes crackled, and he so very nearly tumbled into their darkness that he almost lost his train of thought.

He gripped the stick one-handed and waved it. Pain like lightning shot up and down his arm. "Half a life has no strength." He grasped the stick with both hands and snapped it in two. Worse lightning. "Only a whole life has strength. Power. You need both parts. Good and bad. Strong and weak. Day and night. Cold and warm. Safety and danger. Fierce gar and gentle bream." He thought a moment and added, "If you don't know one, you don't feel the other. You need all of it to feel all of it."

He watched her face. Did she understand at all? And why should he care that she understood? For whatever the reason, he did.

She studied the horizon awhile. "Maybe with some things, it's better we don't feel."

He would agree on the basis of his hands, which he dearly wished he didn't feel, but he knew that wasn't what she meant. He watched her a moment and she would not meet his eye. "Tell me about Kelp."

She shrugged.

So he prodded, "Story."

Was she silently planning how to tell him, or was she simply ignoring his request? She stared off beyond the valley before them, beyond the mountains, beyond the black cloudbank. "Hairies, they are strange People."

Everyone knew that. Gar waited.

"Man and woman, those two pledge."

"So do Real People."

"No. This is different." She should be up and dancing to make herself understood better. Instead she said nothing she could not say while seated, mostly in spoken words interspersed with only a few gestures. "Hard to explain. Pretend that you and I pledge. You bring me meat. Maybe I make a baby for you."

Sounds fine so far! cooed Heart.

She continued, "But I stay with the children's fire, over there. That's my place, the baby and I. Maybe sometimes you invite me to the men's fire. I forage, feed Hare and me and your baby. Hare forages—he is a very good forager. I don't give you any food I find, eh? The proper thing, the man gives the woman meat from the kill, but the woman doesn't give the man food. When the baby gets big enough, it feeds you, maybe Hare feeds you. Maybe you get tired of me, put me aside, pledge someone else, then her children forage for you. Things change. But Hairies, they pledge man and woman tightly. Family."

"Family?"

"Together, two adults, the man and woman. And all the babies—one, two, three, four. All share one big fire."

"Children and men around the same fire?"

"All, the same fire. When the man and woman pledge, she feeds him, he feeds her, and they both feed the children. They all belong together, a group together, this man and woman and their children. Not just clan."

"Eh." Strange indeed. So what did that have to do with Kelp? He waited as light melted out of the sky and the cloudbank grew.

He was being watched again. In the silence here, the feeling came through sharply. Not Mouse and not clan, either. Something or someone else from outside the cave.

Mouse stared off toward nowhere. Did she feel watched also? Gar saw no indication that she did. Her voice purred quietly. "I was eleven winters when the Hairies stole me."

"Why? Hairies hate Real People. Kill us sometimes."

Again, that exaggerated shrug. "Too strange, Hairies. I don't bother anymore to try to understand them. What they do, they do. No one knows why, sometimes even they don't know why. The shaman, he didn't marry, so he t-"

"Marry?" Gar noticed the cloudbank had shoved itself up the sky until it now hovered nearly overhead, bringing its lightning with it.

"Pledge, man and woman, like I just said. So he takes me and I do all the things for him that Hairy women do for men. Feed him, all those things."

Gar gestured, *Union.* "That too?"

"All the time, eh. I hated it. I'd fight him, but no good. It happened anyway."

"Even when you don't want it." Unthinkable.

"He said it was my duty. When a Hairy man and

woman marry, they stay with themselves, union with only each other, no union with others."

Gar shrugged. "Like Real People's pledge."

"No. Stronger than that. By and by I made a baby, and here was Hare. The shaman got mad at me, for he didn't want Hare. He said, 'When Hairies and your kind join, there is not supposed to be any baby." As if it was my fault because I willed it so. Only they don't call themselves Hairies; they call themselves The People and we're The Uglies. 'Here is a baby!' So he blamed me.

"Now the shaman took a real wife, a Hairy woman. He kept me too. He used to be good to us mostly, to Hare and me. But see how ugly Hare was in his eyes. Poor Hare, he's not Hairy, not Real People. Pretty soon the shaman was not good to us anymore."

Ugly in everyone's eyes, mumbled Head, but Gar didn't say it aloud. "No part with the Hairies anymore." He guessed her point.

She bobbed her head vigourously. "The shaman's new woman soon gave him a baby. Then another. For Hare and me, no—" She paused, frowning.

Gar combined *long time* with *safety*. Security.

Again she bobbed her head. "That's it! So late last winter, before spring migration, I slipped away. I was gone two days before they found out, and Hare and I, we got away."

"You went home to Cold Lakes, to your clan of Horses?"

She nodded. "I don't know where the rest of tribe is. The Horses clan are all gone. So Hare and I, we have no clan. Nine winters I was gone with the Hairies, and when I came back, no one was there.

"Along came a Real Person travelling. It was Rat

with two boys carrying salt. 'Where are Horses?' I said to him. 'They are no more,' he said. 'Gone.' Then he says, 'Come with me, by and by we'll join other clans of Cold Lakes.' So we went south."

"And you and Hare helped carry salt."

She looked at him oddly and nodded.

He smiled. "I know Rat."

"Everyone knows Rat. Even Hairies, some of them. Along the way, here is Kelp's clan, Seashore People. Rat stopped and visited with them."

"Elk Clan."

"Elk, eh. Kelp and Rat, they talked. Then Kelp came to me and Hare, told us, 'You'll stay with me now. If you try to leave, try to run away, I'll kill Hare. I'll kill him with spears and I'll kill him with spirits. I have double power, eh.'

"I was very afraid." She emphasised the *fear* by doubling the gesture. "But when I saw a chance, Hare and I ran anyway. We came north. I thought that somewhere, maybe, we could find some Cold Lakes People."

Because of the cloudbank, plus the fact that the moon was entering third quarter, the blackness out across the valley had become very nearly complete. Somewhere in that darkness, hyænas and lions got into a squabble, no doubt over a kill. Their yapping and yowling and roaring carried clearly across the night air. Gar wondered idly how cave lions and hyænas managed to see in darkness so deep.

She interrupted his thoughts. "Four days, no food for you."

"Three. A fast lasts three days."

"No. Four. I saw you return after that rhino kill, after you talked to Saiga and Eel. You didn't eat since then. Three days plus that day. See? Four days."

"Saiga and Eel. Those are the names of those two Elks?"

"Eh. All the women here in your moiety, they swap lots of talk. We women learn everything, you know."

I know that. Heart.

Mouse rattled on, confirming his worst fears. The whole clan, man, woman, and child, knew about his unfortunate and ignominious encounter. "We women heard what you told Newt and Cloud, about finding Kelp's killer. We all talked about it. And I told them the names because I know Saiga and Eel. I lived among them. The very big fellow is Eel. He's a good hunter—smart about animals and hunting, but not so smart about other things. He's probably their warlord now. I know he wanted to be."

"And Saiga is their shaman. So he's not Kelp's moiety."

Mouse grew almost animated. Almost. "Eh! Saiga is Dawn. Kelp was Dusk. The Elk women, they claim Saiga is strong with spirits. He does fasts too. Now your fast is over, eh."

"Eh."

Lightning flashed. Long moments later, thunder rumbled rather complacently.

Mouse leaped up suddenly and trotted off. Gar wanted to call out, "Wait! I have questions!" and he had no idea why he didn't.

The spirits had let him down again. He thought about Cloud's quiet control of the world around. He thought about the Elk clan's shaman, that Saiga, who could commune so comfortably with spirits, even Gar's spirits. He thought about this failed fast. Now what would they do?

Mouse came scurrying. She was so agile, but then she wasn't fat like Kohl—not fat enough to be called beautiful by conventional means, and yet see what grace she possessed. Beautiful all the same. She hunkered down beside him, much closer this time, and spread out a pile of leaves and roasted roots. Gar admired that she seemed quite selective in her foraging, bringing in only the tastiest things. Lazy women, and Gar knew several, tended to scoop up the first edible things that they happened to wander past.

She grunted. "I lived with Hairies so long, now I'm used to feeding a man. It's their way. Here; eat to become strong again." She handed him a bison horn of fresh water.

He stood up only long enough to dance his thanks and sat down to what was a fairly lavish feast, considering that she had received no portion of the rhino. Dreadfully thirsty, he drained the horn instantly and gave it back to her.

His hands aching, Gar peeled back a roasted cattail stalk. Flavourful, but not much pith in it. Wrong season. "What was the colour in Kelp's fingernails?"

"Magic."

The same answer Saiga had given, and it was not the least bit helpful. "Tell me about this magic."

"All I know is, it's Hairy magic. It makes them powerful, eh." Seated so near him, she smelled strongly of mint and woman-ness. A warm smell, and close, and sweet. "And it makes them good hunters."

"They're bad hunters!"

She shrugged in that way of hers. Obviously she didn't agree with him.

Gar thought about this a moment. "You were young when the Hairies stole you. Maybe you weren't yet taught all the ways of Real People. Maybe you never learned the lessons Real children learn. Then Kelp, he probably thought you already knew these things because every adult knows."

"Know what?"

She had mixed duckweed with chopped, tender flower heads of some sort. Very good. Gar paused a moment, chewing as he sorted out how he would explain this. "About hunting and bravery. What makes Real People alive. What brings glory. A child has no glory because a child is not brave."

Mouse bristled instantly. "Hare is brave!"

"More than most, yes. Most children are cowardly. Some never find bravery. They stay children forever. Most, though, they find bravery by hunting and following shamans' rituals. Mostly by hunting. It is why we hunt."

"You hunt for meat."

"Hairies do. Not Real People."

"Hoo."

"Many the time I watched Hairies go by, returning from a hunt, carrying game. Grown men, but they'll kill anything. Rabbits. Ibex. When they go after aurochs, they take the calf and the cow, whatever jumps in front of the spear first. They don't even bother the bull. Horse colts. They kill young horses."

"Tasty and tender, the young animals. Better than tough old bulls."

"But no glory. Ibex? Hmph! We send children to kill ibex. Boys of twelve winters can take a calf. Girls set snares and pitfalls. That's not for Real Men, not any of that. No glory there. Real People, we take only the toughest bulls. Only stallions with harems. We kill the biggest mammoth in the herd. There is the glory."

Gar watched her face for a reaction and saw none. He went on. "I see Hairies throw spears at animals. They corner a bull, then when they're still two, three man-lengths away, they just throw the spear. No glory there. You must move in close, thrust the spear with both hands, feel the bull's breath. There is the glory. Glory is everything. Everything."

"Not many Hairy hunters are hurt or killed. Lots of Real People are hurt, all the time."

"Eh!" Gar reached for a strangely formed root, soft from roasting. Maybe she was getting the idea about what constitutes glory.

Here was a question Gar had asked Rat once. Rat said he didn't know. Maybe she, having lived intimately with Hairies, might. "Why do the Hairies wrap skins around their waists in summer as well as winter? All the time? You know?"

"I know." She spent a while studying the floor. "It's hard to explain. You know what *private* is. Inside you, for you only, you don't let anyone else hear, see, or know what it is."

"Like thoughts."

"Eh! You imagine. Dream. Remember. No one else knows what is going on inside you. It is a world only for you. That's 'private.' They feel that way about men's and women's parts. They don't want anyone to see the parts they cover up. They call it 'modest.'"

"Cover them up all year." Weird.

"All the time my man would say, 'You must be modest. No more running about like some savage.' I had to wear those skirts too."

"Skirts. Skins."

She nodded. "Women's breasts, they are private. But a man's penis, a woman's cove, they are *most* private."

Private parts. *Most* private parts. The phrase charmed him in its odd way, struck his fancy as might some innocent comment from a child, and he knew not why. He shook his head. "But everybody knows what everybody else has. Half of them have one just like it. They called that a secret?"

She continued. "And yet, they talk about union and man-and-woman parts all the time. They hide the parts, then tell stories about them. Sometimes the stories are funny, they say. I don't understand the stories. It's..."

"Funny?"

"When you laugh at them." She wagged her head and met him eye to eye. "It's like, you can hear about the parts and laugh about them, but you must not look at them or see them."

Unimaginably weird.

Slipping and scrambling, the ill-born Hare came struggling up the steep slope to the cave. He half-dragged, half-carried a good-sized beaver. Where would he get a beaver? Gar saw no blood on the fur. Luxurious fur, even when wet. And now that Gar noticed, Hare's odd head hair was as soaking wet as the beaver.

Hare's sneaky little eyes darted all around and spied his mother almost instantly. Here he came, proud as any glorified hunter, dragging his prize.

From who knew where at the back of the cave appeared Gar's cousin's second boy, the nine-winters-old with the front tooth missing. Dor, his child-name was. Dor's brother, a winter younger, limped along right behind him on legs of differing sizes. The brother probably never would walk well. Born that way. Shame.

Four man-lengths away from Gar, Dor intercepted Hare and stopped him. "Ugly boy, what you got? Give me it."

Scowling, Hare tried to duck aside. Dor, bigger if not taller, grabbed the beaver. Hare took a swing at him; Dor swatted Hare.

Gar reached them before they could get into it any deeper. He grabbed Dor by the armpit and yanked him away.

Dor tried to jerk free. "He's ugly!"

"Eh!" Gar lowered his voice. "Ugly. That's what Hairies call Real People. You know we're better than Hairies. We have glory. So you don't call Real People ugly, not even half-Real-People. If you want a beaver, go catch a beaver." He turned Dor loose.

The lad was not the brightest of children, but even he knew better than to big-mouth a shaman. Still scowling at Hare, he backed away.

To Gar's surprise, Hare was scowling also—at Gar. The lad snarled, "I don't need you to help me keep my beaver." And he jogged off to his mother.

Oh, really. If you knew how much my hands ached when I pulled Dor off you... But Gar's pique faded quickly. In fact, the more he used his hands, the more the swelling and discomfort seemed to ease.

Mouse and Hare retreated toward the rear of the cave, as did everyone else, for clumsy, splattering drops of rain heralded the storm to come. Gesticulating wildly and apparently at random, Hare related some sort of adventure to his mother, no doubt the episode with the beaver.

Lightning racked closer, its thunder following quickly. Women scurried to lay out the big, round, willow frames. Although rain or snow fell predictably in winter, a rare summer rain like this was an opportunity to be seized immediately. Over the frames they threw stiff rhino hides. The hides fit just so within the knee-high circular frames, for they had been sun-dried in them. They formed great, concave water-catchers and not a moment too soon. Here came the pelting rain.

Swirling gusts flung rain in under the overhang. A few moments later, water dripped from the outside edge of the ceiling lip. The drips became a torrent cascading off the scarp above them, a dancing, shimmery sheet between here and night time.

Gleefully, the women moved further back under the overhang and watched their water supply grow. For a few days, at least, they would not have to haul water from the creek. By the time the raw hides softened and sagged and turned too smelly, the water would be used.

BANG! and every Person in the cave jumped as brilliant white light washed briefly across the world. The thunder answered instantly from directly overhead. The cave echoed.

Mouse cringed in close to Gar. Very, very close.

What's wrong? You clubbed or something? Heart jeered. And even Head seemed encouraging. *You're certainly not forcing yourself on her, you know.*

Gar reached out and wrapped an arm around her shoulders, drawing her in tightly against him. She pressed against him with an arm around his waist, warm and firm. They watched the driving rain in silence a few moments.

"Hare chased the beaver through the water into its

lodge. He found the lodge entrance and plugged it. Then he tore the lodge apart and killed the beaver." Mouse twisted her head around enough to be able to see Gar's face. "That's glory."

"For a lad, it is. Very. He chased it through the water? You mean swimming?"

She nodded. "Maybe more like followed it instead of chased it. Hare swims like a beaver. On top of the water, down inside the water. Either. Both. He learned to swim when he was very little. All Hairies do. I suppose, that's why we call them Water People."

And it was Gar's turn to say, "Hoo."

6

He Was Such a Fool

Her beautiful tan shaman didn't seem able to sense *her* presence, so *she* felt safe about creeping in closer this time. As dusk deepened and the children returned for the night, *she* climbed a tree very near the south end of the vast cave's overhang. *She* did not fear that adults might notice *her*. They never did. But children see everywhere and they forage widely, so *she* always took great care whilst in the vicinity of an occupied cave.

There he was. He sat out on the edge of the cave floor, eyes closed, legs crossed, unmoving. What patience. A three-day fast as performed by a shaman was so taxing. To sit still, to wait and wait, and all the while to be so hungry. *She* wished he knew of *her* presence, that *she* could bring him a bird or tree rat. They would burn off the feathers or hair in the men's fire and roast it as they talked. Then he would break fast with *her* gift. *Her* gift!

Not yet. Not yet. *She* had moved much too quickly with Kelp, not thinking things through. *She* must be more circumspect this time. *She* didn't want to lose this one, the way *she* kept losing men because of simple mistakes. But then, now that *she* reflected back on the others, they were not nearly so fine as this one. Definitely, this was the man destined for *her.* Gentle. *She* wanted a gentle one.

She sensed a storm coming in behind *her.* Ah well; *she'*d been wet before.

Here came that orange woman. Didn't she know better than to disrupt a fast? Stupid woman! And yet, look how patiently the shaman dismissed her flagrant breach of common sense. He half appeared to be inviting her.

They talked together for a short time. The woman leapt up and ran off. Good.

No, wait. Here she came back. He was going to break his fast with food which that orange woman, and not *she herself*, brought him. Oh, the sting of that cruel twist of fate! It wasn't even meat. *She* saw no meat at all in what the woman was giving him.

And yet, look how mildly he accepted her inadequate offering. He even proffered an elegant thank you. He was a remarkably graceful dancer. Either the orange woman had placed him under a spell or he was being very, very nice to her so that he could have her later.

Something was going on here, something his clansmen were failing to notice. *She* noticed it, of course. With *her* animal cunning *she* missed nothing. First he arranged something with the dark woman. Now he was arranging something with the orange one. It couldn't be mere sexual interest. There had to be something more. He must want something from them—something other than the obvious.

The thought of that burned *her*! It destroyed *her* happiness at a stroke and ignited *her* anger. He shouldn't encourage the orange woman, or the dark one either, for that matter. That was Kelp's downfall—at least, part of it.

That ugly child brought in a dark animal. Otter? Much too big. Beaver. A good look at the tail confirmed it. The shaman interceded for the child. Interesting. So he possessed a good heart in addition to patience. Well, *she* was pretty much coming to expect that sort of thing of him. He was too near perfection in other ways to lack the cardinal quality of caring.

Without warning, lightning struck quite nearby. It startled *her* so badly that *she* nearly fell out of this tree. *Her* whole body tingled. Nearby indeed. Everyone in the cave was moving farther in under the overhang. As they stepped back away from the light of the fire, the shaman and the orange woman became less distinct. Now they paused, so far back they were little more than shapes. *She* could tell they were close together. Much too close to suit *her*.

He drew the hateful woman in against him. They stood pressed so close together, they appeared as one.

Rain pelted the leafy canopy above *her*, drowning out most sound. Lightning streaked. Thunder rolled loudly enough and often enough to frighten *her*. The soaked leaves above, which initially protected *her* from the rain, now began shedding their water. Great, cold blobs dripped upon *her*. They splatted. *She* began to shiver.

Oh, for the solid, unyielding protection of that dry

cavern! Oh, for the shaman's strong arm around *her* own shoulders! Where were the shaman and the orange woman? *She'd* lost view of them.

How *she* hated that woman!

And *she* hated the shaman too, for letting himself be taken in by that orange harridan.

Men.

Fools all.

7

She Says She Didn't Do It

The cloud bank stretching straight across the eastern horizon was thick enough that the dawn sun could not break through. Gar had not left Larch Cave particularly early, but he had nearly reached Alder Cave by the time the sun managed to crawl up and peek over the top. Those clouds, and the slippery wetness beneath Gar's feet, were all that remained of last night's storm.

Ah, the golden clarity of this first daylight! Gar loved its newness, its freshness. He climbed the final path up a scree slope to the trail into his other moiety's cave.

A dark woman approaching him scowled at him as if he had just rubbed nettles on her bottom. Now what was going on?

He nodded to her as he stepped aside off the path, a clear invitation to stop and talk. "Crow."

Fulfilling her name, her skin was quite dark. Not a

lustrous, rich dark like Kohl's. Not the glossy black of an actual crow. Just dark. In a vivid snit of some sort, she brushed past him roughly and jogged away down the slope.

He stood a moment on Alder Cave's lip, thinking about the woman and about all he felt and saw here. He could detect nothing to explain Crow's animosity. But then, rarely could he find an explanation for women's moods and actions. He had long since grown accustomed to their inscrutability and learned to live with it. Besides, Gar had known her her whole life, and Crow had always been volatile that way.

He climbed up onto the gently sloping cave floor. Off toward the back in semi-darkness bobbed a thatch of white hair. Gar headed that way.

Here near the back of the high, gaping cavern, giant chunks of the ceiling had fallen, who knows when. A generation ago at least, Dawn moiety Mammoth People had hauled the fallen rock over to the north side of the entrance and stacked it as a windbreak against winter storms. With the ceiling heightened by sloughing and the fallen rock removed, this concavity formed an elegant sort of alcove. During winter it was the best, roomiest, most protected place in the cave. Now in summer, though, it was just another close, dark hole.

Gar hunkered down across from Newt and Cloud and laid his spear aside.

Because of his crippled leg, the ancient Cloud could no longer hunker. He sat with both legs stretched out straight before him. Gar performed the deference due an old man and nodded to Newt. Newt nodded back. He looked grim.

Gar glanced at Cloud. "Story."

"Nothing."

"Insight."

"None. The spirits are silent. I did not eat last night at nightfall. I kept the fast until this morning. Still, nothing."

Fie on you, Gar, chided Heart. *You even quit a little early last night. Cloud suffers on, while you break fast with good food. Tsk, tsk.*

Head reminded him, *However, for all his added effort, Cloud received no greater insight than did you.*

"As I was coming in here, I met Crow." Gar changed the subject. He looked at Newt. "Are you feeding her still?"

Newt bobbed that white head. Did he look guilty? "Eh. I gave her some rhino. She got an honour piece."

Then Cloud added, "So did Kohl," and the mystery instantly evaporated.

So Newt was taking on two women, Crow to whom he had been pledged for five or six years and now Kohl as well. No wonder Crow was stomping around in such a snit. The woman was fat enough. Newt kept her well, at least most of the year. Why did women so constantly think they had to be the only one?

"Maybe, we should try a longer fast." Cloud shifted his bent leg. "If the spirits still remain silent, we send a messenger to the Seashore People. Tell them the secret must stay a secret."

Gar shook his head. "If I read Saiga and Eel correctly, they won't hear that. They are determined, and Saiga is powerful."

"Kohl says, so is Eel." Newt sat back and stretched his own legs out. "We don't need the spirits to know who killed Kelp. We just send Mouse to the Seashore

People. There's the end of it."

Heart went thump. *I told you he was going to say that!*

Head urged, *Better start talking.*

This was going to be difficult. Gar sighed. "But maybe it's not Mouse. Maybe Hare—"

"A child."

"Who kills. He brings his mother meat. He's a good provider. And he swims like a beaver."

"But weak for his size. Scrawny. Not robust like Real Children. A child that puny killing a powerful man, a shaman? No."

"It could be Kohl."

"No!"

So Newt was already all wrapped up in her. Gar couldn't blame him. Once upon a time, so was he himself. Heart intruded, *What is this, 'once upon a time'?* Crow faced a formidable rival.

And then Cloud gave voice to what everyone had no doubt been thinking, Gar most of all. "Kohl told Newt that Mouse wanted to go home to her People. Kelp said no. Kohl says Kelp threatened to hurt Hare if she tried to leave. Mouse feared he would. Maybe Mouse was thinking, 'If I kill Kelp, I am protecting my child.' Maybe she felt there was no other thing to do. You saw her there with blood on her hands. And the weapon."

Gar nodded. "She smelled blood and came looking. She found Kelp so. The tools were lying there. She picked up the tools, maybe to keep them, maybe to trade them for food, while she and Hare were travelling home."

"How do you know?" Newt eyed him suspiciously.

"I asked her."

After the storm last night.

After their union. Good union.

Newt grunted. "When Eel and Saiga caught you, the first thing they asked was, 'Cold Lakes?' That's Mouse's tribe. Even they suspect her."

Gar shrugged with exaggerated casualness. "Maybe they weren't asking about Mouse at all. Maybe they were asking which territory. They were never up here before and didn't know where they were."

Cloud stared at his toes awhile. "I say, wait. What if it's Hare and Mouse both, together? Or Hare to protect his mother, and then Mouse came along and snatched the weapon away? If Mouse truly is innocent and we give her over, it could be ruin for us. Our spirits don't speak now, but they know. This may be a test. We must be sure. We have some time."

"I'm sure," Newt rumbled.

He would be.

They spent most of the rest of the day exploring the matter, not the least of it the uncooperative nature of the spirits, and found no enlightenment. Speculation. All speculation. Gar, wearied of it all, took his leave. As Newt and Cloud discussed sending the boys out tomorrow for ibex, Gar picked up his spear, wandered to the cave entrance, and headed down the steep path toward home. He noted as he left that Crow, feeding Newt's four-year-old, sulked as ever beneath her dark cloud.

He almost wished he had never undergone the rigorous training of a shaman, the years of memorising lineages, stories and epics, songs and rituals. He wished he were a plain, ordinary hunter, out for an occasional bit of glory. He would come back to whatever cave the clan was using, contribute to the feast, give some meat to a woman, accept her full-time favours, and perhaps even be named a father by and by. No responsibility to summon spirits who do not wish to be summoned. No responsibility to spare a good woman or send her to her death.

On impulse he climbed the steep slope to the ridge crest. He would take the high trail back. It was longer by twice, but this late in the day, it ought to offer some lovely views to savour. Crowded little clumps of firs studded the rocky slopes, sharing the golden late-afternoon sun with scraggly, open brush. In an embayment in the cliff face near Alder Cave, a grove of oaks glowed dark green.

Gar was going to have to pick his three neophytes soon, too. He must not put that off any longer. Frankly, in his Dusk moiety he didn't see three good candidates to succeed him. Dor? Not bright. Dor memorised approximately, delivering the general sense of a story without all the necessary details. The stories and lineages must be memorised exactly. Dor's younger brother? Maybe. A cripple can be a shaman. Look at Cloud. But Cloud earned his handicap seeking glory. Dor's brother was born with his. That made a difference.

Actually, his best prospect was a girl, Sturgeon's firstborn. Sturgeon had died before the child could walk, but she possessed his gift for storytelling. Maybe...

Again Gar developed the distinct feeling he was being watched. Heart? Any comment? Head? Now, when he could use a little insight, they remained silent. The spirits of the hillside, though, whispered to him about eyes following him.

He dropped suddenly to a squat and watched below and behind. Time passed. The sun drifted lower; if he didn't start again soon, he'd finish the walk home in darkness. No movement, no sound, no elaboration of that strange feeling. He stood up and continued on.

Look who's coming! Heart crowed.

Of all the people Gar might meet along this ridge trail, here came Kohl. She broke into a bounteous smile. "Gar." She carried a wolverine skin nearly filled with berries.

"Kohl. That's a lot of berries." Gar nodded toward her skin bag.

"Come." She gestured uphill and led the way to a dark clump of firs beyond some boulders. The women, of course, being the primary foragers, knew every plant and stone in clan territory—so did the men, for all that—but Kohl had been gone so many years. Did she still remember all, or was she learning anew? And what did she know about, that she was leading Gar off around the hill?

Was it she who had been watching? No. The feeling persisted even though she was now ahead of him.

Well up behind the trail, she settled herself to sitting on soft fir duff, her back snugged against a sapling tree, and undid the thong tying the neck of her bag shut. "Not all berries. Some grapes in the bottom."

As she pawed through her bag, Gar flopped down beside her, leaned back against the cold bark of a larger fir and laid his spear aside. "Grapes are berries."

She stared off at the horizon as she groped around in the skin, her arm swallowed by wolverine fur nearly to her elbow. The flaccid paws on the skin flopped about grotesquely. She came up with a glob of half grapes, half berries and handed them to him.

"What is this? Women defy tradition to feed a man." He studied them but a moment and popped some in his mouth.

"You look hungry. Cloud fasted three days. You did too, eh?"

"Eh."

"Learn anything?"

He shook his head. "I heard Newt is feeding you. Are you two going to pledge?"

"Maybe. Every hunt, he earns great glory. He can feed two women. Or maybe he won't feed Crow anymore. We didn't talk about it much."

"Mm. I wondered why you aren't living with us at Larch Cave, with your own moiety. I think I see why you stay up at Alder Cave instead of Larch Cave. Newt's idea, eh? To be with him."

No fool, Newt. Heart.

"Eh. That Mouse, that one is bad! She hates me. Newt thinks we should stay separate, Mouse and me. With her there and me here, it's easier to keep peace. That's his reason, he says."

Gar pondered the many things he might say next, and all the things she might reply, and decided on trickery. "Kohl. Why did you kill Kelp?"

She gasped and stared. "The spirits told you *that*?"

He shrugged. "Why?"

"Jealousy! Mouse! She did it! She was terribly jealous."

"She says she didn't."

"I didn't either. Here." She extended the skin, holding the neck open.

He scooped out another handful.

"You and I, we used sex for fun. You remember those times?" She ate some herself, though undoubtedly she had eaten her fill while picking them, and pawed through the bag for more.

Do I ever. Heart, naturally.

Sex? Now why, demanded Head, *should she bring up this subject out of nowhere?*

She dug out some more grapes, stuck a few in her mouth and popped the rest in his. "Mouse doesn't use sex for fun. She uses it to hold a man. To make him do what she wants."

"Women do that all the time."

"But we didn't, you and I. Fun. That was all. Mouse, she's always so serious. Maybe all those years with Hairies ruined her. She has started to think like them, but she's not one of them, so she gets all mixed up. I feel sorry for her."

"And Hare."

Kohl rolled her eyes. "Hare!"

"By the fire that night, you said you pledged to Kelp. Did Mouse pledge to Kelp?"

"Mouse. All her conniving came to no good. She spends a few years with a Hairy shaman, and pretty soon she thinks she's worthy to mate to shamans from Real People. She thinks, 'If I give him sex, that's a big thing.'" Kohl spat. "It's nothing."

"Did she pledge?"

Kohl shrugged. "Kelp would feed her now and then. But he fed me mostly. He would give me—not her—the honour pieces, and there were plenty of them." She set her bag aside, propping it so it wouldn't spill, and twisted toward Gar. "But you and I. We have a bond stronger than a pledge. It goes far back, even longer than a pledge, eh. I didn't think about it until I was gone. Then when I didn't have you, I missed you so much. Our bond was very special, eh."

"Eh."

"Remember, I used to do this?" She ran her fingertips down his body, and he shivered. "And you say, 'No, this way.'" She altered her touch. "Now I always do it that way."

"Good. Glad you learned something."

Don't just sit there, dull fellow. Heart was too eager sometimes for his own good.

Stop! Once upon a time, this was your woman. But that was long ago. Now she may soon be your warlord's.

Snarled Heart, *Shut up, Head.*

She smiled innocently. "And you learned my teaching too, eh?" He was too slow to respond, for she added, "Show me."

As his fingers touched her soft, soft skin, the fat so firm beneath it, years melted away. They were young again, he and she, exploring again, except that the exploration had been completed long ago. This was the reaping. She snuggled in against him with a sigh. Hers was not the positioning of an experienced woman. This was the way they used to sit in the sunset hours of their childhood, playing together when all was new and thrilling.

The old times were back—come to think of it, just about all of them. In their youth he had to share her with Newt because Newt was already being groomed as the next warlord and thought he owned the world. Gar had heard rumours that she was also consorting with Toad then, and possibly even Sturgeon. He never gave them credence. Since then he'd known other women, but Kohl...

He closed his eyes, not the wisest thing to do at this time of day in carnivore country, and let the gentle pleasure flow through him. Their very first union all those yesterdays ago, right after he killed the bear, had been so ludicrously clumsy in its execution. They decided they both needed practice, and... He could have entered such an arrangement with anyone. But Kohl...

Compared to Kohl, Mouse was so artless. In a strange way, her naivete added immensely to her charm. But Kohl...

She bolted upright suddenly and shifted positions. Good old Kohl. She remembered! This new arrangement had been their favourite back in the old days of their youth. *Why, oh why, Kohl, did you go away?* The distant yesterdays burned bright, multiplying the pleasure. He could not see or hear for the rushing joy.

How excellent was Kohl's technique.

But Mouse...

8

He Trades People

Gar despised travel, though he savoured changes of scenery. He hated walking, though he enjoyed talking to new people. He disliked the half-mile hike from his Dusk moiety's Larch Cave to Dawn's Alder Cave, but he liked visiting his aunts and uncles well enough. As his Head and his Heart so often bickered, at odds, his body and spirit did also.

His feet hurt. His heart ached even worse. In these last four days, wretched, unrelenting travel had carried him north across half a dozen drainages, three significant hills, and a host of small ones. He had no idea where he was going; he was not quite sure how to get back. As he walked farther and farther from the ancestral Mother Earth that had sprung him forth and from the spirits of that place, his resolve faded, weaker and weaker. A fool notion this, ill-thought-out and ill-executed.

He was hungry. Outrageously so. The edible berries were about done for the year and the nuts were still green. He was moving too fast to dig for roots, and anyway, he wasn't carrying fire with which to roast them. Few caterpillars remained this late in the summer, and although sometimes there was a good locust year, this was not one of them.

His legs and feet were tired. So very tired.

Four hideous days.

"I don't think the women are telling us everything," Newt had opined back in the comfort of Alder Cave, referring no doubt to Kohl and Mouse. "They may not realise they know things we need to know." Cloud and Gar had agreed. Kohl and Mouse were holding back information, whether deliberately or not. But what was everything to be told, and did it signify?

"Find Rat," Newt had said, swaddled in his magnificent ease. "He is the link. He is the key. He can tell us many things. Maybe he can even name the murderer."

If Newt wanted to find Rat so badly, he should have sent a hunting group, not a lone shaman. He opined that Cloud and Gar in their fasts had failed to produce a solid word from the spirits of earth and sky, and obviously this was a shaman's next step. Since Cloud was too crippled, it therefore befell Gar to bring Rat back.

Gar sighed. With each breath he took, he nearly inhaled tiny flies that hovered heartlessly around his face.

Hairies made journeys like this routinely. Somehow they had managed to disincorporate themselves from the land that nurtured them—wherever that was. They simply walked away from it. Unthinkable. In spring they trekked north, crossing territory that nurtured Real People, killing game along the way—and occasionally a Person. Rarely did you see Hairies in midsummer. In autumn, here they came through again on their way south, laden with raw reindeer hides and fresh antlers, some still in velvet. A month later, as if holding back to avoid them, the reindeer would come in behind them. And then the Real People ate reindeer as well—without having to travel.

Rivers posed no challenge to the Hairies. They tossed their meat and hides and babies onto a couple logs lashed together and floated them across. Children, men, and women waded or swam without qualm. Unthinkable. They camped on the shores of lakes and let their children frolic in the icy waters. No wonder they were called Water People. Crazy People would be more like it.

And Rat was craziest of all, for although he was Real, he travelled like a Hairy. He walked from territory to territory, from sea to tundra, all year long. And boasted of his travel.

"Try it," he told Real People. "Don't sit in your cave while starvation stalks you and winter blasts you. Travel to where the game is. Travel to the south, to the warmth. You people die of hunger in the lean times. Roam abroad! If the game will not come to you, go to the game! That's what Hairies do."

As if Hairies were a meritorious people to emulate.

Unthinkable.

That was another thing about Rat. He reached no end of words. If there was a spoken word for a thing or concept, he knew it. He could probably talk with his hands tied behind him. In a big way, Gar hoped he would not find the verbose trader. He hated having to contend with the constant torrent of words.

The gentle country rolled away before him in all directions, treeless but for a few straggling braids of willow thickets that laced themselves across vast stretches of otherwise unbroken grass and bog. Here and there, when the sun was right, meandering streams and shallow ponds glowed brilliant gold in the creases and low spots. Much as he liked wooded tracts with their richness, Gar had to admit to himself that there was a haunting, desolate beauty to this land.

He had seen wolf spoor aplenty in the last day. No hyæna. No lion. Very little bear. A region virtually bereft of large carnivores can't be all bad.

He paused on the crest of a low swell and leaned on his spear. How his legs ached. He simply wasn't made for this nonsense. A million mosquitoes plague the feckless Newt, who ought to be out doing this himself.

Speaking of mosquitoes, surprisingly few lingered here now, but the minuscule biting blackflies of summer swarmed around Gar. He itched all over.

Perhaps three miles to the northeast, a thin curl of smoke announced human presence, the first Gar had found so far. No doubt it would be Hairies. Real People did not live out in the open plains. Hairies lived out in the open at times, Rat claimed. Up north here, there were no caves at all that Gar could see, nor even the kind of outcrop hills which provide the simplest of overhangs. Where would one live if one had no cave? Unthinkable. If the Mother Earth did not enclose a person, that one's own spirit could float much too free, possibly never to return.

He drove himself forward, down the slope, across a nearly level greensward, around a bog, across more sward. He must read the land carefully now, and pay attention to the possible presence of hunters. Real People who walk alone into a Hairy camp don't live very long, as a rule. He would have to encounter one or two who were off by themselves. Best would be to find a child. Children knew as much about the whereabouts of Rat as adults would. At the very least, they made good hostages.

He walked a mile or so, seeing and hearing only birds, smelling nothing. He noticed traces of small bog animals, as to be expected. Here were fox droppings. From the hair in them, he figured the fox ate hand-sized creatures for the most part, or smaller ones. The wolves, he noticed, were eating reindeer.

Like the Hairies.

Using the waft of smoke as the marker, he stepped down into a soggy ditch and waded through the slop, keeping himself within cover of scraggly little willows.

And now he smelled people. Real People.

Out on the open bog, a woman bent over, prodding and digging. To Gar's surprise, she was clad in the furs of winter. More specifically, the covering of spring and fall, for the skins were turned fur-outward. Reindeer hide wrapped around her legs, secured by closely wound thongs. A horsehide covered her torso similarly, and her cape was reindeer. Why would a woman wear a cape in summer when it hardly ever rains? Why furs in this warmest season?

He worked around to her side, downwind, undetected. When he stepped out into the open to greet her, less than ten man-lengths separated them.

He gestured *friend* and repeated it for emphasis as he declared tribe and clan.

She stood motionless a few moments, glancing all around, as if expecting the rest of the party to appear. "Tribe of Dark Mountains, Wolverine Clan, Dawn moiety."

"Eh. I am seeking Rat." He combined gesture and

words. Did these Dark Mountains people use the common language in the same way most did? He'd never met one before.

"Rat does not bother with us." Common language. "We do not trade enough."

"Is your shaman nearby?"

She looked at the gatherings in her hare skin bag. Apparently she decided *enough.* She turned and walked away.

Was he to follow? He did so.

Despite the winter garb, she went barefoot. Gar would give these People the benefit of the doubt and assume they knew what they were doing with their erratic costume. But through the eyes of an outsider, they appeared as crazy as Rat.

They slipped and squooshed across soggy ground, he and she, splashing in frigid water. The land finally rose enough that grass replaced bog, and Gar could get something like a decent gait going. Here and there across the casual slope, a few women and children stood up in the tall grass to look at him. They too wore furs. From the number of them, he guessed that this moiety, perhaps even the whole clan, probably contained no more than twenty.

Surely this was merely a temporary hunting camp he was entering. Much as he disliked deep, narrow caverns where sky light never reaches, Gar would much prefer that to this. These people lived, essentially, like horses or reindeer. Even hyænas and foxes dug dens. The only dwelling here consisted of a few reindeer hides thrown over branches, antlers—anything to raise the skins high enough off the ground to creep beneath. Did all twenty crowd down into it each night?

Their fire languished unprotected, out in the open. No men's fire and separate children's fire. A single fire, and that not robust. They were burning willow and dried scat. Gar could just imagine the flavour of a haunch roasted over this pitiful thing.

Four men sat about here and there. They made no move to greet Gar, offered no welcoming dance.

The woman said simply, "Buttercup," and flopped to sitting beside two other women.

Buttercup?

A man with a bent left arm stood up. His shoebark pouch said *shaman*. He was younger than Gar, but he couldn't walk as well as Cloud could. His welcoming dance parodied the efforts of even the graceless Toad.

Despite that he was no doubt the senior, Gar performed a dance of obeisance and respect much as he would for Cloud, leaving out a few parts. He ended by gesturing *friend* and got a halfhearted *friend* in reply. Slowly, carefully, meticulously, Buttercup arranged his body to sitting again on a horsehide.

Gar saw not one bear hide or skull in the whole place. Not one. Unthinkable.

Although this shaman did not invite him, he sat down awhile to the man's left, encouraging silence, as was polite. Biting blackflies swarmed around him relentlessly and he now perceived the wisdom of wearing furs in summer. To his extreme discomfort, the little terrors seemed to find his most private parts particularly tender.

Where should he take this?

Buttercup made no attempt at conversation. Certainly no invitation.

So Gar began. "I must find Rat."

"Rat." The shaman spat. "Don't like Rat."

No news there. Who did? Gar waited.

The dyspeptic shaman grumbled, scowling. "Rat is like a leech between your toes—no good use, and no glory."

"Eh."

"He's a coward, won't hunt. He's lazy, won't forage. Besides, that's woman's work, he says. Lazy coward. Useless. Leech."

"Not always lazy. It's a lot of work, to travel so much. He goes down to the sea and clear up to here, every year. Follows the warmth north in spring and the geese south in fall. Trades salt with Real People, mint with Hairies. I think mint. Maybe. He is here now, eh."

Buttercup signed *no* and *fool* in quick succession.

Rat was many things, unreliable not the least of them, but fool? No. "Why fool?"

"He trades slaves."

"What are slaves?" It was a spoken word not in Gar's memory.

"People. Real People mostly."

"He trades People? How?"

"He seizes a Real Person and goes to the Hairies. He says, 'Look! Good worker, good forager. You give me some stiff hides, maybe flint and salt, and I'll give you this Person.' Then he catches a Hairy, says to Real People, 'You give me chewed hides, mint, crowberries, and I will give you this Water Person. Good with his hands, this one. A good stoneworker, makes fine spears.' Sometimes, even, Rat trades Real People to Real People. Fool!"

"Eh." Unthinkable. "Where is he now?"

"South. He found a couple slaves and took them

south."

Gar's bones chilled. He had journeyed so far, was tormented by these clouds of blackflies, and for what? "Rat doesn't usually go south this early. Usually he is here now. That's why I came."

"He stopped by here. He wanted us to feed him. Him and his slaves. He said he knew a Person in the south who would want the slaves. But that was a long time ago, then. Before good summer."

"Eh."

Gar never would have had to come, had only he known that Rat had abandoned his habitual routes. The only value of this journey, and a pitifully tiny one it was, was that he had somehow shaken that sense of being watched. It relieved him.

He tried out his new word. "Did Rat have Real People slaves with him, or Hairies?"

Buttercup shifted on his horsehide. "Real People. One, a red woman. Orange. Good woman. The other, though. Why not make him a slave? Feeble, that one. Scrawny. And ugly. Horribly ugly."

Gar's heart quailed. "Stripling. Maybe nine, ten winters."

"You know that one." Buttercup nodded again slowly. "That one, only a mother could love."

······9·············

He Up and Disappeared

A wild panic gripped *her* and *she* could not quell it. Where was he, that beautiful tan shaman? *Where was he?*

He simply disappeared. *She* could not understand how he could do it, or why he should want to. When *she* followed him that day in which he travelled to the other moiety's cave and then returned, he was easy for *her* to follow. Nothing out of the ordinary. On the way home he met that horrid dark woman—obviously an arranged meeting, the woman lying in wait for him—and joined with her. In a hideous way, that was normal. Men seemed to think the dark blob was special. And now suddenly he was gone.

He and that dark woman were working in collusion somehow. That much was obvious, the way they kept meeting. Maybe he and the orange woman were also. How else to account for the observations *she* had made over these last several days?

Although the two women acted like enemies, perhaps that was a ruse of some sort. Maybe all three of them together had some sort of plan going. What kind of plan? Certainly powerful magic was involved, though *she* could not begin to guess. But there was the evidence right there.

And now suddenly, he had disappeared. Gone. Not in his cave, not at the other one. No one seemed to question his absence. No one seemed upset. And yet, Real People don't travel, except that Rat. They stay where they belong. *She* desperately wanted to find *her* shaman.

For two days *she* hid in trees near either one cave or the other. *She* watched these People as they went about their business, coming and going, laughing and squabbling. *She* studied the two women carefully, the orange one and the dark one both, and could see nothing unusual in their behaviour. *She* curled up in thickets and brush to listen to the chatter of foraging women as they passed, and *she* could hear nothing about the shaman. Surely if his absence were unexpected, there would be some sort of gossip. Maybe, if it were a hot topic, they had finished exchanging all the pertinent gossip before they got this far out into the field. No. Women never finish with really good gossip.

She must find him. *She* must observe him and decide how to make *her* approach. But how could *she* learn his whereabouts without letting this clan know a stranger prowled in their midst?

And then the Big Idea came to *her*. It tickled *her*. It charmed *her* with its effrontery. As People go, *she* was on the pallid side anyway. And thin. In fact, Kelp had called *her* gaunt. The plan should work just fine.

As soon as *she* could safely assume that the women and children had headed home, *she* hurried down to that stream the beavers had dammed. On the southwest side of the beaver pond lay a partially submerged grey clay bank. *She* went there.

Carefully *she* smeared *herself* all over with the whitish clay. *She* even remembered to coat the insides of *her* ears. *She* scooped another few handfuls into *her* ditty for touch-up on the morrow and went to sleep in a beech.

Next morning before first light, *she* skittered down to the ground, nimble as a civet. *She* re-coated the scuffs and dark places, picked a likely path on the pond's north shore—probably an elk track—hunkered down behind a dense bush, and waited.

By and by *she* heard footfalls approaching. A woman passed by. Another.

And now, here came odd footsteps, two persons, lightweight and rapid, and one of them shuffling. No doubt this would be the lad the foraging Mammoth women called Dor. *She* knew his name because *she* had heard it called days ago. His little brother, the one with a short leg, usually accompanied him rather than their mother. Apparently, the small one foraged with him today.

This couldn't be better! Lads were so much easier to fool than were little girls. *She* waited. And waited.

Slowly, slowly *she* rose up from behind *her* cover, *her* hands forming the *sit* gesture.

Dor it was indeed, and his brother. They froze in the track, gaping wide-eyed. The smaller child gave a muffled little yelp. They sat.

"Dor!" *She* intoned breathily, "I am the spirit of this place. Where is your shaman?" *She* stared right at Dor.

The lad's whole body vibrated. His terror delighted *her*. He urinated right there and didn't seem to notice. He stammered, "Gar—Gar—Gar went north. V-v-visiting Dark M-mountains to find Rat. B-b-back soon, back soon, eh."

The crippled lad bobbed his head.

So the tan shaman's name was Gar. *She* tried to remember what the word meant. A fish, perhaps. No matter.

"When you see Gar, you tell him to come to *me* here, to this place."

Violently nodding heads.

Her voice a harsh whisper, *she* ordered, "Tell no one. The business of spirits is no one else's but yours and mine." *She* gestured *go*.

They went, stumbling in their haste, falling over their own feet.

So easy! It was so easy! *She* nearly laughed aloud, but that of course would have spoilt the whole effect. *She* hurried back the elk track and down to the shore of the beaver pond. Beyond a clump of rushes at the north end, *she* slipped into the water and spent some time washing this miserable grey clay off. It itched. *She* ended up having to dip *her* head beneath the water to soften the film in *her* ears, and *she* hated that. Hated it!

Her own self again, *she* started north. So he was travelling north. *She* would pass quite near the cave of the other moiety but *she* must risk detection. *She'd* lost too much time already. He was so strong, he'd be hard to catch up to.

And his name was Gar. Eh. That was some fierce sort of fish—*she* was pretty certain, as *she* thought about it—known only in legend now. He was certainly gentle to be named for something so tough and dangerous.

The more *she* considered this, the gladder *she* was that he was travelling. In fact, *she* was elated. Now that he was out away from his clan, he would not question the appearance of a stranger. This was, after all, a strange land. In fact, he would rather expect *her.* That would weigh heavily on *her* behalf. And now that he was away from those two women, he would have to seek his sex elsewhere. *She* would be that elsewhere. Naturally, *she* would not mention the discharge which plagued *her* constantly.

She travelled three days due north before *she* began looking for him in earnest. Again the fates smiled upon *her,* for *she* left the hills and wooded bottomlands behind. Much of the country now consisted of open tundra and vast bogs laced with gleaming cords of water. *She* could see great distances, often in all directions at once. Sooner or later, *she'd* spot him. And he wouldn't see *her,* not until *she* was ready. *She* was looking for him; he didn't know *she* existed.

Blackflies abounded. The fourth evening, *she* clubbed a spawning salmon, but it was too near death, its flesh too mealy and soft to be palatable, especially without fire. When *she* spied a wolf following *her* along the ridge, *she* tossed the whole thing in his direction and continued on.

How would *she* approach Gar? *She* would sign *friend* first, of course. But then what? Which tribe and clan should *she* claim? Perhaps *she* ought to just make one up, and then *she* would be certain he had never heard of it and knew no one from there. That had been *her* downfall the other time; Kelp knew the clan *she* cited and saw through *her* lie.

West. *She* would claim to be from the extreme west. *She* had once heard that elk with particularly huge antlers were common out that way. *She'd* call *her* tribe Elk Plains. Now a clan. It must be a powerful animal. Wisent. Bison. That was it. *She'd* identify *herself* as Bison clan. Dusk or Dawn didn't matter. *She'd* have to say one and stick with it though.

When another day passed, *she* began to worry. What if *she* never found him? *She* was deep in Dark Mountains country now and hadn't seen any living Person at all yet. *She* might have to find a clay pan and do *her* "I am a spirit" trick on some child again—except that there was no child about.

She was perched in a stunted little alder like a crane in a nest, scanning for predators, when *she* saw him afar off. Very far off. What was he doing away over there angling south-southwest? Maybe that was not he. Maybe it was some other Person travelling.

She scrambled down from *her* ærie and hurried in his direction—rather, a direction with which *she* would close on him, eventually to intercept him if he continued as he was going. The figure was his colour, that lovely rich tan. It walked like a male. It had to be him! *She* wished he carried fire; then he'd be easy to find come nightfall. He did not, for *she* spotted him twice before dark and he was slogging resolutely onward without attempting to gather wood.

Probably, the simplest, most effective way to approach him would be sexually. There wasn't a man alive who didn't pay undue attention to women. Besides, if he'd consort with that dark one and the orange one, he'd consort with anything.

All right, so *she* wasn't fat. Fat was highly overrated.

She had survived just as many starvation moons as had the dark woman. Thin women provided their babies with milk just as rich as fat women's. Surely he wasn't so foolish as to use fat as a criterion for beauty.

She was certainly sturdier and therefore more beautiful than the orange woman. Whatever did he see in that orange one? Surely when he compared *her* to the orange one, he would forget the orange one and fall in love instantly with *her*.

Next morning *she* thought *she'd* lost him. *She* foraged as *she* went, assuming he was going to have to also. *She* didn't spot him till nearly midday, and he was still very far off. Try as *she* would, *she* could not close the distance between them. *She* knew this country. *She'd* been here before. Still, *she* couldn't catch up.

And then he entered the Seaside People's territory. This was not good. Some of the Seasides knew *her*. Perhaps *she* would have to wait until he headed back toward home. Oh no! He was aimed straight for Elephant Clan! Now *she* didn't dare catch up to him. They'd kill *her* if they found *her*. Ah well. *She'd* move in as close as *she* could and watch and wait. Every spirit in the world knew *she* was accustomed to waiting, to biding *her* time.

By nightfall they had worked down into the scarp country, with caves and overhangs aplenty. No more spending the night in a tree. *She* did not belong in trees.

As day melted into darkness *she* became a hyæna, swift and dangerous. *Her* eyes opened to see the night. *Her* muscles sang with power. *She* moved across the rough terrain at a lope, sure of stride. Like a hyæna, *she* knew what *she* wanted now.

She had chosen Gar.

10

He Took Death Well

Was the Beyond a continuation of the present circumstance, or did special delights and perhaps rewards await? If so, on what basis were rewards disbursed? Bravery? Suffering? Discomfort? Honesty? Pure chance?

If the Beyond contained unguessed-as-yet rewards, Gar had definitely earned a few. This travel was becoming a horrendous trial.

He had retraced his route south from Dark Mountains back to Reindeer Country, or so he thought. He had now travelled longer southbound than he had travelled northbound, and so far, he had seen not one familiar landmark. That terrified him. What if he never found his way back? Without the land that kept him, he would wither and die.

Even worse, if he did not return betimes, Newt would throw Mouse and Hare to the hyænas. The Seashore People would not be put off with excuses.

He should have brought Mouse with him.

Seven days now, since he left the lugubrious company of Buttercup and Dark Mountains. He was back in well-wooded forest country, crossing bear, hyæna, and lion sign frequently. So far, the few caves and overhangs he'd passed were occupied only by bears or lions.

It surprised him—perhaps even shocked him—that he hungered so powerfully for the sight and sound of another Person. How he wished he were journeying with someone, anyone, even the gimpy Buttercup. He had nearly reached the point where he would almost welcome the company of a Hairy. Or even Rat.

Nightfall soon. He angled in closer to a crumbly ridge running roughly east and west and began looking for a good place to spend the darkness. He found an unoccupied overhang, little more than a niche, half an hour past sunset. He dug it out somewhat, crept back inside against the wall, positioned his spear, and stacked rocks in front of him. Prowling carnivores would have to do a little digging to reach him, and by then he could pierce an eye or a heart.

Strictly as a precaution, he marked his own forehead with powdered blood and sang the cant for the dying for himself. He had no idea if it worked in that manner—that one could sing one's own way into the Beyond ahead of time, as it were. Well ahead of time, one would wish. He did know that if he did not see home again, he would die. Nothing lost in trying.

The cant cast a particularly melancholy mood upon him.

Mouse. Poor, star-crossed Mouse. Her story meshed neatly with Butterfly's claims when you compared them. Did she understand that Rat intended her as a slave? Did she hide that part from Gar, perhaps thinking he would not believe or understand it? Possibly. Possibly she did not understand it herself. Possession of one person by another, as one would possess a skinning blade or bear hide, was, after all, unthinkable.

So Kelp made some sort of arrangement with Rat and as a result owned her. What then was all this about family relationships among the Water People? Mouse seemed so determined to make certain Gar understood it. No hint why. Now that he analysed her story, Gar saw all sorts of unspoken parts. Things hidden.

Mouse. Her body and his in the darkness of the Larch Cave as lightning played and thunder rumbled. How he missed her.

Buttercup thought Rat travelled back south very early because he knew of someone who would want Mouse as a slave. That someone, presumably, must have been Kelp. Why? What if it wasn't? What if Rat had someone else altogether in mind and Kelp forcibly usurped her? And then, for Kelp to lose his head...

Mouse. Her lingering smell.

He awoke to the sound of distant voices. People! The first yellow streaks of sun brushed the treetops out there. Hastily he shoved rocks aside and moved out beyond the overhang. He wasn't on a hilltop, but perhaps he could make some connection.

He tilted his face upward toward stars now snuffed by morning light and raised his arms. Real People were closing on a bison, driving it to water's edge. A lake.

He was that bison. No, he wasn't. The spirits would not permit it. Maybe he was too far away, or not high enough. He tried to join the hunters, to see what they saw. The presence and person of the bison were all he could feel. He could not actually see it, could not connect with the People at all. He snatched up his spear and headed due west. The spirits weren't being very cooperative, but they did allow as how this was the direction he should go. He hurried.

The bison hadn't died yet. There was some chance it would escape by swimming. No, apparently not. Great glory was being won; Gar could feel it. And death. The presence of the bison lingered.

He thrashed his way through alder thickets and tangles of hazel. The ground turned soggy. He should have stayed higher up the hill. He could see nothing ahead, but he felt water. Now he could smell it. He broke out of woodland into a willow thicket on a lakeshore.

When he finally worked his way around the willows and brambles to open water, he could see the hunt site on the north bank a quarter mile away. Splendid animal, that bison bull, sleek in his summer coat. His horns, each the length of a man's leg at least, jutted straight out to each side. He need only swing his head to skewer a man nearly a spear's length away. And look at those bulging neck muscles! Gar could see the power from here, and the curly rosette of hair on the beast's forehead.

The bison dropped to its knees in the lake perhaps a man's-length offshore. The drama was nearly played out, the bison almost dead, for they were all grasping ears and horns, and laughing.

Heart gloated, *Real People! Six or seven of them!*

Gar broke into a run toward them, overjoyed.

You have no part in the taking, Head warned. *You must avoid giving the impression that you want any bit of the glory.* True. Gar slowed to a walk as he approached.

So intent on the People was he, he nearly stumbled

over one of the hunters. A Person lay face down in the lake near water's edge. Silent, ruffled waves lapped against the mud bank, carrying several loops of the Person's intestines in and out, in and out. A shaman's pouch, still on its thong around his neck, bobbed by his ear.

Rather than idly wait for the glory to be completed, Gar would make himself useful. He dragged the Person up the bank far enough that neither the shaman nor his intestines floated, laid hands on the fellow, and began the cant for the dead.

Roaring, the hunters mounted the great shout goodbye as the bison entered its death throes. Their warlord sang the bull into the Beyond with a voice much deeper and stronger than Newt's. Gar and the warlord completed their duties at just about the same time. In theory at least, the shaman and the bison entered the Beyond together.

Each hunter yelled out his nomination for the supreme honouree. Usually, a cacophony of names on the first vote became two or three names on the second vote, settling to one on the third or fourth. Today, as one they shouted a single name. Civet.

Head pointed out the obvious. *Clearly, this dead shaman is named Civet.*

Ah, Gar, Heart pouted, *you've never come close to being honoured like this.*

Head sniffed. *You've never come close to being dead like this. Disembowelled? Hard way to go.*

Gar stood, declared his lineage and signed *friend.*

Despite the splendid kill, the warlord looked absolutely crushed. Defeated. "Sturgeon, Elephant clan, tribe of Seashore, Dusk moiety." He stared at his departed shaman. They must have been good friends.

He pointed off upshore several man-lengths. "Cant that one too, eh."

"Eh." Gar would be glad to do them the favour, for he was about to ask a favour himself. Nothing encouraged cooperation like obligation.

The recipient of Gar's third cant for the dead or dying since yesterday, if one counted his own last night, was a lad of perhaps fifteen winters, lying at a sorry angle on the sward and gasping red froth. He smelled of death. He looked terrified as Gar approached. When Gar marked the boy's forehead with powdered blood, an expression of genuine happiness washed across the lad's face. Gar took the lad's hand in his, a substitute for simply laying a hand upon him. When he concluded the cant, he gave the hand a squeeze.

The lad melted closer to the ground, lax. He could barely breathe, so shattered was he. The blood pooling beneath him was turning dark. He must have been gored early on. "Shaman dead," he whispered. "I think, 'Now I can't get to Beyond. Die, can't get there. No song.' Then you." He was well past performing any dance of thanks, but he made a few of the accompanying hand gestures. Eloquent thanks from one so near the Beyond.

Would Dor or the other youngsters of Gar's moiety produce stoicism like this lad's under similar circumstances? Gar almost doubted it. But an interesting thought flashed through his mind. Hare would.

Gar looked at Sturgeon and gestured toward the dying boy. "Name."

"Civet."

11

No One Listens to Him

"Rat!" Sturgeon, the Elephants' warlord, spat. "Don't like Rat."

You seem to be getting that a lot, mused Heart. *Rat certainly brings out the spit in people.*

The warlord continued, "Rat says something but it's not true, then he says another thing, that's not true. He says one thing and means another. No one listens to him now."

They sat beside the fire, Gar and Sturgeon, watching idly as women and children prepared the night's feast.

Out beyond the yawning mouth of this high, shallow cave, clouds obscured the late afternoon sun and turned it orange. Already lightning played around near the horizon. Perhaps this night would look and sound like the one when he held Mouse.

Mouse.

Gar was being treated as an honoured guest, and not without cause. He claimed no part in the kill, of course, but he helped the clan haul meat. He helped them bury their dead. Before he left here he might well bury one more. One of their babies was so sick that she would probably die soon.

"But we'll get him." The warlord waved a hand toward a little fire off by itself at the far end of this cave. "Beaver over there. My Dawn moiety shaman, he hears spirits well. He will find Rat for you. He is calling Rat now." Sturgeon wagged his head. "Never would I ever think, 'Today I will try to find Rat.' Crazy! Nobody wants him. Except you."

"I don't want him. I want what he knows."

The shaman identified as Beaver sat cross-legged as Gar so often did, staring beyond his little fire. Even from here, Gar could see sweat glisten on the man's brow. This Beaver fellow was working hard.

Sturgeon drew his knees up and draped his arms over them. "So Kelp is dead and Eel wants the killer. Interesting."

"You knew Kelp."

"Some. I try not to meet the Elk clan much. Kelp, he was too strange. He didn't think right. So he lost his head, you say. Not much lost. Eel is very big and very dull. He's their warlord now. Too bad. Now their hunts will not bring much glory."

"So you stay away from the Elks, eh." Gar could not conceive of avoiding someone's own tribesmen just because they were a different clan.

Sturgeon nodded. "Lots of power there. Dangerous."

"Their shaman, Saiga. He has strong power."

"Eh! And Eel, he's strong in a different way. He's

vicious and doesn't think. Can't think, I'd say. A bad mix, that."

"How about this idea? People from Kelp's own clan killed him to take his position and power, and now the killer wants someone else to die for it." Gar watched Sturgeon for a reaction. He had spent most of the afternoon explaining the situation and politics up in Scarp Country.

Sturgeon mulled the prospect only a few moments. "I don't think so. Saiga, no. He's a good shaman. He doesn't need to get power that way. Eel? Probably not him either. Not smart enough. Others in Elk, no reason. Except maybe the woman."

"Kohl."

"No. The new woman. The woman Rat brought to Kelp. Something was going on there, but I don't know what."

"Eh." Questions swarmed through Gar's mind like a reindeer herd on the run. He could not decide what to ask. So many things to know, and Sturgeon probably ignorant of most of them.

Gar needed time to let his heart and mind mull this latest, so he shifted subjects. "When I was young I had a very good friend, also named Sturgeon. We were eleven winters old—it was starvation moon—and he went out to snare birds. Wolves killed him. If he had lived, he'd have been a fine man. He was brave already at eleven winters. You carry a good name."

Sturgeon grunted. He didn't dance his thanks for the praise, but he made the hand signs for gratitude. He pondered the slithering fire a few moments. "Your clan. Mammoths. That one is still strong?"

"Eh. In the two moieties we have three babies, fourteen children. We have some good young men coming. Maybe not as fine as Civet, but good."

Sturgeon pointed out across the floor toward a very light-hued woman. "That woman. She had three babies, they all died. That woman over there, the dark one." He gestured toward another who was nearly black. "For ten years she's been getting fed by this man, that man, and still no baby. We don't know why. Women don't have babies much anymore. We're dying. You see it all around. And now, Hawk is gone." He wagged his head morosely. "We're dead."

"Hawk. Your shaman who died today."

Sturgeon nodded. "He knew the genealogies back ten generations. More. Now he's gone, before he trained anyone young."

Gar scowled, incredulous. "No one knows your genealogies now?"

"No one."

"But the shaman over there. He knows the whole clan. The past is still alive in him, eh."

"No. He knows only his own moiety."

Gar and Cloud both could recite each other's genealogies, and not just ten generations. Back long before that, when Scarp Country People lived north of their present territory. They both knew all the stories that make a People a People. Cloud knew the histories of both Mammoth clan moieties. Gar knew the histories of both moieties. It was the way things were supposed to be done. Cloud had trained his three neophytes. Gar would pick three youngsters soon. The clan's past was secure in four other minds even if Gar died in this horrid wasteland, torn from his soil.

Sturgeon stared off into nothing. "It used to be, the

Seashore tribe was the biggest among Real People. Our Elephant clan was the biggest and best of the Seashores. Now the old men, the wise old women are all gone. People die. Starvation moons rise, more die. The Elephant clan is little now. Worthless." He snorted bitterly. "Even elephants are all gone. For many generations, there have been no elephants. Just the name. Now it's lost too."

Gar felt a woman's presence behind him, beckoning his attention. He turned.

She was fairly old, probably thirty-five at least. Her face might be pretty if it were not warped with sorrow. Her body was certainly not beautiful. Bones stuck out here and there. He remembered her as one of the chief mourners when they buried Civet among the rocks this morning.

She stepped forward cautiously, drew a deep breath and danced her thanks. She looked at Sturgeon briefly and hastened away.

Gar frowned.

Sturgeon's deep voice purred. "Civet's mother. If you had not come yesterday, Civet would have died with no cant, no Beyond. The same with Hawk. She speaks for all of us. We are all grateful. So you want Rat? We'll find Rat for you! In gratitude."

The shaman named Beaver stood up. He summoned two youths and began dancing. Gar recognised it as a dance describing a two-day journey, but many of the gestures were new to him. These people communicated in the common language to some extent, but they had their odd little mannerisms.

The two lads picked up spears and skin bags and left. Beaver walked away.

Gar gestured, “If he sends them away now, they’ll miss the feast tonight.”

“There will be other feasts. They want to find Rat, because they’ll get big glory.”

“Glory for bringing Rat?” Ludicrous.

“Eh. Glory and hard work.” Sturgeon smiled. “Beaver says, Rat doesn’t want to come.”

“Eh.”

Gar perceived how warmly he was regarded when they gave him a piece of the honour haunch at the feast that night. After the obligatory dances, including his own as he told his story, a pleasantly plump woman approached and signed *union.*

He thought of Mouse and almost declined. But refusing the gift of a woman’s attention was an insult, and this was one clan he did not want to irritate. So he rose and took her hand.

Whew! Heart, of course. *I thought for a moment there you were going to be stupid.*

She led him to the dark, southwest end of the cave, to Gar’s bed. Was this woman obliged by clan ties to serve the stranger and couldn’t wait to get back to her favourite? Was she being fed by anyone? Almost always, women offered to strangers were not pledged, but you never knew. Was she hungry for union? Wearied and eager to get it over with? So many uncertainties.

And for no reason whatever, an inane thought crossed his mind. Why were the attentions of a man not offered to visiting women?

Afterwards, he spent quite a bit of time that might have been spent in revelry and dance, thinking instead about why he cherished the memory of Mouse when his unions with Kohl, past and present, pleasured him so much. Kohl had always been the woman in his heart, or at least in a part of it. Until now.

The shaman was supposed to understand the heads and hearts of the People he served. Gar did not even understand his own.

The lads returned not in four days but in three, late in the afternoon, herding Rat between them. Sturgeon greeted them as heroes and equated finding Rat with making a major kill. Gar danced to them as honoured heroes and then danced thanks to them for their sacrifice. They were quite full of themselves by sunset.

The half moon rose before dark, so there was no darkest time. Lightning flitted carelessly through the clouds to the southwest, but no one thought fresh water would come of it.

Gar hunkered down with Rat and invited Sturgeon and Beaver to join them. Between them, Beaver, Sturgeon, and Gar probably knew enough to be able to catch Rat in at least a few lies, should the wily trader decide to try them.

Gar was not particularly robust, nor was Sturgeon. Average. Next to the scrawny Rat, they were giants. The little trader wore a perpetual scowl, as if life never delivered quite as much as he wanted from it. His colour, an ashen sort of brown, did nothing toward making him attractive.

Rat still wallowed in the morose pout he had brought with him. "I am very tired." He transferred his glower from Gar to Sturgeon. "Those boys travelled day and night without rest."

"They were afraid. If they stopped and rested, you might slip away."

Rat bobbed his head. "I have things to do, and other

places to go. I should not be here now."

Neither should I, grumbled Heart. *No sympathy.*

Gar wanted no more time with this annoying little man than was absolutely necessary. He drove straight to the centre of the matter. "Why did Kelp want Mouse?"

"Good woman, that one."

Heart cooed, *Maybe this fellow is not so bad after all. See how we agree there.*

Head warned, *That can't be the only reason.*

"More."

"She was the wife of a Hairy. He was intrigued."

Another new word. Gar didn't mind learning things, but he hated Rat teaching them. "Intrigued?"

"Interested."

"Then say that." Gar pondered the whole thing a moment. "No. Kelp was south of Scarp Country. You were moving north. Mouse was moving north. You met Mouse and took her south to Kelp." He looked at Rat. "That's right?"

"That's right."

"Then how did you know Kelp wanted her? You found her after you left him. He didn't know Mouse is a good woman. He didn't know about her link to the Hairies. He didn't know about her at all. Why did you think he wanted her? Why did you take her to him?"

Sturgeon nodded sagely.

Rat explained with mock patience, the way you chide an errant child. "Everywhere I go, I say, 'What do you need? What do you want?' Then I remember all that everyone tells me. Also, I observe carefully. I see everything. Sometimes, I see that you need something before you even know you need it. When I find what People need, I take it to them. You know this. It's what

I say to Newt. I often say it to you, Sturgeon. Kelp said, 'I want power. I want more power than the Hairies even.' So when I found that, I took it to him."

The implication addled Gar. "Mouse is power?"

"Apparently."

There was another word not in Gar's vocabulary. It sounded from the tone of voice like a positive response, so he let it slide by. "Why did Kelp come up to my Scarp Country?"

Rat scowled. "Gar, you went far north. Then you came away down here. Now all these questions about Kelp. What is happening? What are you doing? Are you trying to take power over all the Seashore People? Is Newt up to something?"

"How do you know I went north?"

Rat flicked a finger toward Gar's arms. "Blackfly bites. They itch, so you scratch them. They keep itching, you keep scratching, claw them open, and they're not healed yet. Anybody who goes north ends up with blackfly bites."

"Every year, you go north too. But not this year. Why is this year different?"

Rat studied him a moment and spat. "Kelp!"

At least someone isn't spitting about Rat this time, Heart sniggered.

Rat waved a skinny finger. "I warned him, don't go to Scarp Country. Things are best just like they are now. The Seashore People stay at Seashore, those People in Scarp Country stay there. Don't mess it up, I said. He did it anyway, and now I have problems. No one listens to me now."

"Why did he go to Scarp Country?"

"He wants to try his new magic. His new power."

"Power from Mouse."

Rat looked at him in the patronising way he would a child whose silly question had an obvious answer. "Where else? He can't try it with the Seashore People because they're already his People, and Saiga is strong. Saiga is their Dawn shaman. He needs somewhere else, some other People, other spirits to try out his power. Dark Mountains are too far away, have too many mosquitoes, blackflies. Also they are feeble now, a sorry People. So he didn't want Dark Mountains. Cold Lakes? He surely doesn't want to go there."

"Because it's Mouse's country, and she knows it well enough that she could easily escape from him."

"Eh. So Scarp Country is just right, he says. Now see! Here you are three days from home, asking questions."

Three days from home! Heart rejoiced. *You're not as far as you thought. Despise Rat if you will, but he knows where you live; he can take you there.*

Head cautioned, *That's how he enslaved Mouse. He promised to take her home. You can't trust him.*

Sturgeon was scowling just as much. "Mess up what? What problems do you have?"

For once Rat seemed at a loss for words. "You know what I do. The Hairies need lots of salt." He held out a hand. "They travel afar to the north, butcher reindeer. Meat spoils in the summer. So they salt it and smoke it, and it's still good to eat come winter. There's no salt up north where they need it, but the Seashore People make lots of salt." He held out the other hand. "Seashore People need flint. Cold Lakes People, they got lots of flint, but they need salt like the Hairies. See? Everyone needs things, everyone has other things. I take this to those

People, that to these People." He clasped his hands. "Everyone is pleased, and I eat well. Life is good.

"Kelp, he's going to change that. He wants to link the Seashore People in power with Scarp Country, maybe even Cold Lakes later. All one big tribe. Now they can give each other salt, lion teeth, flint, chewed hides, all that. People to People. Now all those People don't need Rat anymore. Poor old Rat starves. It's best to keep everything like it is, eh. Anything more brings me problems."

Gar understood, more or less. He'd work it out later. "Kelp's new power from Mouse. How does that work?"

"Ask her. I don't deal in power. I deal in salt."

12

He Should Have Known Better

"Are you coming?" It was the tone of voice a mother would use on a pouting three-year-old. Twenty man-lengths up the hill ahead of Gar, Rat the Trader paused and twisted to watch the weary shaman struggle.

Once upon a time, Gar's own mother used that tone of voice on him. And he was definitely pouting now. Not to mention panting. He slogged uphill through stiff, knee-high heather. Sturdy little branches gouged at his shins and calves. He had adopted Rat's habit of using the butt end of his spear as a walking staff, letting his shoulders and arms do part of the work of pulling his weary, weary body up this interminable mountain. Like most of the palliatives Gar came up with, it helped but did not cure.

With an impatient snort, Rat turned on his heel and pressed onward, up the hill.

Why can we not go around it instead of this slogging up, over, and down the other side? Stay with a ridge and just keep walking on virtually level slope? For once, Head and Heart agreed.

Head answered the question. *Because Rat is leading, and he is insane.*

Gar couldn't agree more. Gar himself had been insane to coerce Rat into this. He should have known better. He had no idea where they were or where they had been during these last three days of miserable travel. Rat could be conducting him directly to some lair of the Hairies.

Rat topped out on the crest and turned again, scowling, to watch Gar's tortured progress.

Gar caught up. "Sit."

"Again?"

Gar sat, giving Rat little choice.

The trader flopped down beside Gar and grumped, "It takes too long to get anywhere, the way you sit all the time." He waited, probably for a response Gar wasn't going to bother to make, then added, "And there's not much protection for me when you lag so far behind."

"Who protects you when I stay home?"

Twice in his life, Gar had climbed to the crest of Ibex Mountain on the western fringe of Scarp Country territory. Both times were in his youth, before he became a shaman, when he still hunted ibex and snared small game. He remembered the view as being much like this. Beautiful.

What few trees there were stood about in huddled clumps, all stunted and gnarled. From this rocky tor, he could see in all directions. The land stretched away, in some places broad and sweeping, in others, creased into intimate folds and gouges. Partially hidden by forest patches and knolls, sparkling streams and tarns splashed sky light across the ground. And see all the ragged, layered scarps! At least he wasn't back in that accursed caveless Dark Mountains country.

"Now you see where you are?" Rat waved a hand northeastward, toward a mountain hard beside this one.

"No."

"Ibex Mountain there."

"Ibex!" Gar studied the profile drawn against the evening sky. He could see that it was, now that Rat identified it. "Ah. The back doesn't look like the front."

"So? Your back doesn't look like your front. You know where home is now. I completed my part of the bargain. Give me the spirits and I'll go my way, eh."

"Eh." Gar drew his legs in and crossed them. He had asked the spirits' permission before he made his promise to Rat. It was not a rash one.

He marked Rat's forehead with dried blood and noted in passing that Rat was not at all sweaty from exertion. Gar was. He drew a deep breath and held it. Buzzy flies found his perspiration and went wading. He noted the tickle of their movement on his face. His chest tightened, begging him to breathe. He held on. The flies' tickle disappeared as his awareness shifted into other realms.

The spirits snickered. *Hypocrite. You ask safety for this Person you despise.*

Gar argued, *He is a Person. And he did as he promised. Honour my request on that basis.*

He listened and felt. His chest ached as if it were somehow a great distance away.

They whispered, *Done. And not a moment too soon.* He exhaled and sucked in air almost simultaneously, grateful that he didn't have to wait longer. The tickle of flies returned.

Sitting beside him, Rat stared in terror beyond Gar's shoulder, his eyes open as wide as his gaping mouth. Gar twisted to look.

A lion, horrible in her tawny tightness, crouched not five man-lengths away. Easy pouncing distance. One leap. Unblinking, her yellow-green eyes studied them.

"Where's the other?" Gar snatched up his spear and squirmed about to scan the berry brush and hazel scrub around them. Lions always hunted in pairs or threes. He saw nothing, but that didn't mean much. That only meant that a lion was better at concealment than Gar was at observing.

Rat relaxed by slow degrees. Eventually, his look of fear melted down to a smug, casual half-smile. "Why the spear? You doubt your own magic's protection, eh?"

"Eh." Gar thought he saw movement fifty feet away, but he wasn't certain. "It's the same thing as you asking everyone what they want. They already know they can tell you if they want things. You ask anyway."

Rat grunted. The half-smile became a whole one. "I feel your protective spirits. I feel them!"

"They're yours now."

"Eh." Rat stood up. He picked up his spear, but he swung it to perpendicular for use as a walking staff. He wasn't defending himself with it. "Tell Newt, when the leaves turn red and yellow, I'll come by bringing dried crowberries. I'll trade them for chewed hides."

"You going to Dark Mountains now?" If, perish the thought, Gar had to find this man again, he wanted to know which direction to follow. He stood up also, his spear at ready.

The lion lifted to her feet in that curious way lions did, not like an aurochs or horse by gathering her legs beneath her but simply by straightening them. Silently she moved off. What power.

"Dark Mountains, Blue Lakes, eh. Maybe I'll wait for Hairies at the river island. Bring a few musk ox horns down to Kelp. He'll be back home by then. He always wants musk ox horns."

"Musk ox horns?"

"Good stuff. Powdered, it makes you a better lover. Maybe I should bring you one sometime, eh?"

Gar snorted. "Bring me it, I'll show you how you use it."

With a merry cackle, Rat started down the hill at an angle, headed north. He must have had a sense of direction like a Hairy's, always knowing where he was.

Now that Rat travelled under the protection of spirits, did that mean Gar was abandoned? How many spirits were there, and how many of them went off with Rat? In fact, did one even count spirits with numbers the way one counted toes or clansmen or mammoths? Did they multiply themselves the way People and animals did? Was there a calving season?

So Rat thought Kelp was still alive. By design, neither Sturgeon and Beaver nor Gar had told him any different. Gar rather hoped Rat would somehow slip up and reveal that he knew more about the matter than he ought to. Then Gar would trot him right over to Saiga and let the shaman's spirits examine him.

Now there was an idea. Gather up the people who might have reason to kill Kelp and bring them all to Saiga. Let the old man sort it out. He had the spiritual faculties to do it.

"Here is your murderer, Saiga, delivered as you demanded, and also a fair number of innocents. Surely you'll know who is who."

The mountain was so steep here that he had to descend by traversing at an angle, wading through tangles of prostrate willow. He hated switchbacking; it only added to the time and distance travelled.

Rat was clever, Gar knew. How clever? Gar didn't know. Rat had reason to rid Mother Earth of Kelp. He had to preserve his own twisted way of life. If the wiry trader was indeed the murderer, might he not on purpose say that last about taking horns to Kelp? Then Gar would not suspect him. Gar found it suspicious in itself that Rat mentioned Kelp at all.

Behind you! Spirits shrieked. Gar was not abandoned after all.

Instantly he shinned up the beech trunk beside him with two knees and only one arm, because he had to drag his spear along. Three or four man-lengths above the ground, he draped himself over a limb and looked around below.

The lions had decided to take Gar after all. So much for protective magic. The lead female poised crouching at the base of the tree, her tail tip twitching as she contemplated the wisdom of climbing after their prey. Her hunting partner cowered in the brush downhill. Had Gar continued on, he would have stumbled right into her open mouth, her welcoming claws.

What was this? Afar downhill, swarming across an open lea, a pack of hyænas came hunting, grey in the dusk. They usually travelled behind lions, letting the lions do the heavy work of stalking and killing, then stepping in to lay a claim to the spoils. They did the same thing with Real People, come to think of it. Were they wandering some other track, trailing other lions, or just unusually far behind the pride of which these two were part?

And then Gar saw the fire.

Halfway to the crest of Ibex Mountain on this side, a small, bright fire glowed in the waning evening. There could conceivably be a cave there, though the vegetation suggested there was not. But what People? Gar's Mammoth clan did not venture to this side of Ibex Mountain, Rat and present company excepted. Neither Rhino nor Fox, the only other two Scarp Country clans anywhere near, was likely to roam there. Hairies? Never had they come through there before, and besides, it was the wrong time of year.

I'm sure; I'm absolutely convinced. You must go to that fire! Heart speaking. *And the spirits of the forest agree with me.*

Heart often claimed the corroboration of other spirits when he wanted his own way badly enough.

Screamed Head, *Quit mooning and pay attention to the lion!*

With a sudden lunge, the lion covered over two manlengths straight up. Her claws gritching and gouging in the smooth bark, here she came, and scrambling.

Gar braced tightly against the trunk. Much depended now upon those hyænas.

She hooked one great, flaccid paw over the lowest limb. She now possessed the leverage to make it all the way up here. With the other, she lashed up at him, snarling. Her clawtips raked his ankle.

He rammed his spear downward. Its fire-hardened point drove down through her mouth into her throat.

Glory! Now he need only hang onto it and keep his perch.

Only? She very nearly wrenched him out of the tree as she thrashed. He clung desperately to tree and spear. Then she fell away and almost pulled him down with her.

Her voice gurgled as she thrashed. Good. Good.

It took the hyænas but a few moments to hear and smell and come a-laughing, though it seemed like a long time. Gar crawled a few limbs higher, seeking a comfortable crotch. Hyænas didn't climb; they didn't even leap well; but his clawed-up ankle was dripping blood. They'd notice him.

They had no trouble driving off the second lion. Without her hunting partner, she possessed no heart for the chase. They fell upon the injured one, answering a question Gar had debated with Toad from time to time. Hyænas often steal a lion's kill, but would they savage the lion herself, were she compromised? Toad said no, they didn't dare. *Told you so, Toad*, chortled Heart.

Useful they might be at the moment, but Gar despised hyænas anyway. Their very appearance invited ridicule, with those long legs and that spherical head attached to so short a neck. Their coat never lay flat and sleek like a bison's or horse's, not even in the warmest summer. Grizzled and rough, it stuck up in raggedy cowlicks at their shoulders, at their tail. And the voice! Hideous! But most of all, Gar despised their slinking and their dishonesty. Cowering, they pretended to weakness and fear, when in truth their jaws easily splintered the sturdiest elk bones with no effort. Cowardice was the antithesis of glory.

As bones crunched beneath him, Gar picked a dozen

beech burs and settled down to wait. The burs were much too green and fleshy yet to yield edible nuts. He prised one apart with his thumbnails to make sure, but the nuts were useless. So he amused himself by pegging the remainder, one at a time, at the hyænas below. If he popped a hyæna just right near the base of the tail, it would wheel and slash at the innocent animal behind it. Gar drew a little blood that way.

Assuming he survived this, which seemed comfortably likely, and danced the story of his exploit, could he claim he killed the lion unaided? The hyænas helped out considerably by finishing the job. On the other hand, he could hardly consider them hunting allies, since they would rip him just as eagerly as they dismembered the lion. And she probably would have died eventually anyway, hyænas or no.

Finally, the hyænas left. Gar waited. Unaware of the Person in the tree, a wolverine moved in to pick over the few scraps left. Good. That meant the hyænas had indeed quit the kill, for wolverines took no chances. Gar climbed down cautiously, listened a short while, and headed eastward toward Ibex Mountain.

He entered a clearing and checked his bearings. From here he could tell that the distant fire still glowed; he had to scramble up into some rocks to see over the brush. And he reflected that had he not climbed that beech, he almost certainly would never have spotted the fire at all.

Perhaps he should not have spent so long waiting after the hyænas left. He pushed the track as hard as he could—he wanted to reach the fire before daybreak—but he wasn't making very good time. Protective spirits or no, he disliked travelling at night through this alien land. At home on the far side of Ibex Mountain, he knew where the lions and wolves and hyænas denned. He knew their habits of coming and going. On this side, he knew nothing. Any major carnivore might be waiting for him and he did not completely trust the spirits around him to tell him so. He did not know the voices of this region, and they did not know him.

He crossed the soggy bottomland and started up the rocky lower slope of Ibex Mountain.

The clouds that had shrouded the sky through most of the day and evening were breaking up. From time to time, stars and a gibbous moon shone between them. The added light helped speed travel considerably.

He passed a shallow, unoccupied cave and moved out onto an open slope of berry brambles and scree. His footfalls in the sharp, loose stones sounded louder than they ought in this floating night. He hated crossing this kind of stuff in summer when he was bareskinned top to bottom. The scree hurt his feet, and too many body parts caught on brambles. However, he had seen this slope from his ærie in the beech and knew it was not far at all below the fire. He was nearly there!

A line of low, dense heath marked the upper limit of the scree slope. Gar need only find a place to break through that hedge, climb a few more yards, and he would walk into the ring of firelight. Perhaps this low spot right here would let him through. It looked thinner than most places.

The moon slipped behind a cloud.

Ghostly pale, a phantasm squirted straight up out of the hedge in front of him. It screamed with a lad's human voice and flailed. Out of nowhere, a spear gouged into Gar's ribs. The sharp end stuck. With slow, elegant grace, the butt end sagged to the ground. Gar stood there staring at it, stunned speechless.

Having escaped lions and eluded hyænas, Gar had foolishly thought that quite possibly he would survive this horrible trek. He really should have known better.

13
He Doesn't Know What's Happening

I think I hear a woman. Hope springs eternal in the human Heart.

Is that all you can think of? We're dying! snarled Head.

Gar lay on the scree more or less propped on one elbow as he studied the half-sized spear in his hand, a child's weapon. And that was indeed a child who attacked, he was certain. The come-again-gone-again moon revealed that the piece was very nicely trimmed and sharpened. Good handwork.

A plethora of smells confused him—some almost Hairy, some not, familiar, male and female, and a cave bear. He was too dizzy to sort out the odours or to think. And thirsty. And very, very weary. He must get back down to that unoccupied cave beside the base of the scree field. Despite that it was so shallow, he could better defend himself there. He needed the Mother Earth to embrace him now.

A familiar woman's voice, as in a dense cloud, floated in from somewhere.

Heart teased, *Come now! You're not so far gone you don't recognise that one.*

Gar flopped onto his back on the scree. His eyes were dimming; he couldn't even see the pearlescent clouds well. He must gather up both these spears and take them along. The child's short piece would serve well for defence in a confined space. He was bleeding profusely. That was sure to draw animals. What if the hyænas...?

In a few moments. Right now he would rest and catch his breath. Wait. He smelled someone...

Both weapons leaped out of his hand. He grabbed at them much too slowly. Then he saw...

"Hare."

In the sallow half light, that misbegotten lad discarded his own spear. He hefted Gar's, bracing it tightly against himself by an elbow, and aimed it at Gar's belly. The child need only drop forward and his weight would skewer Gar to the scree slope. And Gar could not rally the strength to resist.

Mouse's voice from that distant cloud called out in an incomprehensible language.

Hare replied, "Gar."

The two commenced arguing. From Hare's body motion, Gar perceived that the lad was deadly serious about finishing the act of murder which he had begun.

Gar managed a spoken word. "Why?"

"Enemy! Newt sent you!" the child hissed.

Out across the scree came irregular footfalls, as if the person were staggering. Mouse? In a violent paroxysm of effort, Gar pulled himself up onto one elbow.

Mouse. She made her way on one leg, balancing and supporting herself with two shoulder-high sticks gripped in her hands. Her other leg was bound rigidly from thigh to ankle in sticks and rawhide. She paused and leaned one of her handheld sticks against a breast so that she could gesture toward Hare. She sounded furious. "Not him!"

"He's one of them!" Hare sounded just as furious. "You can't trust him. It doesn't matter that he was not there. He has to choose between you or his clan, and he'll choose the clan. Now he knows where we are."

"We need help."

"Not from him! I'm enough. I'm all you need."

"You're a child! We need *him*!" She resumed her one-legged lurching hops toward Gar.

Apparently Hare decided he had lost the argument because he lowered the spear and backed away. He glared at Gar. "Tomorrow, the next day, he'll betray us. You just watch. Clan ties are too strong."

The loose stones just about upset Mouse with each tortured step. Adjusting that bound leg, she settled beside Gar onto the sharp stones, looking very worried. The moon, uncooperative, stayed behind clouds. Gar would have liked to see her face better.

"Come to our fire. Rest there."

"Cave?" Gar kept an eye on Hare.

"No. It was getting dark, and we didn't find one."

"Down there, that way, very close, a small one." Why did he have such trouble speaking? He looked at Hare. "Easier to defend than a fire in the open." That reason the lad could understand.

Mouse gestured to Hare. "Find it and move the fire,

eh."

Hare glowered at them a moment and jogged off across the steep scree slope. How could the child move so fast, barefooted, in such miserably sharp talus?

Until now, Gar's side had remained more or less numb and unfeeling. No longer. Bleeding had abated, however, so he didn't have to grip the wound so tightly any more. He began to poke around a little, assaying damage. "Story."

"You don't know?"

"Know what?"

"Newt has been listening to Kohl. He decided I killed Kelp. So he was going to grab me and Hare, take us to the Seashore People. Crow came and warned me. Hare and I ran. A big escape. Newt is seeking us up north. He thinks we fled north to Aspen Lakes. But we came west instead, so here we are. I can't travel fast, eh." And she patted her bound leg.

"Eh."

Hare came scrambling up the scree slope and paused by Mouse. "It's a bad cave, too shallow. No good. And a bear comes there by and by. I smelt him. I suppose we have to go there anyway, eh?" He said it accusingly.

"Eh." Mouse bobbed her head.

Looking disgusted, as if Gar had just vomited on his winter furs, Hare slogged off across the scree and squeezed through the hedge.

Lying still a while helped. Gar didn't feel dizzy anymore. He pointed to Mouse's bound leg. "Story."

"Kohl saw Crow leave Alder Cave and come down to Larch Cave. She followed and watched. She found out Crow warned me, and thought I might run. When I went out for pine nuts, to see if they were ripe yet, she followed me. I climbed up in a tree." Mouse made climbing gestures. "I didn't know in time that she was there. Suddenly, here she is climbing the tree below me."

"Up into the pine you were in?"

"Eh. I tried to get below her, but I couldn't. She made me fall. My leg caught in the branches and went snap. She laughed. 'Now you won't run,' she said. I was hanging there. She couldn't reach me, and I couldn't reach the ground. Then Hare came along, and she ran home. He wanted to go kill her, but I wouldn't let him. He broke some branches away and I got to the ground without falling more."

Gar knew they despised each other, but he couldn't picture Kohl going to those lengths. There had to be more to the story, but he didn't know what to ask.

Hare paused again beside them, bearing a bundle of sticks with flaming ends. "Sunrise soon. Make the fire ready to travel?"

"No. We'll stay there all day, all night, then travel the next day."

He shook his head.

Whatever he would have argued, she interrupted. "We need rest, Hare, and we need to think about what we should do next."

He trundled off down the hill, tracking smoke and light across the waning darkness.

"Good choice, rest." Gar closed his eyes.

For you maybe. Not for her, Head reminded him.

He opened them again. "But maybe Newt will learn you went west instead. He has good trackers. Toad, Goose, they're fine trackers. Maybe Hare's right. You should leave."

It pained him to say that. Now that Mouse sat here

beside him, he wanted desperately for things to stay that way. Only now did he realise how very much he'd missed her. But her safety, and even Hare's, was primary.

Mouse was grinning. "They can track good through the water, eh."

"Through water..."

"Down by the beaver pond there are thick rushes, at the north end. You know where?"

Gar nodded. All the Mammoth clan knew that area.

"We hid there, Hare and me. Newt and all were sniffing around the shore."

"Hide in the water?" Gar couldn't imagine that. And yet—

"Eh. With only our heads out, down among the reeds. We heard everything. Newt and Cloud sat on the shore very near there, arguing. Six or seven men were with them. Cloud said, 'This is wrong.' Newt said, 'No, it's right.' Newt thinks that because I ran, Hare and me, it proves that I'm guilty.

"Hare gave me a reed—hollow, eh—showed me how to breathe through it. We sank all the way under the water then, breathing with the reeds, and those men were kneeling on shore right there, this far away from us, filling their water skins, and they never knew about us."

Unthinkable.

And fiendishly clever.

Hare joined them, staring at them with distaste.

Mouse looked just plain smug. "We stayed in the water all the way around the lake and over to the beaver dam. We came out on those rocks, left no tracks. And when you're in the water a while, there's not much smell to you. Like a bath. Then we came over the mountain." She added proudly, "Hare did it all. Lots of glory, eh?"

"Lots of glory then. Not now." Gar reminded her accusingly, "He threw his spear. There's no glory in throwing a spear."

"Of course he throws a spear. He grew up with Hairies. They all do that."

Hare grinned wickedly. "It works, eh. I, a child, almost killed you, a shaman. Almost. I would have, too, but she said no."

That was what was wrong with the boy, even more than his repugnant appearance. He thought like a Hairy.

Hare completed moving the fire and their remaining firewood. He helped his mother to her feet. He offered to drag Gar to the cave by his heels so that he wouldn't have to stand up. Gar declined. The little ass.

Hare might think he was big stuff to come close to killing a shaman, but a child's spear thrown by a child does not break bones. Gar had ascertained that much. It had ripped the fat and skin. Such things heal, once the infection subsides.

Gar demanded his spear back and received it. He made it downhill to the cave by leaning heavily on the spear, and he doubted seriously that he would have been able to go those few man-lengths were it uphill.

With his nicely wrought child's spear, Hare dug out a part of the sand floor to make a bit more room. Gar and Mouse nestled back against the wall, the solid, comforting breast of the Mother Earth. Hare stretched out between the fire and the whole world.

Cold and refreshing, the silent peace of predawn began to blot the dimmer stars. It chilled the waning light of the third-quarter moon and washed it away. The spirits hushed their breathing as they were wont to do.

Gar, drifting very close to sleep, watched the erratic

dance of a mosquito on the soft air. "Mouse? Everyone I talk to—Saiga, Rat—say you have magic. Tell me about this magic."

"Magic? I don't have any magic. No."

Hare interrupted by picking up Gar's spear. "Here's fresh blood on the point here. Whose blood?"

"Lion."

Hare stared at Gar. No doubt he knew better than to question a man's claims. Surely Hairies, like Real People, held to the tenet that to stretch a claim or to prevaricate was an unthinkable transgression. "How close?"

"Closer than I like." Gar pointed to his ankle and twisted it around a bit for a better view. The blood had crusted in thick dark lines defining the clawmarks.

"Hoo."

Mouse stared at him open-mouthed. "You have the magic! Not me."

Hardly! Head and Heart together.

Gar pressed. "Kelp wanted power. Rat traded you to Kelp, and I think he told Kelp you would help Kelp get more power. How?"

"Rat took me to Kelp on purpose? To trade me?"

"Seems so."

"He said..." She watched the fire a few moments. It glinted yellow in her eyes. "He told me he heard that Horses were living down south now, joined up with Seashore. It didn't sound right to me, but I couldn't find them in our territory, not anywhere. So we went south to Seashores." The firelight intensified her wonderful golden-orange colour.

Gar went back to the first question he had ever thought of when he got into this mess. "The colours in

Kelp's fingernails. What is it?"

"Magic." She gasped and looked wide-eyed at Hare. He stared at her.

The lad nodded slowly. "There is the magic Kelp wanted, eh! He couldn't get it anywhere else except from Hairies—or from you."

Mouse was thinking hard; Gar could see it in her tight, frowning face. Gar closed his eyes and let the Mother Earth cradle him. What a predicament. Go home or stay with Mouse. He couldn't do both.

Mouse's leg would disable her for at least a moon yet. By then the Seashores or the Scarp Countries would have surely found her, were they at all diligent in their efforts. And the determination which Saiga and Eel displayed suggested strongly that they would be diligent. Mouse was condemned and therefore Hare as well.

There were other women. Gar ought simply to let the spirits sort out what was to be and let Mouse's fate unfold itself.

No. Glory came in stepping past fate. Fate was taking the calf and yearling. Glory was taking the bull. Finding the truth in this matter regarding Kelp could not by any stretch of imagination be called glory in the usual sense. And yet, in a special way, it was. Absolutely. He would never dance the exploit. There was no haunch of meat to be distributed to favourites and honoured guests. Still, he must pursue this. He must earn his own glory in this new way, by finding Kelp's true killer.

Besides, there were no other women.

14

He Prefers to Throw His Spear

Gar and Mouse floated below the surface of a deep lake, its water as warm as they. Breathing was not a problem despite that they were submerged. They coupled, but somehow it was not a happy union. From a distant place, a shrill voice called, "I think the bear is back."

Gar awoke with a start, snapping the fragile spell of dreamy pleasure. He was pressed back beneath this little overhang hardly large enough to be called a cave.

Drowsily, Mouse raised her head. "Huh?" She lay squeezed against Gar, her back to his chest, the fire before her. Apparently, she had been sleeping as deeply as he, for she sounded groggy and disoriented.

Hare, seated beside the fire, silently picked up his spear. "Downslope there, four man-lengths. Five. See?"

Very carefully, Gar rearranged his sore body to sitting. The gouge in his side was inflamed, naturally, but not yet to the point of robbing his ability to think, as infection might do. He listened and sniffed.

It was nearly dark now; it had still been light when he fell asleep. The nightjars were out, two of them careening about overhead with their nasal *goo-eck*. Crickets chirped all over. No, not all over. Not down in the brush where Hare was pointing. Something had disturbed them to silence there.

Gar pulled his feet under him and at a crouch stepped over Mouse's bound leg. He scooped up his spear and tucked it against his good side. He settled to a squat. He exhaled, then inhaled deeply, picking up nuances of odour. "Sow of two or three years. Not a big one."

"Big enough."

Gar smiled. True. When you were the size of Hare, even a sub-adult she-bear looked monstrous.

Hare frowned. "I don't hear it now."

"Listen to the crickets. Where they stop chirping, there is the bear."

"She won't come in to the fire, eh."

"Eh."

Mouse was sitting up now, her bound leg stretched straight out across the powder dirt. "Kill her for meat, eh. We need to eat more before we go."

Good idea, but Gar might not be up to the task of tackling that bear single-handedly. The day of rest had renewed him greatly. Hare was an excellent forager, bringing in a tasty variety of roots. Gar had drunk three skins of water and most of a fourth. He was beginning to feel fully alive again. But to face down a bear?

He wagged his head *no*.

Smugly, Hare stepped out to where he could stand erect and moved downslope. "I'll get her." He raised his child's spear above his shoulder and drew it back. It was the stance People used when hurling a rock, the stance the Hairies used when throwing a spear.

Gar snorted. "Sit down. Either get stronger or quit throwing it."

Hare glanced back at him. "If you don't like it, I don't care. It's smart to throw it. You don't get so close."

"Smart!" Gar spat. "Attacking me wasn't smart. If you do it right, your first spear-thrust pierces a lung. It did not even break a rib. If you throw your spear at that bear now, it will bounce off the hair. It's too lightweight. Then your spear is gone, but the bear isn't. There you stand with no weapon. The bear's long hair, that's good protection. If I throw a spear at a lion and she ducks, I have to start climbing fast, eh."

"Hare, listen to him," Mouse cautioned, "He's been a hunter for a long time, with many kills. You are a child."

Gar softened the jab at Hare's pride. "You can kill many things with that spear, but not a bear. It's too short, your spear."

Reluctantly, awash in a spectacular snit, Hare returned to the fire and flopped to sitting. "Bears aren't much. Not like lions or hyænas or wolves. Bears don't hurt you."

"Unless you poke them with a stick." Gar settled to cross-legged, but he kept his spear at ready.

A mosquito buzzed in his ear. He batted at it. A sharp, itchy prick told him where it landed. He grabbed his hip, squashing the insect. And he thought about the Hairies, who wrap skins around their hips because they consider such places private. Then talk about them, yet. Hairy women did not wrap their babies and small children—except in winter, of course. Apparently small children were not private. And yet, small Real children dreamt dreams and imagined things, and those thoughts were just as private for a child as for an adult. At least Real People were consistent.

Mouse scooted over and nestled in beside him. "I've been thinking about magic. Maybe Hare is right. When I was a wife, when I belonged to the Hairy shaman—" She licked her lips. "Probably a slave of that one, you think? He would not really marry a Real Person."

Gar nodded. He wrapped an arm around her and drew her in tighter.

Mouse continued, "Wife, slave, no matter now. When I was his, he worked his magic in the Eagle Mountains, in a vast cave there. A deep cavern that goes way back."

"Eagle Mountains."

"It's a—a whole clan of mountains clustered together, south and west of here, beyond the Seashore People. He used red, blue, yellow, black, brown. Colours like flowers, colours like animals. It takes great wisdom to make these colours. It's a secret art."

"Art?"

She studied the fire for long moments. "Hairy word, *art.* I don't know any word or gesture for art among Real People. Nothing like it in our common language."

"Secret. Private."

She bobbed her head. "They have only one shaman in a clan. They don't split as moieties. They split as families."

"You said."

"Eh. This shaman, he chooses lads, shows them his art, and teaches them how to make it in the cave. I watched him do that. After they finish doing their art, everyone, the whole clan, gathers in that cave. They eat, laugh, dance a lot. I saw it all along with them. And I helped him make the colours. Maybe that is the magic."

"Rat knew all this."

"Yes." Her whole body worked gently against him with her breathing.

"So Kelp wanted the magic in the colours. Rat knew that, so he gave you to Kelp. Then Kelp had you make colours for him."

She bobbed her head. "But he could not use them well. I thought I should show him how, but then I thought, no. That is Hairy magic. Leave it with the Hairies. Now, I'm not so sure I did the right thing."

"And Kelp thought your Hairy magic could make him strong."

"Stronger." She looked sad. Sad and confused. "He had so much power already. Enough power. Why did he need more?"

At least, unlike Hare, she still thought like a Real Person.

And Gar could not answer her question because he could not conceive of the kind of hungers that seemed to have driven Kelp.

He listened to the bear move around out there in the darkness. He thought he saw a shaggy shadow once or twice, the voluminous hair reflecting their firelight.

Hare dug a hole, raked in some coals, covered them loosely with scree stones, and arranged the last of the roots. He tossed more stones and some dirt in on top. By the time the moon came up, they would have a good meal.

They needed water, but with the bear in the immediate vicinity, that would have to wait. Were all three of them hale, they need only go out together and safely fetch the water. A child and two invalids, though, would invite the attention of any hungry meat-eater on this side of the mountain. Even a half-sized bear.

They really needed to get more firewood too. The fire no longer danced with open flames. Blue glow and yellow glow slithered about across the dying red coals. Pretty, but of minimal use, should animals drop by. Perhaps later Gar would venture out and pull some dead limbs down.

Gar would have scooted himself back so he could lean on something or perhaps lie down, but Mouse still sat against him. He'd suffer anything to avoid moving before she did. "Mouse? The Hairies. That thick hair grows on their faces, sometimes on their chests even."

"The hair on their faces is their beard."

"Their beard. What does it feel like, this beard? Coarse like a bear's? Fine like a beaver's? Like our head hair?"

"It looks stiff and harsh, but it isn't. But not fine, either. Hard to say. Mostly like musk ox, I guess, or mammoth."

"Mm." He tried to shift a little without disturbing her. "Inner hair or outer hair?"

"Inner." She hugged tight around his waist. "Now what are you going to do?"

"I don't know. You?"

"I don't know. I can't go south. That's where the Seashore People seek me. And there the Hairies will be soon, when they come down from their summer territory. I can't go north. Scarp Country People are looking for me there, and there are no Horses left anyway. I can't go—"

"Maybe that's not true."

She arched her head back to look at him. "What's not true?"

"That all the Horses are gone. Maybe if Rat wanted to sell you to Kelp, he would tell you that—another of his lies. If you quit looking for them and went with him, Rat would profit."

"Profit. What is profit?"

For once Gar knew a word that she, for all her travel and sophistication, did not. "Rat uses the word a lot. It means something you can get that you want, and you didn't have it before."

"Mm." She didn't seem particularly interested in profit. "Before I met Rat, I didn't find any Horses. I don't think they're in our territory any more."

"But maybe not gone. How about other clans of your tribe?"

"Aspen Lakes has five clans in all. Do you think I should go up there, look around? Think maybe some Horses are up there living in other clans? What about Newt?"

Gar shrugged. "How about, we just wait right here. Nobody is going to look for us here. It would be a nice turn, eh—Newt travels all over north looking for you, and here you sit right on Ibex Mountain, next to him the whole time. In a month or two, you can walk better and I'll be well. Hare will grow more. Come the first starvation moon, we'll all be strong and we can travel north. Eel will be back home then, Newt will be back home then. The Hairies will be back south then. No one will bother us. We can seek out other Aspen Lakes clans, and maybe find some of your kin."

"We. Us."

Gar tipped her chin up, the better to hold her eye to eye. "You don't like that 'we'?"

She laid a warm, firm hand on his. "'We' is good! I hoped. But I didn't know." Her eyes got a little wet. She bobbed her head smartly. "We!"

Hare hissed, "Bears build fires, eh?"

"Where?" Gar wrenched himself to his feet and stepped forward to stand clear of the niche.

A yellow dot, a big yellow dot, glowed near the crest of a low hill to the north-northwest. A robust fire. A men's fire.

Hare moved in beside him and leaned on his spear. "Real People, eh. This is still Scarp Country we're in. Your Mammoths?"

"No. Not Mammoths. Not this side of the mountain." Gar reconsidered. "Wait. Eh, Mammoths. Newt! It has to be." In his mind's eye, he put the story together from bits and pieces. It all fit together well. "I think Newt was out hunting you, up north. Rat left me and headed north. Newt has fire with him, so he is easy to see each night. By and by, Rat sees his fire and joins them. Newt says, 'Gar seeks you, Rat. Where is Gar?' Rat says, 'West of Ibex Mountain with a lion staring at him.' Now here comes Newt to look around. Maybe if Newt is very smart, he'll think that maybe you and I will find each other."

"Newt?" Hare snorted. "Not that smart."

Gar smiled and wiggled a finger. "Better bank the fire, make sure they don't see us."

"Maybe we'll eat bear after all, if we have no fire to keep her away." Hare dropped to his knees and began scooping dirt.

Mouse had struggled to her feet. She pressed close.

"Kohl's that smart. Do you think maybe Kohl is with him?"

"When you were hiding in the lake, did you see Kohl with him?"

"No. But we didn't see everything."

"Mm." Gar tried to picture Kohl being so vindictive as to accompany Newt on the search for her avowed enemy. Possible. Not probable. Would Newt take Kohl along? In an instant, just as Gar would, and for obvious reasons.

Now what?

Mouse tipped herself back down to sitting. She sighed heavily. "I am doomed. I did nothing, and I am doomed."

Gar sat down beside her and balanced his spear at ready. Hare was right. With the fire banked, they would become an item of much greater interest to the bear. On the other side of their smouldering fire, Hare hunkered down and readied his spear, watching the night.

"When the moon comes up," Gar said, "we'll leave here. Maybe Newt has seen our fire, and maybe not. We can't take the chance. We'll get down the hill somewhere to hide."

"Then what?" Hare would have to ask.

"I don't know."

Mouse twisted. "You speak to the spirits. You can..."

"Sometimes."

"You can learn who killed Kelp, then we'll go to Seashore and tell them, eh."

"Cloud and I tried that. The spirits decided not to tell."

Undaunted, she pressed on. "Then we'll go south, we three. We'll go back to my old home with the Hairies, where Hare was born. Hare and I, we know that country. We'll go to the deep cave in the Eagle Mountains."

Gar frowned at her.

Her voice became animated, almost hopeful. "I'll make the colours. Then we'll go into the cave. You will listen and speak. The spirits like that spot, deep in the Mother Earth. The magic is so strong there, it will give you a better ear to hear the spirits. They'll tell you what you have to know. Then we'll go to the Seashore People and tell Eel and Saiga."

He thought about it awhile. "Talk to Hairy spirits? I don't like that."

"They attended Kelp and he was Real People. Maybe it's not Hairy spirits and Real spirits. Maybe it's just spirits, eh. For anyone." She pressed on. "A shaman can do what most people can't. You can hear what others do not. Add that magic to yours, and it will give you the power to save me." And then she whispered, "I don't want to die."

15

He Makes Foolish Decisions

Gar sat cross-legged on a rocky little outcrop near the crest of Ibex Mountain with the world spread out before him. From here, he could not see the slope where he and Mouse and Hare had met and rested for two days. That lay behind. He could, however, make out away to the west the hilltop where he and Rat had parted company. To his right lay the length and breadth of home, Scarp Country. And over there to northwestward was where Newt built his fire last night—if indeed it was Newt.

Somewhere behind him, Mouse and Hare were working their way to the southwest. By and by he would catch up to them. For now, he must find out what Newt was doing.

Mouse! Reunited with Mouse! What a happy turn of events.

The mid-morning sun caressed his back with its warm, smooth fingers. Already the alder leaves were turning bitter and brittle, and curlews were flying south. Soon, aurochs and horses would turn shaggy. There wasn't much summer sun left. When this moon waned, the nut moon of autumn would be the next to rise, and then the starvation moons so bleak and grey, snow-choked. The clan lost People every winter. Whom would they lose this time? No wonder white was the colour of death and mourning.

He smiled as Head crowed, *You were right. It* is *Newt out there.*

Here came the party up the slope now, a straggling band of familiar Mammoth clansmen headed home.

Interesting. Mouse was right too. Kohl travels with them. Heart sounded miffed, certainly jealous.

Gar couldn't smell a woman yet, but if Heart sensed her, she was probably there. Heart tuned in to spirits Gar usually didn't bother with.

Gar's People had spread out into a loose search formation as they moved uphill toward this outcrop, here a Person, there a Person, more or less abreast each other with maybe a dozen man-lengths between them. Searching for Gar? For Mouse? For both? They were almost certainly foraging as well as seeking.

Gar scooted forward, down off his perch, to squat beside a stunted fir. With the rock at his back, he laid his spear crosswise across his knees and waited. Clumps of barberry and fir blocked his vision, so he relied upon nose and ears.

Footfalls and leaf-rustling told him four clansmen approached within hailing distance. And he recognised the clumsy, laboured tread of the Person four or five man-lengths to his left. Toad. Good old not-too-bright Toad. Gar assayed the band's mood. If they were anticipating outlanders—the Seashores, perhaps—they were certainly being lackadaisical about it. When one hunted a grown man, he was hunting the most dangerous of game and needed to keep his guard up better than these People were doing. Therefore it was safe to assume that outsiders were not part of the scene.

Gar mumbled, "Eh, Toad."

The footfalls ceased. "What? Who?"

Gar raised his head slightly, to see.

His eyes fear-filled and wide enough to glow by night, Toad stood gaping, looking all around. He dropped his saiga-skin pack bag to grip his spear with both trembling hands. Gar could even see white knuckles.

Smiling, Gar straightened his legs, rising slowly.

"Don't do that!" Toad snatched up a stone and flung it at Gar.

Gar ducked almost in time. It caromed off his shoulder. "You've been up north. Looking for Mouse and Hare, eh?"

Toad stared at him a moment, then relaxed the rigid grip on his spear. He ululated with a voice to be envied by trumpeting mammoths. From the distance, someone returned his call and passed it on. He came slogging through the heath, so Gar climbed back up onto his craggy perch.

Toad crawled up on the rock and hunkered down beside him. "That's why you are shaman. We don't have to tell you anything. You know everything already."

Gar snorted, outwardly disdainful and inwardly quite proud. "So Newt's here, eh."

"Eh."

"And he's got Kohl with him."

"Eh." Toad twisted to study Gar. "Newt decided we should go north. Kohl said, 'I've been there long winters ago. I know the area. Take me along.' And Newt, he's happy to take her along. But how do you know all this? How did you know we've been north?"

Gar shrugged casually and pointed to Toad's arms. "Those blackfly bites look like they itch."

"Eh!" Toad snorted. "Miserable up north. I don't know why Newt thought he'd find anything in that ugly place. She didn't go there. No sign of her."

"Did he talk to those Dark Mountains People?"

Stoat and Trout came crashing out of the brush. Newt's white head appeared amid the brush below, coming this way.

"Up north there, we caught a child. The child said you were there by and by, but not Mouse." Toad shrugged. "So we came home."

"And met Rat on the way. He said I had been south with the Elephant clan, Seashore People, and now a lion was chasing me, eh."

"Eh! He said all that. He said the lion was going to catch you because you didn't have any protecting spirits. Then Newt says, 'Ah, Gar's spirits are no good anyway.' You should have seen Rat's face. Surprised. Worried. And he said, 'Are you sure?'" Toad gestured toward the gouge in Gar's side. "The lion didn't catch you, eh. But almost."

Gar drew Toad's attention to his ankle before the hulking hunter realised that this was far more likely a spear wound than a lion slash. "Almost."

"I hate travel! You're gone, you don't know the country, you don't know where to look to find food and good water, you don't know where animals lie in wait. You don't know where the caves are. Sometimes there aren't any at all and you spend the night out in the open. Walk, walk, walk. Walk farther than women foraging in winter. And there's Rat, saying we must walk more all the way south. Newt says, 'Good. Let's go.' We all said, 'Not good!' and started home, so Newt had to come home too. Rat went off his own way. Good riddance." Toad spat.

"Kohl. Did she say she knows where to find Mouse?"

"She said Mouse can't go south, with Hairies there. She won't go west. Nothing west except maybe more Hairies. Kohl says Mouse's old People lived up north. Cold Lakes are the only ones who have to take her if she comes. Anyone else would chase her off, kill her maybe. For sure if she runs into her old Hairy tribe down south, they'll kill her. That's what Kohl says."

Here came Flint up through the rocks, and Otter and Goose. They practically staggered, utterly spent. Indeed, the whole clan looked on the verge of collapse.

Gar propped his elbow on his knee, his chin in his hand. "Toad. Cloud said this was a bad idea, eh."

"Eh. His counsel was, wait for your return. Newt didn't do that, eh."

"Can you think why Newt is so eager to find Mouse?"

"He's afraid of Elk clan, the Seashore People."

"He's not smart enough to be afraid."

"He acts so."

"Mm."

The weary travellers gathered in around Gar's perch. They flopped on the stony ground, sat back against the rocks, sprawled in the duff. A sorrier band of grumpy hunters Gar had rarely seen.

Newt looked just as bedraggled as everyone else. Only Kohl at his side showed any spirit at all. The white-haired one paused but a moment to stare at Gar. "Who speared you?" He tossed his pack aside and stretched out on the ground beside Stoat. Kohl sat down beside him, watching Gar curiously.

Gar skirted the question. "Not much safety when you travel alone. Not many People welcome you. For sure, no pleasure travelling alone."

Stoat snarled, "Not much pleasure, travelling with Newt." He tapped his chest. "Believe me. I know."

"Speared?" Toad studied Gar with renewed interest. He smirked. "Speared by that lion, maybe."

"Speared by a clever hyæna, maybe. Maybe the same clever hyæna that snared that colt, eh."

Goose cackled. "Toad still gets mad about that, every time he sees that ugly lad."

Toad rumbled, "We'll find those two, and soon."

Newt raised his head to look at Gar. "Rat says you came off the Far Mountain. As you travelled east this way, did you see any sign of Mouse, Hare?"

"I didn't look for them. I didn't know you want them."

Fie! Heart chided.

More or less true, Head returned.

Newt's eyes narrowed. "Took you a long time to come that short distance."

"Why hurry?"

"There, see?" Stoat aimed his riposte at Newt. "'Why hurry.' Now that's good thinking, eh. This push, push, push, scurry all over, wears everybody out, and no good comes of it."

"We'd do better if Cloud were along. But he stayed

home. He said it's no good to chase Mouse." Obviously, Newt would prefer a different shaman just now.

Gar noticed that Newt had brought the eldest of Cloud's three initiates, a gangling youth with bones showing, Dragonfly. The callow lad could cant the dead and dying, which would be his primary function on a journey, but wisdom, maturity, and experience were required to commune with foreign spirits.

Newt spat. "Rat should be helping lead us home. Instead, he pointed in this direction and said, 'Go that way.' Then he showed Rain and Dor how to go the other way. Rain and Dor, they can get lost in a bear skin. He should have taken them too."

Gar frowned. "Rain and Dor? Where are they going?"

Stoat was scowling royally, obviously dissatisfied with most of life. "Newt sent Rain and Dor down to Seashore, to tell Eel and Saiga that Mouse is hiding. They're supposed to say that if the Elks want her, they should come help find her. Another bad move, I say, inviting a hostile clan in. Too many bad moves, you ask me."

"Didn't ask you." Newt lurched to sitting. "This is big country. We don't know it, but she does. She knows many places to go, and we don't. Elk clan knows the country. If they help, we'll find her quicker, eh."

"You don't know she killed Kelp!" It burst out of Gar. This was all getting away from him, and he could see nothing except Mouse, poor Mouse, dying one way or another.

"We know!" Newt lurched to his feet. "She ran away, eh. If she didn't do it, why would she run away?"

"Too many things happen with no reason." Stoat

stretched mightily. "Here we are chasing that Mouse when Cloud says don't, no reason. We brought Kohl along, no reason." Stoat dipped his head toward Kohl. "Newt killed Crow, no reason. Too often, we travel after dark, no r—"

"Killed Crow!" Gar stared. His Head and Heart babbled incoherently.

"Newt got mad at her, called her traitor, and beat her."

Newt glowered. "She warned Mouse. If she hadn't warned Mouse, we wouldn't have to travel all over like this."

"See." Toad prodded Gar's ribs. "You don't know all that happens after all."

Crow! Dark and furious Crow, moody Crow, a noble woman. Strong. So many years, Gar wished he had a child, wished he were named a father... Crow gave Newt a child, and Newt...

Newt shouldered his bag. "This is Ibex Mountain, so home isn't far now. Here we go."

The hunters stood up and stretched amid a chorus of moans and grumbling. Gar remained sitting.

Toad slid down off the rock and picked up his pack. He stopped and looked at Gar. "You're not going."

"You don't need me. You've got Dragonfly."

Newt came scuffing over and stood squarely facing Gar. "Maybe you found your Mouse already, eh. Maybe you're going to go to her now after we leave."

"Maybe. Maybe not. But if that was true, why would I sit here, and wait to meet you? Why not just flee, I and this woman? I'm wasting a lot of escape time, sitting around here talking to you, eh."

Newt's eyes narrowed with suspicion. "What other

reason would you have to stay out here?"

Now, of all times, Gar must think clearly, but he could not. All he could say was, "Fool! Crow was feeding your son."

16
She Is Definitely a Hyæna

Gar was going to have to remain seated on this craggy little outcrop where he had met his Mammoth clansmen late this morning, at least for a while yet. For one thing, Newt seemed certain that Gar knew Mouse's whereabouts. So the warlord most surely had posted a watchman to see where Gar went. Gar must wait until darkness to elude the spy. But for another, even more important thing, he must pause long enough to listen and think.

There was much thinking to do, too. But it all remained ajumble.

The true murderer. Why did Saiga insist so strongly that it must be the actual killer and no other? Obviously there was a reason, but it eluded Gar. Among Gar's People, it would not matter. When someone died by the hand of an outsider, the whole outside clan shared guilt.

That's what clan was all about. The Elks should be after any handy Mammoth clansman in return for the death of the Elk clansman. It simply was the way it was done. Why weren't they?

And who was their culprit?

Newt? He would kill in a minute to protect what he called the balance, to keep anything from changing. Had Kelp decided to add the Mammoth territory to his own, Newt would have been facing a terrible problem. Besides, Newt held life in far too scant regard, as evidenced by the murder of his own woman. Poor Crow.

Rat? Yes, to protect his trade routes and contacts. And he certainly would use all his cunning to see someone else take the blame when he found his trading partners irate and up in arms.

Kohl? The Kohl Gar remembered from their youth would not, but maybe she had changed somehow in her years away. But why? Jealousy perhaps. But if jealousy, would she not go for Mouse's throat rather than Kelp's? Perhaps she killed him because of some promise broken, a matter between the two of them. If so, why wait until Kelp was far from home? Revenge, denying him the cant and thereby denying him the Beyond? Could anyone be that cruel?

Eel? Possibly, despite what Sturgeon thought, if the lure of power be strong enough. Sturgeon himself allowed as how that whole clan was cuckoo.

Mouse? Gar would have to admit that she very well could have killed to escape Kelp's clutches, perhaps to protect Hare.

And yet, why would she want to escape? Pledging with a man or being possessed as a slave was largely a matter of semantics. The end result of either was to be fed by, in this case, a powerful Person. Women vie for that kind of status. Indeed, Gar knew of a few times when some successful hunter, full of glory, would pit two women against each other just to watch the fight.

Did Mouse's elaborate explanation of family signify? And if so, how?

Questions, questions, questions.

And he became aware again that he was being watched. If the watcher be something carnivorous, he was in deep trouble, sitting out on this rock like a pimple on someone's backside. No trees near, nowhere to escape. But the watcher felt human. It was the same watcher who had raised Gar's goosebumps when he sat in Larch Cave. It was the same watcher who had tickled the back of his neck as he was travelling south from Dark Mountains.

He closed his eyes and took a deep breath. He held it and waited, feeling beyond senses, scanning the spirits of the hillside all around him.

She was a woman, this watcher, a troubled woman, her spirit in turmoil. Though a Real Person, she was skinny to the point of being scrawny, like Hare. And she was pallid, paler by far than Mouse, a bit paler in fact than Gar himself, and he was considered tan rather than brown.

Her spirit churned like a mountain stream tumbling down through riffles. Her spirit sensed his as he assayed her and she seemed surprised that he detected her. He couldn't understand that. What was so surprising? He'd been detecting her for days and days.

Was hers a powerful spirit? It seemed it could be, were it not weakened by its turbulence. It was certainly not powerful enough to follow him north to Dark Mountains, south to Seashore and back while she remained in one place. No, she must have been following him around physically, tagging along behind him beyond easy ken.

The impression he received through all this was *Hyæna.* For some reason, she was adopting the persona of a hyæna. It must be a totem of some sort.

This raised another, more immediate question. What should he do about his watcher? He sensed her moving cautiously this way.

Meet her, Heart argued. *It isn't every day that some woman follows you all over the known world.*

Head objected. *She's not a part of the problem, so she is not part of the solution. She has no connection to Kelp or to Mouse. You must find a solution quickly. Were you at leisure, you could pursue this, but you are not. Mouse's well-being depends upon sticking to the problem.*

He let out air and drew it in again.

Someone else was out there. That one must be Newt's spy. It felt like Goose. Yes, definitely Goose.

Head was right. The watcher, whoever she was, would do nothing but lure him off the trail he must follow. He would elude her, or at least avoid contact with her. That might be difficult; she was certainly clever and persistent to have followed and watched thus far.

He would elude Goose as well before joining again with Mouse. That wasn't too difficult. Goose was good, but not that good.

And suddenly, he didn't want to wait until dark. He didn't want to have to bother thinking about some recondite outland woman behaving unfathomably. He wanted to get back to Mouse.

And then what?

He knew what. Forget this find-the-murderer chore.

Rat survived year in, year out without drawing nurturance from his ancestral clan country. Women from time to time migrated with impunity to other territories. Kohl had done so successfully. He could, however, not think of a single man or boy who lived more than a season or two once he separated from his ancestral home. And yet, legends and even some genealogies told of people who lived much farther north in the remote past, in lands now gone. They moved successfully.

Perhaps Gar could step into a new life elsewhere without wilting and dying from the uprooting. In fact, he could live among Sturgeon's People, serving as shaman, any time he wished. He would shake off the past, as exampled by this Hyæna woman and Newt's feckless spy Goose, and move forward into a simplified life with the best woman he'd ever found.

Probably Newt and Cloud, or Eel and Saiga—somebody—would eventually ascertain the identity of Kelp's killer and the matter would end, one way or another. Let others undertake the task. As soon as they succeeded, Gar could bring Mouse home. Until then he would be a sojourner in others' territories. He could do it.

Gar applied eye, ear, nose, and spirit to exactly where Goose lay in hiding, and also how far that Hyæna woman had come in her approach. The breeze shifted slightly, bringing Goose's vague scent. The spy cowered close by, in those bushes up behind this outcrop.

And the Hyæna woman? He concentrated on her again. Her back to the North Mountain, she was moving this way along a ridgeback, perhaps to make initial contact. Yes. That was her intent. She believed him to be alone, but then, she wouldn't be expecting Goose up there. She would think all the clan was returning home.

She was close and getting closer.

Was Goose sensing the Hyæna? Hardly. Goose did not feel spirits. To get Goose's attention you had to hit him with a stick.

If Gar started walking due west, exactly in that direction right there, Goose would take the easy way down the hill to follow him. That easy route would carry Goose past a little moss-choked seep all abuzz with flies. The Hyæna was working her way south along the ridge right now. She would pass that seep also, and soon.

Gar smiled to himself. It was worth a try.

He hopped down off his perch, stretched his back and flexed his bottomside muscles. Then he took off deliberately toward the west. Ten man-lengths down the slope he adjusted his direction a bit, making certain he remained visible to Goose. He upped the pace slightly.

He continued past the seep, calculating when Goose would reach that point. He tried to imagine the effect on Goose, should a pale, scrawny woman pop into view totally unexpected. The thought tickled him. Whatever Goose's sudden appearance might mean to the woman, he could not care less.

Long moments later, the seep now behind him in the uphill brush, he heard Goose's terrified shriek.

At a new angle, he broke into a run. Then he followed a small drainage, keeping behind willow thickets. By the time the sun passed midday and began its inexorable fall westward, he was off Ibex Mountain and headed south-southwest. Toward Mouse.

He no longer worried about Goose, but had he managed to elude the Hyæna? When next he paused to rest, he tried to detect her. Either the spirits were playing the mischievous little games in which they sometimes indulged, or he had succeeded.

17

Hyænas Are Out There

Curious, the way day dissolved into night so daintily. Rather than watch the flaming sun slide downhill into the western hills, his usual habit with sunsets, Gar sat tonight on a little knob of white quartz and admired the changing colours of the northern horizon. Even as they shifted from pallid off-white through palest pink to blue, they turned from limpid to milky. Autumn skies were milky that way.

Winter was coming early this year. See? The red deer and the elk were growing out their cold-weather coats already, and their gigantic antlers still in velvet. And the red-and-black banded fuzzy caterpillar rippling in slow deliberation across Gar's rock here—a narrow centre band portended a mild winter. This caterpillar's band was very wide.

Gar was tempted to split and eat it, but there were a

lot of caterpillars less acrid than that one. He would pass.

And he would worry. Here at the confluence of two streams west of Ibex Mountain, he was supposed to meet Mouse. Three days ago. Was she merely slowed up because of her leg, or had something untoward happened to her? Had Hare, who hated Gar anyway, convinced her to leave the area and forget about him? Did she still have fire? He'd hunt up some meat if he thought they could cook it when she got here.

Blue darkness drifted from east to west until the light all dissolved away. Autumn haze ate most of the stars. With the sun down, the air cooled quickly. He waited until the darkness grew too thick for her to travel in. He had spotted a bit of an overhang up behind him. He would spend the night there.

Twice today he had crossed fresh lion scent. He paid particular attention now to the world around him as he made his way up toward the overhang, for lions loved to settle in at the base of some scarp and survey the world below them for their next meal. Partway there he paused for breath and looked about.

A small yellow dot glowed on the hillside half a mile downstream on this larger river. Surely that wouldn't be Mouse. What would she be doing away down there? Perhaps they somehow missed each other. Just a little uneasy about the prospect of lions and hyænas, Gar braced his spear at ready and changed directions. He headed parallel to the scarp along the slope, hastening toward that dot.

Why would she build such a large fire, a men's fire? He could just as quickly find her with a much smaller fire. Why was she advertising her presence like this?

She wasn't. As he approached to within good seeing, Gar discerned the hulking Eel, the wizened Saiga, a couple other Elks, and his own clan's youths, young Dor and Rain, all seated around the fire. Good! Good! They were quietly contemplating the two back haunches of a saiga that sizzled and crackled above coals glowing beside the main fire.

As Gar approached, Dor stretched forward with a stick and raked some more coals aside from the flames to the cooking pit. Smoke, fat, and juices were putting a glossy brown finish on the meat. Gar's arrival could not be better timed.

Brush rattling uphill of him reminded him he wasn't there yet. Leaves rustling downhill did too. Not lions. Hyænas. Hyænas weren't careful about how noisily they moved. The first sound a hunter heard from lions was the crunch of his own bones after they'd pounced.

Half-grown Dor and hulking Eel heard the rustling too. Man and boy, they picked up their spears and studied the blackness between them and Gar.

Gripping his spear, Gar bolted forward toward the ring of yellow light. The hyænas abandoned any pretext of stalking and came crashing after him. They hauled up short of entering the light ring; the one uphill laughed in disappointment. Three others joined the hilarity. Gar plunged full tilt into the light circle, a less-than-dignified entrance but a safe one.

He glanced back. Beyond the circle, green eyes glowed in ghostly round, grey faces. He gave a respectful greeting to Eel, did obeisance to Saiga, acknowledged his clansmen, and flopped down beside the fire, utterly wearied of life.

His nerves jangled, and he hated that. By his age, he should be accustomed to close calls. He was so rattled he could scarcely control his breathing. Protective magic be hanged.

Eel smirked. "Interesting. Here you are very far from your home, well outside your territory. And you do not seem surprised that we also are far from our home."

Gar shrugged. "Newt sent Dor and Rain to you, asking you to come to Scarp Country and help seek Mouse. Newt believes she is the murderer you want. I think he is wrong."

Eel nodded. "At first, I thought, 'This Gar, his magic is weak.' Not so. You see much."

"I do not see enough." Gar looked at Saiga. "If I bring a Person before you, you and your spirits will know if that Person is the one, eh."

"Maybe."

Gar's heart thumped. "Maybe? Not for sure? Your closeness with spirits is very strong. To be envied. Now you say maybe."

Saiga nodded. "Maybe. The messages I get are very confused here. I cannot read them."

Maybe wasn't good enough. The moment Gar spotted the men around this fire, he assumed he could find Mouse and simply let Saiga pronounce her innocence. That would end her peril. He could then take her home to Larch Cave and...and...eh!

But now what? What if the old sage misread the spirits or they misled him? What if he pronounced her guilt when it was not true? Gar did not dare bring her into the picture unless Saiga's gifts could confer certainty.

The aroma of the roasting meat tantalised his mind's eye and made his stomach gurgle. Its richness reminded Gar that raw roots and a few berries were poor sustenance for an extended journey. Hunger leaped up to dance with Anticipation. Nothing tasted better than saiga.

Off to the side lay the saiga's ridged, golden-amber horns. He wondered who would claim them when the group moved on. The antelope's yellowish summer coat on the stripped hide was turning thick for winter. Saigas were creatures of the tundra, spending the summer far to the north. Were they travelling south unseasonably early or had these people been north? He saw no black-fly bites, but the light wasn't good.

He watched Dor a few moments. Although he was by far the youngest here, the lad seemed self-possessed and competent. Mature. Perhaps Gar had tested him when he was still too young, and Dor was one of those fellows who takes a little extra time to come of age. Possibly he should make Dor one of his three apprentices after all.

Gar looked at Saiga.

The old shaman was watching the lad also. "Your clan makes strong young men."

"Dor is a good one."

The lad glanced at the two of them, embarrassed and pleased.

Saiga rumbled, "Our clan makes fine young men also, but not enough of them. Not enough babies to make up for those who die. Winter takes them away; spring brings too few new ones."

"I hear it's the same all over with Real People."

"Eh." The old man sounded so sad.

Silence, save for the crackling fat, the sputtering haunch.

Perhaps he could find some answers here. No harm trying. Gar addressed Eel and the old man. "A pallid woman, very scrawny, powerful spirit, troubled. Your clan?"

And as one, they all stared at Dor, for he had just let out a muffled little yip. He next made a concerted effort to melt into the earth, as would the first snowflake of winter.

"You met her." Saiga seemed to be addressing both Gar and Dor.

Gar replied, "No. I have not seen her yet. I know she's been following me." He stared at Dor.

Dor scrambled to his feet. "Go, pee, eh."

"No." Gar wiggled a finger. "Sit. Story."

"No story."

Gar dropped his voice to a rumble. "Story." What was distracting this lad?

Dor's eyes flitted about, alighting nowhere, seeing everyone. "Not a woman, that one. She's evil, an evil spirit. She frightens you. It's no good to talk about her, eh."

Gar frowned. "You've seen her?"

"Beaver pond, eh. She appeared out of nowhere. All grey and white. She was not there; the next moment, now she was. She said my name."

"How does she know your name?"

"She's an evil spirit! She knows everything about me. She said, 'Where is your shaman,' and in another moment, she was gone again." The lad was stammering.

"She said my name too?"

"Eh."

Gar looked at Saiga, at Eel. "You two know her."

Eel grimaced. "She's not from our tribe. I don't know her line. Dark Mountains maybe, or farther west."

"She feels like a Geese Lakes," Saiga offered.

"Eh. One day she came toward our home cavern at

Three Streams, but the women drove her off." Eel doubled the *chase away* gesture for emphasis. "Not long later, we went out, a party of a dozen maybe, to seek glory. We saw her far off. She lingered half hidden, like a hyæna, watching us. We took a mammoth, a nice bull. I looked up afterward and there she was, standing there. We had a young one, Beech, on his first big hunt. Beech pitied her and gave her meat."

"Honour piece?"

Eel shook his head. "Chunk from the neck. Beech, he got no glory on that hunt. She offered him *union,* and there he went, eh, following after her up the hill. We started hauling meat. When we came back for the next load, there was no Beech anywhere. We found his left leg and guts a day later. Hyænas had pulled him apart."

Saiga sighed. "I canted the leg and guts, but I don't know how much of Beech is Beyond now. Good lad. Not bright. Good."

Dor, Gar noticed, had broken into a sweat. Gar waved a hand toward the lad, a motion of dismissal. "Go, pee. Be careful, there are hyænas out there, eh."

With two shamans and a powerful warlord chuckling at him, Dor had not much choice but to carry his anger and shame without venting them. He moved downslope of the fire to relieve himself, remaining well inside the light circle. Gar felt a brief pang of guilt for embarrassing the lad. Dor, after all, had seen their mysterious Hyæna and he had not.

They divided the darkest haunch amongst themselves and let the other one roast longer. The saiga must have carried a lot of belly fat, for the Elks had larded this meat liberally. Still another portent of a difficult winter.

With his boning blade, Gar hacked himself off a

generous portion and settled close beside the fire. Nights were getting chill as summer waned. Where was Mouse now? Comfortable?

Saiga returned from a relief expedition downhill and sat down beside Gar, knee to knee. Eel cut the old man a portion from the centre, the tenderest part. The sage licked the juices and paused a moment, his eyes closed, savouring that first matchless flavour. He relished life as much as Gar did, obviously.

Gar cut off a bite. Before he popped it in his mouth, he turned to Saiga. "The day you joined our spirits on the rhino hunt, remember? I marvel yet at your skills."

Saiga smiled. "No wonder Mammoths are strong. You, your spirits, your hunters, your warlord all work together well. When you joined that rhino, you could direct its actions and protect your People. That isn't easy. Your skills are just as formidable."

"Hardly. I cannot tell who a murderer is. I can't hear the spirits whisper the name. Surely they know."

"They know. And I cannot always tell either. He could be sitting among us this very moment."

Here among us. The immediacy in Saiga's idle comment jolted Gar.

Saiga doubted his ability to hear. Cloud couldn't hear. Gar couldn't hear. Might it be that the spirits did not know? Spirits were supposed to know everything. And yet...

They ate in silence, the seven of them, each wrapt in his own world.

Where was Mouse?

Rain finished first. Beside the fire, he got up and danced the story of meeting up with Eel and of his and Dor's adventures crossing the river. There were no streams of comparable size in Mammoth territory, for which Gar was grateful. He hated having to get from one side of water to the other, whether that water be flowing rapidly or simply lying there. He thought again of Hare, wading across the creek with his elbows held high, of swimming underwater to track a beaver to its lodge.

Unthinkable.

Gar danced his visit to the Elephants, the tragic loss of their shaman and the history that had died with him, the impressment of the reluctant Rat, and Gar's subsequent meeting with the Mammoths. He neglected to mention anything whatever about Mouse, and no one asked him about the spear gouge in his side. He danced his exploit with the lion and mentioned only that the hyænas tore her apart. He did not give them credit in the kill.

Eel danced the taking of the saiga from which they were eating this evening, a relatively uneventful hunt, for even the largest such antelope was a timid creature conferring no glory. The group slipped into silence.

"Saiga." Gar tossed a couple of dry fir limbs on the fire. "When Kelp loses his head in Mammoth territory, the usual thing is for you and Eel to kill any Mammoth. A life for a life is good enough. Why do you insist on retaliating against one Person, the killer, and not just any Mammoth? Why that one only?"

Saiga's eyes bored into him. "Elk reasons belong to Elks. Not you. They are thoughts."

In short, private, to use Mouse's word, and therefore beyond any discussion. You do not display thoughts for the world to see and judge. That would be obscene, revealing so private a part of you. So that ended it. They were surely powerful reasons, though, for Saiga to respond so intensely.

Every time Gar asked a question or otherwise sought an answer, he got more questions and the puzzle became more complex. Perhaps if he were to work this out at all, he would have to stop asking questions.

The moment Saiga responded with "maybe" instead of "certainly," Mouse's plan to seek out that deep cave became the best plan again. Now all Gar had to do was to spirit Mouse away before lions, hyænas, wolves, Water People, Newt and his Mammoths, or these determined Elks got to her.

Of course, first he had to find her.

······ 18 ·············

The Hideous Child Should Be a Beaver

She lingered to memorise the spectacular view from beneath this overhang near the mountain crest—voluptuous hills shimmering in the breathy air of late summer, water glistening, the blue-white sky clear this morning. There were not many mornings this fine.

She might have assumed hyæna spirit, but *her* Real-People nature still savoured vistas and memories the way Real People did. During none of the many times *her* spirit joined with hyænas' did *she* ever detect that kind of pleasure in them.

Below to the south where this small stream met a larger one, a band of elk browsed. These were bachelor bulls, most of them less than three springs old. Even so, they had huge racks, each antler over a man-length long. Any day now, the bulls would get serious about the fall rut and begin fighting each other. The rut made *her* sad, for when the elk bulls cleaned their antlers off and attended their harems, snow would soon fly.

A skein of geese passed overhead in a ragged, undulant vee, southbound. *She* could hear their honking conversation long after they themselves were lost from view.

The last time *she* saw *her* Gar, he was passing that seep on the north side of the mountain. He appeared to be headed down toward that stream, but so far, *she* had not seen him anywhere along it. *She* had good eyes, too.

Why was he avoiding *her? She* was certain he had detected *her*. It wasn't as if he didn't even know *she* existed. And he knew that *she* was following him. Why would *she* follow him about except to catch up to him and meet him? He couldn't be so dull that he'd fail to figure that much out.

She picked up the spear, left *her* ærie and started down to where the streams met. There *she* would sniff around and seek out tracks. If he passed anywhere near that place, *she*'d know. The more he eluded *her*, the more hungrily *she* yearned for the day when they would meet and be together.

She wondered what kind of sex he provided, though it didn't matter particularly. It looked pleasant enough when *she* observed him in union with others. *She* was not one of those women who took pleasure in union. Sex was a tool with which to get what one wanted from a man, just as a flint adze was a tool with which to get meat from a kill.

She wondered too about that other Person at the seep. Did Gar know that the fellow was in the area? *She* thought he probably did; they were from the same clan. He must have known also, therefore, that the fellow was following him, just as *she* was. Did Gar time his departure from his rock perch so that *she* and the other fellow would arrive at the seep at the same time? Surely not. Why would he do something like that? Much as that seemed to be the case, *she* knew he would not be so cruel.

Oh, well. It all came out in *her* favour. *She* pictured again in *her* mind's eye the look on the fellow's face as *she* popped up suddenly, right in front of him. Talk about terror!

One thing about the fellow: He knew how to trim a spear into perfect balance. The spear hinted at much in the fellow's personality, for its butt end had been whittled into the representation of a phallus. The spear, its ornamentation notwithstanding, might prove useful to *her*, particularly because *she* smelled lions every now and then. Hyænas didn't worry *her*. Lions, hyænas' traditional enemies, posed a threat.

She waited until lions would have bedded down for the day before commencing *her* journey. Re-commencing it. How long had *she* been travelling now? *She* scarce remembered *her* clan territory, so long had it been. *She* angled sharply downslope, listening, watching.

She reached the smaller of the streams and simply stepped out into the creekbed. It was easier travel than fighting one's way through streamside willow and larch. The water of late summer gurgled sleepily, not over its stony bed but through it, among and between the pebbles. *Her* memory sang for *her* the wild, rushing song of spring freshet. What a difference between the beginning of a summer and the end of it.

She paid close attention all around with nose and ears as well as eyes. Dank smells of rotten vegetation stranded on the creekbank... Crisp whirs of grasshopper wings and the prolonged, strident scream of a cicada...

No hint of Gar.

Gar, Gar, Gar, why do you resist your fate?

Ahead there!

She stopped and slipped off to the side among willows arching over the water.

Ten man-lengths downstream, a tall alder wavered, paused, and, with a sort of resigned majesty, toppled. Beaver, no doubt. *She* stepped back into the streambed and continued.

The water deepened. It covered the stones and its gurgling ceased. It filled the streambed bank to bank. The pool widened out. *She* was up to *her* knees in it. Above *her* knees. The beavers were damming downstream, and their pond rising along this creekbed. *She* sloshed ashore and continued downstream along the west side. This was easier going; *she* wound among fir, sycamore and alder, for the growing beaver pond had already crept up past the stream's drowning shoreside vegetation.

She came to the stump of the fallen alder, beaver-gnawed and the muddy ground around it heavy with beaver smell. Its lower three man-lengths lay in the mud, but the upper part with its leafy branches extended out into the water half submerged.

She detected another smell as well, vaguely familiar.

That ugly half-creature, the orange woman's child! He had crawled away out onto the fallen tree trunk. Hidden by leaves, he stood with spear poised, motionless. He was a clever lad, in a twisted way. Two beavers—no, three—were harvesting the fresh branches by cutting them, dragging them down, and stashing them underwater near the lodge in the middle of the pond. The moment one of those beavers decided to cut that branch right there at the boy's feet, the one extending out into the pond, the lad would have a good shot at spearing it.

Out near the lodge, a great round head surfaced. Here it came, submerged from the nose down, cutting a wake through the flat water. The head *plipped* below the water and the huge, wet back arched briefly and disappeared, but the tail did not slap. The beavers suspected no danger.

She tucked *her* travel bag behind a boulder. *She* would do the world a favour by ridding it of that misbegotten half-breed, but not yet. Let him spear his beaver first. The point of his spear buried in the animal, the lad would thus be rendered defenceless. *She* would skewer him with this spear so recently and conveniently obtained from Gar's terrified clansman, take the beaver, and go off in search of the mother.

For the orange woman surely lingered nearby. And the orange woman had fire.

She would eat sweet roasted meat tonight.

Alone.

The whole tree jiggled a bit. It jiggled again.

The lad plunged forward even though no beaver had appeared. Fool child! Didn't he know that when you looked at an object beneath water, that object was not where it appeared to be down there?

As beaver tails splacked here and there around the pond, the lad's spear flayed in his hands. He twisted and pushed, shoving it against a branch. The water churned frothy red.

The struggle subsided. The lad reached down toward his kill, stretching.

Now! She leaped up from *her* hiding place in the bushes, poised *her* spear, and ran forward out onto the fallen tree.

The feckless lad snapped erect, still kneeling. He gaped at *her* dumbstruck, and no wonder. *She* had the child trapped! With nowhere to go, no way to escape, he would back out into the branches as far as they would support him. *She* weighed more than he, but he couldn't get anywhere *her* spear could not reach. Glee bubbled up in *her* at the thought of driving this spear into so loathsome a creature.

With a funny little cry, he folded over double and plunged head first into the bloody water. He disappeared. The troubled water closed over the lad, the beaver, everything.

"No!" Frustrated, *she* stabbed at the water at the place where he had plunged in and nearly lost *her* own balance. There was nothing down there. And yet, the pond could not possibly be that deep. *She* dropped to *her* knees and thrust *her* spear deeper. *She* hit muddy bottom. Again. Again.

The tree bobbed up and down harder with each thrust. It bobbed when *she* did not thrust. It bobbed sideways as well as up and down. *She* looked around wildly, seeking something solid to hang onto. The abysmal child's head appeared briefly out at the end of one of the limbs. He was pulling and jerking on the branch, making the tree dance!

She tried to brace *herself* with the spear to no avail. The tree dipped out from under *her*, and *she* plunged into the chill water. Panic! *She* could see nothing, for *her* eyes would not open. *She* could hear nothing; the horrid water instantly clogged *her* ears. *She* could not breathe, but with slinging stabs of pain, the water entered the whole length of *her* nose. *Her* mouth opened and *she* gagged on water.

Her flailing arm struck wood. *She* grabbed at it. A branch. *She* hauled herself up; *her* head burst forth into air *she* could not breathe because *her* nose and mouth were waterlogged. Water from *her* hair cascaded down *her* face in a choking sheet. *She* coughed. *She* hacked. *She* vomited. *Her* lungs and nose and throat burned with unholy fire.

Somehow *she* managed to hand-over-hand *herself* to muddy footing and the shore. *She* crawled up the bank still choking.

That miserable snot of a dung-infested lowlife maggot! That putrid excuse of a purulent asshole! That—

Where was he?

Where was *her* spear? Somewhere near where *she* fell in, no doubt. And *she* was not about to go back out that fallen tree to retrieve it.

Furious beyond words, *she* sat for quite some time shaking violently. Though *she* watched the pond carefully, *she* saw no sign of either the lad or beavers. The beavers no doubt cowered in their lodge out there, but where did the child cower? He must have somehow made it to shore while *she* struggled in the frigid water. He could not have swum about below the surface, like the beavers do.

The beaver the lad had speared was bigger than he and certainly weighed more. No way could he carry it off as *she* watched. Could it be that the lad himself was some sort of malign spirit? Surely not; *she* would have detected that in him immediately. On the other hand...

She arose eventually to seek out the despicable woman who would give birth to such an atrocity of a child. The orange woman was ultimately to blame. The orange woman would pay.

She retrieved *her* ditty from behind the boulder and chose *her* flint bone-adze for this. *She* didn't like spears anyway, for *she* was not accustomed to using them. Shaped like a penis on the butt end indeed.

She slung *her* ditty and set out. If *she* encountered no sign of the woman or child on this side of the beaver pond, *she* would cross the creek below the dam and search the other side. One way or another, *she* would find these hideous People.

Near the dam *she* discovered the beaver. The lad had not taken time to skin it out or even to butcher it properly. Slashing and ripping, he had cut the quarters free and carried them off, leaving the hide virtually unusable. The steaming entrails lay in it. He had taken the liver but not the kidneys.

That was the final insult, for *she* loved liver. *She* hated kidneys.

The lad was easy to follow. His scent, his tracks, the bloody meat he carried all led *her* up this hill hard beside the main river. Those elk *she* had seen earlier had bedded down on this slope. *She* startled them as *she* passed and they crashed their way down the hill toward the river.

Wait! The lad passed this point also, and only moments ago. Why did he not startle the elk? *She* must pause and think this through. *She* continued along the spoor, following by rote and in no hurry, as *her* thoughts mulled this whole situation.

He obviously communed with beaver and water spirits. He apparently communed with elk spirits too, to avoid disturbing the bulls like that. Whether he himself was an evil spirit or not, he worked closely with the spirit world to be able to hunt so successfully and to pass safely through the land, not to mention through the water.

How ever did he manage to transport his beaver all that way without *her* noticing him at all? The lad had gifts, that was for sure. Therefore his mother must be endowed with spiritual insight and magic beyond the ordinary as well, for such things were usually inherited.

She smelled People close, so *she* climbed up into a boulder pile at the base of a steep scree field.

There in the distance, protected by an overhang high above the valley, the orange woman sat. If she still had fire, she had buried the coals, for no glow or aroma suggested it. She scanned the vista below and beyond, watching the river vale intently. No doubt she was awaiting the return of her son.

No, that wasn't it. There went the lad scrambling up the steep hillside, huffing and puffing beneath his load of meat. He carried his child's spear, and look! He also had the spear with the carved butt. In fact, he had tied two quarters to each end of it with strips of wet beaverskin, using the men's spear as a carrying pole on his shoulder. Clever. But so twisted!

The lad joined his mother and still the woman kept watching out across the valley. She was expecting someone else. That someone else must be Gar. Of course! It all came clear now.

How fortunate *she* was that *she* had not run right up to that overhang and murdered the orange woman, for the orange woman was, in effect, the gateway to Gar. She sought Gar. Gar no doubt sought her. They would find each other. Then, and only then, after Gar was back in *her* sight, would *she* destroy that insane orange woman who so constantly interfered with *her* dreams.

19

The Snake Ate the Moon

Only twice in his life had Gar ever seen a snake, they were that rare. The first time, he was hunting salamanders down at the beaver pond. The snake whipped through the grass beside his foot and plunged into the water. Gracefully undulant, it swam away to nowhere. The second time, he would not have seen the animal at all, had he not heard a bird's startled chirp beneath a bush. He investigated immediately. Already a snake had seized the luckless bird and, its loose jaws working, was forcing its prey down the bulging gullet. The bird was twice as wide as the snake's mouth and throat; yet there it went.

Those two occasions seared vivid impressions onto his memory. The serpents' slack and slithery sleekness fascinated him.

Many winters ago when he was a child, he had

watched a great, round bite be bitten out of the full moon; his mother had told him a giant black snake was eating it. He hadn't doubted that for a moment. And then the snake had turned around and spat the moon out again, and he hadn't doubted that either.

He wished now that he had caught one or both of those snakes and examined them more closely. Yet, at the time he saw them, he would have rather captured a wolverine bare-handed than touch the ominous creatures.

Tonight the giant black snake in the sky struck again.

Gar was sitting alone beside the fire Saiga and Eel had left for him when they continued their journey this morning. He told his Elk and Mammoth compatriots he would seek Mouse by magical means, since they were pursuing her in the flesh. In truth, he planned to sit right here beside this bright fire, glowing at night and smoking by day, until she found him. She knew he was in this area. Sooner or later, they would connect up, surely.

Unless, Head grumped, *her attachment to you is less than yours to her and she decides to disappear. She can do that, you know. She's travelled through this country before. She knows where and where not to go.*

Bear dung. Heart. *Shut up with that. She knows she needs you. Besides, she's thrilled with you. You're a good lover.*

You're also the enemy. Head.

The arguments plagued him; he refused to entertain them. They persisted.

Bloated in its fullness, the last moon of summer cleared the firs and crags of the eastern horizon. But it looked just a wee bit crooked, as if it had been flattened slightly by lying too long on one side. The deformity grew, or, more precisely, the deformed moon diminished.

The snake, Gar realised with astonishment, was back again and taking another bite.

He repositioned himself, hunkering down to the south of the fire so that its brightness would not affect his eyes. With horrified, morbid fascination, he watched the round chunk of blackness grow. The moon slipped bit by bit down the gullet of a snake Gar could not see, try as he would.

The snakes Gar had observed made nary a sound in their passage, but this giant snake was shouting (with its mouth so full?) in the far, far distance. The working of its jaws sounded like someone pounding on a hollow log.

The moon climbed steadily with its usual deliberation, no doubt frantic in its efforts to evade its nemesis. The black circle that was the snake's deathgrip grew, but the snake's shouting came more from Gar's left, around the side of the hill.

How he would love to join the spirit of that black snake! Think of the new experience! Did he dare?

His eyes on the dark chip in the moon, Gar raised his arms and inhaled slowly. He was that snake. He was that snake. He closed his eyes.

Mouse! In his mind's eye, she came upon him as vividly as if she sat at his side. He felt her screaming, terrified. With a great stick, she pounded mightily upon a log. Beside her, her son beat on the log and shouted just as lustily.

He opened his eyes. The voice he heard was not the snake's. It was hers! Where...?

He picked up his spear and left the safety of his circle of light.

Had he called Rat insane? This was insane! He was

exposing himself to instant death in the jaws of a lion or hyæna, and he didn't even know where he was going. His nerves dancing like gnats on a summer eve, he worked his way around the side of the hill.

The shouting and pounding grew louder and he definitely recognised the voice as Mouse's. He looked back. He could no longer see his fire; the curve of the hill hid it. But ahead, he noticed a dim red dot. Mouse's fire? He hurried forward, wishing large carnivores were cowed by the snake's ravages upon the moon, knowing that they almost certainly were not. They preferred to hunt in the dark of the moon, and the world was rapidly becoming just that. If anything, this sorry happenstance would draw them out.

What if the dreaded serpent succeeded in swallowing the moon? Every night an unlit night, alive with eager hunters. What a terrible thought. And however would People mark the seasons if the moon disappeared? Gar felt helpless to do anything about it. No one had instructed him in serpents. He had no experience in bending the minds of snakes. Apparently, he couldn't even make contact, at least not in the usual way.

It *was* Mouse and Hare beside their fire! And indeed they were beating upon a fallen log. He called her name as he hurried toward her dull orange circle of safety. Her waning fire needed attention; she was neglecting it at her peril.

No joyous reunion. No cheerful greeting. Not even his name. She yelled, "Scare it! Help scare it!"

"Scare what?"

Hare snarled impatiently, "The thieving evil spirit who's stealing the moon!"

"It's not an evil spirit; it's a snake. A big black

sn—"

"Look! I think it's working!" Mouse paused briefly to point to the moon. She and Hare renewed their noisy efforts.

And it certainly did appear to be working. Long, long moments passed but the moon shrank no further. And then the bright arch which still remained outside the mouth began to widen perceptibly. Perhaps the snake was again disgorging its prey. If the moon was so predictably unpalatable, why did the snake bother to attempt to eat it?

Gar attended the fire, tossing on the last of the branches stacked beside it. He made one more attempt to initiate contact with the spirit of that snake and failed utterly.

By slow degrees, the moon was emerging from that horrid maw. Not until the moon slipped free and regained its full, circled brilliance did Mouse and Hare cease their din. With a heady little smirk of triumph, Mouse flopped down beside Gar and her fire, her bound, sorry leg stretched out.

Hare scowled uncharitably at Gar. "We saved the moon, but you didn't help. No shouting, no noise, no nothing."

'Nothing' is right. Not even spirit contact. Heart cringed with embarrassment.

We tried. Head reminded.

"How does noise and shouting work? Tell me about it." Gar held Hare's eye. He was asking enlightenment of a half-grown child. If that didn't ease Hare's surly attitude, nothing would.

Mouse started to speak, but Hare grabbed the opportunity to get one up on a shaman. "An evil spirit tries to stick the moon in his ditty bag. Such a big moon, eh. He is pushing on it, trying to shove it into his bag, but we make lots of noise. He is afraid of the noise. By and by he gives up, lets the moon alone, and flees."

"Eh." For a moment, Gar weighed this against his mother's claims. With abundant gestures, he countered with, "A giant black snake of the sky, with mouth shaped so, like this, seizes the moon. The moon is greater than he, but no matter. His mouth wraps around it so, and his slack jaws work so, trying to swallow the moon. But the moon is a bad shape to swallow, and it has a bad taste. The snake thinks twice about it and spits the moon out. By and by, he forgets how bad the moon tasted and tries again."

Hare shook his head. "In a bag!"

Gar cupped his hands in a convex shape. "Then the moon would be shaped this way as it slipped into the bag, not this way, like a bite was taken out."

Hare looked perplexed. "You've seen this snake?"

"Not the giant black snake. No, you can't see the snake in the sky, just as you don't see spirits in the sky. Some things are too great to see. I've seen snakes on the ground, though. They are this shape, long and—"

"I know snakes. Seen lots of snakes."

Oh you have, have you? Heart sniffed. *Uppity brat.*

Gar changed the subject. "How come you're carrying Goose's spear there?" He gestured beyond Mouse's ditty bag. The phallic symbol on the butt end was one of a kind, and Goose had been trailing Gar. So he knew part of the situation already.

Hare danced his story and Gar sat in rapt amazement at the lad's prowess. This was assuming that Hare, like Real People, held to the tradition of truthfulness in the description of exploits. It fit exactly with what Gar knew. And even if it were enlarged a bit, the story in its bare bones amazed him.

He asked Hare to describe his attacker. The Hyæna woman. Of course. It fit. It fit.

And a dark thought crossed Gar's mind. How did the pallid woman end up with Goose's spear? Goose certainly would not have thrown it. He might have dropped it, but that was not likely. Did she attack him too? It would seem so.

The thought clarified one thing for him: He was not going to entertain her for a moment. She was dangerous, possibly a murderer. He hoped he was wrong, but until he returned to the Mammoths and learned the truth, he would not take any chances with the Hyæna.

Would he meet her? Most likely, for obviously, this strange, pallid woman was still persisting—following him for whatever motive he could not imagine. More to the immediate point, she must be somewhere around here. A lad carrying beaver meat would be ridiculously easy to follow.

So. Not all the hyænas lurking near were four-legged.

20

So Gar and That Woman Are Together Again

Stupid, stupid orange woman! She obviously failed to realise that you couldn't frighten a snake away by making noise. Yelling and pounding on things was an erroneous Water People notion. A snake would do as it damn well pleased. Only when it decided the moon was inedible would it disgorge it. Shouting at it availed nothing. Anyone halfway intelligent knew that.

She sat in a very tall beech tree five man-lengths beyond the orange woman's circle of light and watched her and her misbegotten child make utter fools of themselves. Utter, *utter* fools, for the woman was neglecting her fire. How would *her* Gar find them if that woman let the fire go out?

The beaver was nearly cooked. It looked so, with a

dark sheen on the meat. It really did require attention though, and basting. It was overdue for basting.

Wait! What was this? *She* pressed *her* eyes shut, the better to concentrate on senses beyond the physical. He was near! *She* could feel his presence approaching! He was coming! Probably it was the noise which drew him, for the fire had melted down to embers, virtually unnoticeable. Yes! There he came, out off the far side of the hill. *Her* mind's eye saw what *her* natural eyes could not. Look at him striding in his magnificence!

She opened *her* eyes and watched the darkening hillside from *her* high vantage point above the lesser treetops. When he emerged from the brush into the dim circle of light, *her* heart gave a little tickling jump. He was so strong; he walked in power. Had he not assumed the role of shaman, he would have been a spectacular hunter.

Smart one, too. His first order of business was to feed the dying fire. At least he kept his priorities straight. He even basted the beaver, turned it, and raked some more coals under it.

She watched, then, a curious phenomenon. The orange woman and he did not meet the way lovers do. They had been apart for several days, yet they did not initiate union. Had they quarrelled? Were they at odds? Bored with each other already? Hope sang in *her* breast, for they did not even speak to each other.

Only a sliver of moon remained. Then the snake finally decided that enough of a bad thing was enough and commenced the difficult process of spitting the circle back out. The hideous woman and her lad renewed their ridiculous display. Thankfully, *her* Gar watched, no doubt with disgust, and did not take part. The hillside grew lighter, brighter. The moon broke free of those dark jaws and soared again in its familiar bloated brilliance.

Now at last the three below began talking. They paid better attention to the fire and the beaver. They ate, then, consuming most of one haunch. The lad dragged in some more firewood from off in the trees on the downhill side. They cleared a floor beside the slithering flames.

The lad danced the story *she* already knew well. He described *her*, called *her* pale and skinny. He should talk! He said he could dive and swim like a beaver and that was how he eluded *her*—by swimming beneath the water. Oh, hardly! Lies! He must have escaped in some other way.

Boastful little snot. But look. *Her* Gar appeared to believe him. He did not act at all surprised by or incredulous of the nasty lad's claim of underwater swimming prowess. Was *her* Gar, a mature shaman, actually so gullible? And if so, could *she* use that gullibility for *her* own purposes somehow?

Her Gar next danced his story, but he revealed nothing that *she* did not already know. He left out parts. He did not say anything about being followed by the feckless fellow with the carved spear, and he said not a hint about sensing *her,* even though *she* was certain that he had. Was he ashamed? Forgetful? Afraid he would make the orange woman jealous? It would seem that *her* interest in him meant absolutely nothing to him. *She* couldn't believe that.

The ugly child then did a highly curious thing and actually succeeded in it. His mother sat with that bound leg outstretched. Beside her danced the lad, who told the parts of her story expressed by legs and steps as she told the parts using her arms and upper body. Finally the three hunkered around the fire and lapsed into informal conversation.

By and by, *her* Gar and the ugly lad stood up and headed this way toward the tree in which *she* perched. They stopped at the base of it a moment, arguing about the relative merits of beech as firewood. Why did an experienced shaman even bother with the opinion of a half-grown child?

Now *her* Gar gave the lad a boost up the trunk. *Her* trunk—*her* tree right here! Misshapen though he might be, the child had good eyes and a good nose. He was sure to notice *her* up here. *She* remained very, very quiet and absolutely motionless. The lad paused at the first major limb and called down to *her* Gar, something about a hyæna. His voice hard, *her* Gar barked an order to break loose some firewood and climb back down immediately.

They definitely knew. They were aware of *her!* Now what should *she* do? *She* did not particularly want to present *herself* to *her* Gar until *she* had got the orange woman and that hideous child out of the way. The orange woman would constitute a distraction and a complication so long as she remained. And the lad would defend his mother until he was removed.

The lad was craning his neck, trying to see higher into the foliage where *she* hid. *She* listened to the crunching and cracking as he pulled dead branches free and tossed them to the ground. *She* could not see him for the black leaves and shadows. Then he shinned down the trunk and said something to *her* Gar that even *her* fine hyæna ears could not quite make out. The two gathered up their dry wood and returned to the fire.

Down there beside the fire, the whole tone changed. A short time ago, those three below had been chatting casually amongst themselves. Now they huddled close, heads together, and talked with tense, abrupt gestures. They were discussing *her*. *She* knew that. They were making plans of some sort.

And yet, how could they know what *she* was going to do when *she* herself was not yet certain? They could not make their plans regarding *her* until *she* formulated *hers*. *She* intended, of course, to eliminate the odious orange woman, but details of how *she* ought to go about it still escaped *her*.

She must wait until they went to sleep before settling *herself* into a comfortable situation. *She* didn't want to make any noise up here. They suspected *her* presence but had not yet seen *her*. Let them continue to doubt.

The lad fed the fire and took first watch. *Her* Gar joined in union with the despicable orange woman, so apparently they were not totally at odds with each other. Kelp had never been that tender and considerate a lover.

Kelp. The memory of his sex flooded *her*. So did the memory of him sprawled out headless. And all the other memories of him.

Perhaps the lad would fall asleep as well, affording *her* a chance to climb down there, pick up a spear, and run it through at least one of *her* two nemeses. If *she* speared the lad first, *she* could probably get the orange woman as well, for with that bound leg, the woman was pretty much doomed. But no. The lad eventually stood up and walked about, keeping himself alert. As the moon coasted into its descent toward the horizon, he awakened *her* Gar. The shaman took over watch and the lad curled up near the fire.

She needed sleep too. Cautiously *she* worked *her* way down to a three-way crotch and wedged *herself* among the limbs. Safe from predators and gravity, *she* allowed *herself* some rest.

She awoke to the vague aroma of burnt beaver drippings. They must have reheated leftovers from last night. If *she* was fortunate, they would leave behind some tasty leftovers as well as coals and the cracked bones. *She* climbed up out of the crotch, stretched to relieve *her* stiffness, and made *her* way to higher branches, to where *she* could see *her* Gar.

He was gone! All three were gone! Nothing remained except the black fire site. *She* clambered down to the three-limb crotch, pausing to listen and sniff. No one. *She* hurried to the ground.

They had scattered their fire. *She* laid *her* hand on the warm dirt where coals once roasted a beaver. The embers had cooled past reviving, dark and useless. Those miserable People did not even leave fire for *her*. Surely *her* Gar knew *she* travelled alone and cold and would have welcomed fire.

All was not lost. Beaver bones had been tossed into the bushes all about. The chunks of meat left upon them would still provide *her* with an excellent meal.

The hair at the base of *her* neck prickled. Someone lurked near. This must be a trap, and yet *she* couldn't—

Hyænas! *Her* totemic sisters, no doubt lured by the aroma of those beaver drippings just as *she* had been, were closing on the spot. Already several of the pack had cut *her* off from *her* beech tree. In desperation *she* scrambled up into the flimsy cover of a hazel thicket. One hyæna, two, three moved out into the clearing. Sniffling and snuffling, they investigated. Then one after another they laughed joyously as they dragged cracked beaver bones about. They would eat all the succulent leavings. They would rip up the tendons and the tail. They would eat the bones as well, for even the largest of beaver bones were not too hard and bulky for a hyæna to chew up and consume.

She knew better than to try to join them or even to purloin a bone or two for *her* own use. *She* was not of their pack. No hyæna family welcomes a newcomer, not even a spiritual sister. No. *She* would go hungry while *her* sisters feasted.

As *she* huddled among the uppermost branches and twigs of these hazels, watching hyænas eat what was supposed to be *hers, she* had ample time to ponder the whole situation. If the situation were reversed—if *her* Gar were following *her* and *she* wanted to put him off the track—*she* could not have devised a better, more diabolical ruse than to scatter beaver leavings about, especially if *she* knew hyænas prowled this area. *She* could not imagine *her* Gar being so cruel and unfeeling as to do that. Surely it was the orange woman and her wayward son who were influencing him badly. Maybe they sent him ahead to scout and did this behind his back; perhaps he did not even know what they had done to lure hyænas in and thwart *her*. Yes. That had to be it.

That horrible, horrible woman!

She would pay for this!

21

The World Is on Fire

Before the beginning, a particular spirit existed, powerful and vast beyond ken. He lived forever in both directions at once, past and future, and yet he felt at loose ends, and very, very lonely. Floating adrift in forever was not pleasant. And so he built a place to be.

He piled up mountains, broke them up here and there and wove streams among them. He dug lakes. He raised up trees in some places and scattered myriad flowers across other places. He did all this abundantly, exuberantly, enthusiastically. Then he settled himself amidst all this splendour. At last he had a place to be.

But he still felt at loose ends, and lonely.

He decided to make creatures that would entertain him by doing interesting things. By the time he was finished, a wonderful variety of animals graced the world. Some moved quickly and some slowly. Some were very noisy and some virtually silent. When they began to grow faint, he gave some permission to eat of the vegetation he created and a few to eat other creatures. As an added touch, he imbued each of them with a portion of his spirit, that they might enjoy the world as he did. He did all this abundantly, exuberantly, enthusiastically. At last he was not alone.

And yet, see! He still felt at loose ends, and lonely.

So he broke up some of the animals and with the portions he made People. Strength from the rhino, aggressiveness from the aurochs, gentleness from the dove, wisdom from the crow, eyes from the eagle... And as each part was incorporated into People, a little bit of the spirit from those creatures entered also. Lastly, he imparted to each of his People a portion of his own spirit, so that he, a non-physical spirit being, could interact with them who were physical beings. He did all this abundantly, exuberantly, enthusiastically.

At last he was not lonely.

Not long thereafter, however, he realised a flaw in his world. He had lost his privacy. These People communed with him at will. No longer could he move apart and reflect upon his own heart. Indeed, neither could they. He enjoyed their clever thinking and their élan, but he could not escape their pettiness and complaints, their selfishness and frequent, unthinkable cruelties. Because they shared one spirit, they all thought alike.

In the end he had to take care to give each Person and all Persons thereafter an individualised spirit, no two alike, with individualised inner thoughts and dreams. He made these to be holy, sacrosanct, not to be shared and communicated. Thereby he restored privacy. He did all this with misgiving, knowing he would suffer great loss.

And exactly as he feared would happen, he became lonely again, but not unbearably, for observing Real People was immensely more entertaining than observing animals. And he savoured his privacy, as do all People also, to this day.

Gar completed the story, sat down, and tossed a few more sticks on the fire.

Beside him, Hare watched the sparks prance around the new wood. "Water People, their stories say nothing about all this."

"When Real children are small and they hear this story, I leave out many things. Small children hear one short story. Then as they get older, I add things, making the story longer. When you are a man, you learn things about the same story you never heard before."

Mouse nodded. "You just told parts of it that I didn't hear before, because I was gone so young."

Gar had to keep reminding himself that the lad was half Water People and therefore cared much more about what the Hairies might think and believe than did Gar. But not Hare—not even Mouse—pressed constantly upon his thoughts. That pallid Hyæna woman did.

Sooner or later, he was going to have to come to terms with that inscrutable woman. But Mouse's safety loomed more important, primary in fact. That remarkable episode with the great snake had brought him and Mouse together again; he must let nothing separate them or slow their quest. The Hyæna woman was certain to do both, should he turn aside to seek her.

Since Gar had encountered hyænas and the lad too had read hyæna sign, they agreed that the predators probably denned on that hillside not far from the camp. It was Hare's idea, however, to lure them in by scattering bones and burning some drippings. Bring them near and use them as a shield and buffer against the pallid woman up in the beech tree.

Head reminded him, *This lad, ugly or not, will be one of the three you train to serve as shaman when you are gone. He's smart—very quick and smart—and appearance be hanged.*

And of course, Heart pouted, *You don't fool me. You're testy because he came up with a splendid idea and you didn't.*

Perhaps Gar was not the only one perplexed and worried about the pallid woman. Mouse asked, "Two days now we've been gone from that place. Do you think she is lost, maybe?"

Everyone knew which *she* Mouse was talking about.

"Don't know. She certainly has been persistent." Gar dipped his head toward Hare. "You want first watch or second?"

The lad shrugged elaborately. "First is all right. You rest awhile, eh."

"Eh." From their shallow overhang here halfway up a south-facing hill, Gar stepped out to where he could stand up straight and scanned the world one last time. The hillside dropped away precipitately at their feet. But then it smoothed out into a gentle downslope to a narrow, boggy valley. Across a feeble stream rose another hill, sombre and fir-studded. It drew an irregular line across the southern horizon, sky above and darkness below. In all that countryside, Gar detected no signs of large game or predators.

He curled up beside the fire, not too tired to hunger for sex, but tired enough to melt immediately into sleep without it. Every muscle in the upper half of his body ached. He was surprised his legs did not; they were the only part of him that felt half decent, and they had been working quite as hard.

Actually, he was rather messed up anyway. In order to make good time escaping from the hyænas of both stripes, he had hitched Mouse up onto his back and carried her pick-a-back. How many miles had they travelled with his fingers laced together behind him supporting her? For how many miles did her body nudge gently against the small of his back with each step? Half a day of that had pretty much cured most of his reaction to her weight on his back. Now he had no idea what his responses were going to be.

As they journeyed, they had to stay in the open, for her bound leg stuck out at a gross angle and tangled in brush and trees if they tried to pass through dense vegetation. That little problem aside, the pick-a-back method worked splendidly. According to Mouse, they were now winding their way down the last major drainage to the sea.

So she thought. For toward the close of day, her comments had taken an unsettling turn. The landmarks didn't seem right. She could not clearly identify any of the features she had noted on her way north all those months ago. They found a comfortable overhang under a steep ridge, there to spend the night.

As they watched the sun disappear, their backs pressed against the Mother Earth, their faces breeze-kissed, they talked in hushed voices about the journey's next leg. They agreed between them that once they reached the great mountains, they were essentially there. Hare reminded them that his Baboon clan of Water

People claimed only a limited territory among crags that extended forever, perhaps, in both directions. If they could find no bearings, they would not know whether to head east or west once they climbed into the great nest of mountains. It was a glum note upon which to end the day.

Now Hare settled himself cross-legged facing away from the fire. Off to the side, his mother finished up her chore of breaking the seeds out of a ditty bag full of pods. She tossed the bitter pods into the fire one by one as she emptied them. Each sizzled as it dried. It curled and charred. The day was over, and not a moment too soon. Gar closed his weary, weary eyes.

"Fire! Look out there!" Hare's voice, as from a great distance, jolted Gar.

He raised his head. The moon hovered just above the fir tips; he'd been sleeping longer than one would suppose, as tired as he still felt. Close against him, Mouse stirred and grunted.

Gar sat up. The horizon glowed, a thin orange line that limned the hillcrest to the southwest. It could almost be a sunset, did the orange glow not hug the horizon so snugly, did the gibbous moon not hang so high above. The fire looked to be nearly half a mile across, somewhere beyond the crest of the far hill.

Hare stood just outside the overhang, watching that bright orange line.

Gar lurched stiffly to his feet and stepped out beside the lad. "Lightning brings fire at times, but there was no lightning tonight."

Hare grunted. "Water People bring fire, too. Sometimes they burn the dry grass on a whole mountain. Then new grass comes, and that brings the grazing animals in close, the aurochs and saiga. Makes it easy to hunt meat."

"Hoo." Once in a while, a night's camping fire might get away from a party, particularly if they were travelling across tundra before the winter rains. But to set fire deliberately to a place not meant to burn? Unthinkable.

The moon disappeared behind a wall of smoke, black against black. They could smell the fire now on the night air.

A bead of brilliant yellow light burst forth on that hillcrest. The fire had topped the mountain. It began inching down the hill on this side. Fascinated, Gar watched the ragged line squirm down toward the valley between them and it. Here or there along that thin, rickety orange line, something would flash into a ball of fire—a cluster of firs igniting perhaps, or a thick reed clump. The flare-up would momentarily light up a small portion of the black smoke wall.

Mouse struggled to her feet and pressed in close against him. "You think it will come up here maybe?"

"Eh." He wrapped an arm across her shoulders and drew her in. Her skin felt very cool. "The wind is right, from the south. And see the trees and grass? See how dry they are. There's been no rain for a while. They'll burn easily, burn quickly."

The fire crept down the facing hillside in its broad, thin line toward the valley, close enough now in places that they could discern flickering.

"But the bog's too wet to burn." Hare pointed to the valley floor.

"The bushes and reeds down there might."

Mouse's voice oozed worry as she pointed southwest directly toward the fire line. "Where the fire is out there—that's just where we ought to go. That direction."

Gar felt a bit disconcerted about this turn of events himself. "We can't go that way now."

His memory retraced their route over the last half day. Nowhere behind them was the country rocky enough or barren enough to hide from wildfire. Even this overhang here was not large enough to protect them from heat and smoke, should the fire catch them. Their best chance, perhaps their only chance, was to run downhill toward the stream. Sink down into the water. Cover themselves with water. He shivered at the horrid thought.

Fine turn of events, Head mumbled. *To flee, we have to run* toward *the fire.*

Ah, Heart countered, *but see the bright side: Large carnivores don't like wildfire and run the other way.*

"Hare, bring the spears, eh. And the ditty." Gar stepped in front of Mouse and wiggled his fingers. "We must hurry!"

She hitched herself up onto his back and he laced his fingers behind. How his arm muscles burned! He heard a little *oof* behind him as Hare shouldered the travel bag.

Gar led the way at an angle down the slope. He sincerely hoped Heart was right about the carnivores, but Heart was so frequently wrong. What if wolves, lions, or hyænas roamed nearby? Despite his apparent prowess, Hare was nowhere near big enough to repel major predators, not even with three spears to wield. Gar despised travelling by night.

For the most part, the stream on the valley floor trickled across riffles. From up by that overhang behind them, Gar had not noticed any pools deep enough to cover a Person's body, but then, he hadn't been looking. And they just might have to resort to fully submerging themselves to escape the flames, too. The very thought terrified him. Hare, the insane child, probably relished the prospect.

As they neared that meandering stream, Gar could clearly hear the burning brush crackle ahead of them. Bright yellow hot spots glowed all over the mountainside, colonies of flame left behind as the line swept downhill. Somewhere in that black-and-brilliant fury, a tree crashed down. Pungent smoke assailed his nostrils. Before, the churning wall of smoke seemed to be lifting straight up. Now it was definitely leaning forward this way, billowing out ahead of the fire. Either the wind had shifted or the fire was making its own wind. Regardless, the flickering yellow line surged toward them faster now.

On the hillside behind them, hyænas chorused.

Lovely, Head noted. *Fire before and predators behind.*

Ever sanguine, Heart mused, *Perhaps the fire will be stopped at the stream.*

Gar stumbled in the darkness, his ankle hung up on brush. Mouse's weight drove his knees into the ground. He almost pitched flat onto his face. The fall bumped Mouse's bound leg; she yelped. He regained his feet and staggered out across the bog, lurching, sloshing, panting heavily.

Mouse screamed, "Drop me! Save yourself!"

I trust you're ignoring that fool notion. Heart.

On the other shore not far downstream, an alder ignited; the whole tree burst into flame all at once. It toppled across the water, carrying a great, dazzling ball of flames and sparks with it, and fell heavily to earth on this side. The fire had just jumped the stream.

And there was no way that Gar and Mouse would be able to get away from it.

22

Terror Changed Her Mind

For hours she had dozed, stretched out on her side in the sun. Now she rolled onto her belly and elbows and began licking between her toes. Her sister's surviving son, born half a year ago, clambered up onto her sloping back and batted at her ear. Impudent cub. Heavy for his age, too. He was going to be a big one, almost as big as a female, probably. She shook her head. He persisted, so she swung her head back and shoved him. Thrashing to regain his lost balance, he slid down her coarse grey fur to the ground.

The other hyænas were stirring now. The sun, very red-orange this evening, perched on the horizon and began to ooze down out of sight. Time to go. She lurched to standing and stretched mightily, yawning. Downslope a ways, her son of last year braced, all four feet splayed, and shook himself as if he had just come out of water.

She understood her son's irritation and agreed; the fleas seemed especially annoying this year. Much as she hated winter, she would welcome the hard frosts of autumn that killed off those pesky fleas and ticks.

She yapped a *Let's go* and led off over the ridge, more or less southwesterly. To either side of her, the pack ranged out, scattering yet moving together.

Out on a scree slope, her year-old son and her sister's cub put up a hyrax. They managed to cut it off from its den, but it took the two of them working in concert to catch it before it lost itself in the rocks. They fought over it noisily. Her son got the most of it, but the cub came away with the head and a foreleg. Already his jaws were strong enough to break open an ibex skull without his mother's help. This hyrax posed him no problem.

To the west, her sister yodelled *Horses!* and the pack drifted in that direction. Before long she picked up the horse scent too. It was too old, yesterday morning at least. Her sister never could distinguish between aged and fresh scent. She barked, calling the other hyænas off it.

Along this slope she detected human smell also, very fresh. Three humans travelled together and a fourth human more or less followed behind them in the same direction. Humans stank and were generally distasteful except for young ones. However, they were usually easier to catch than four-legged prey, being so pitifully slow. They were much more dangerous, though, particularly the males with their long, sharp sticks. And one of these was a big male.

The others picked up the trace now and fell silent. They tightened their formation, moving downhill in the usual pursuit pattern. The scent grew stronger, less than half a day old.

That fourth human, a female, was bleeding without being injured, as human females sometimes did. The occasional drop of blood along the way tantalised. It excited. The males in this pack became agitated.

Wait! What was this? A vague smell. Smoke. And see how red-orange the moon appeared as it hovered above the trees on the far mountain. This didn't smell like an ordinary human fire and it spread out extremely wide. Human fires were little spots, frightening but quite limited in scope. Something unusual was occurring, something she had never before experienced. The moon turned dirty brown and disappeared behind clouds.

The rest of the pack picked up on her edginess. They paused frequently with noses high, sniffing, watching.

The fourth human, the laggard female who bled, must have detected the hyænas behind her, for she was moving faster now, perhaps to catch up with the other three. But the other three had sped up as well.

She must step up the pursuit. She yodelled, *Hasten!* Her sister on their left flank and her cousin on their right voiced their response. Since the humans now knew she was behind them, the pack could abandon any attempt at silence. They crashed through the brush at a dead run, out onto the swale of the valley floor. She began salivating in anticipation. Ahead in the bog—she could smell them directly now, not far off! How she loved the chase! Besides the male, she detected the bleeding female, another female, and a child. Tasty!

As one, all the pack stopped and moved in closer together, for a flaming tree fell across the creek ahead. That burning tree was a much larger fire than any humans' fire she had ever known. Her son pressed in hard beside her. The pall of smoke overhead glowed, and look at the sparks! Never had she seen so much fire at one time. A flickering, dancing line of yellow light stretched in both directions across the bog before them, beyond the stream. And now the flames were leaping and playing on this side of the creek, where that tree had apparently set them free. A reed patch smouldered a few moments and flared up. Her pack fell back. She paused, confused, trying to think, having no experience upon which to draw that even remotely resembled this.

Just downstream, a herd of horses sloshed out across the bog, running ahead of the fire. They paid no attention to the hyænas, though they surely knew the pack was close. Three bellowing aurochs bull-calves, the young of last year, slammed out across the bog mere yards ahead of the flames. They leaped the stream and thundered directly toward the hyænas. They practically ran right over her and her pack, so terrified were they. Small animals scurried all over, fleeing the fire.

Flames snaked toward her; the smoke rolled up and over them. It scudded along the ground and gagged them.

Fear seized her. She abandoned any thought of pursuing the humans, the horses, the aurochs. She wheeled and broke. They raced back uphill, the pack of them, leadership falling to the fleetest. The smoke roiled, thicker. It choked. It seared the nose and throat and lungs.

They ran for their lives beside the fleet horses and the lumbering aurochs, and left the sluggish humans to their doom.

23

The Spirits Are on Her Side

She despised water, one of the reasons *she* never bathed. And here *she* lay buried in it. By lying flat on *her* back in the creek, *she* could just barely keep herself submerged. It had been plenty deep enough to start with, but the water level was going down. What if it dried up completely?

Of course, *she* had to lift *her* face out of it every time *she* took a breath. But *her* face burned so hot whenever it left the water that *she* breathed as infrequently as possible. And because *she* had to pinch *her* nose shut, *she* had to breathe through *her* mouth. What was worse, the air that *she* took in wasn't worth breathing—smoky, searing, unsatisfying. This was terrible. Absolutely terrible!

Her lungs burned horribly. *She* felt very sick and headachy.

Probably because *she* was female-bleeding, *her* stomach cramped up mightily in the chill water. *Her* feet and fingers ached. With water clogging *her* ears, *she* could hear nothing of what was happening around *her*.

She was beginning to fear that perhaps *she* might not survive this.

As *she* lay in this abject misery with *her* fingers pinching *her* nose closed and *her* eyes squeezed shut, *she* tried to identify the source of *her* suffering. It had to be that orange woman somehow.

And *her* own reaction to this crisis surprised *her*. Apparently *her* Gar had become more important to *her* than life itself. Instead of doing the right thing, the smart thing, *she* had followed him, risking *her* own life.

She let *her* memory rehearse what happened when the fire first appeared on the horizon as an extensive glow. At that time *she* did not know where Gar and the woman were. In fact, *she* had lost *her* bearings and did not even know where *she herself* was. After losing the three because of that ugly situation with the hyænas, *she* had continued to the southwest in the general direction they had been going so far. *She* had groped along blindly, with no idea whether *she* were behind them, ahead of them, or going *her* own merry way whilst they had diverted down some other drainage or course.

She had seen no sign or scent of them when *she* settled for the night in a nest of boulders on the hilltop. But a short time later *she* detected hyænas on the slope behind *her*. *She* abandoned *her* nest and moved downslope to find a good tree. And then, the fire.

When it topped the hill and came slithering down the far slope right toward them, a sensible person—as did all the animals, in fact—would flee to the northeast, away from it. But wait! Far and away down the hill, there stood *her* Gar on a rough little ledge, illuminated with a small campfire at his back! No doubt the campfire—and he, until just now—was tucked away in an overhang which opened out away from *her.* No wonder *she* could not see him before. And now *she* noticed the ugly child. They were watching the fire on the mountain ahead. *She* had been near them all along!

But then *her* Gar immediately left his own fire behind and hastened *toward* the glow. Toward it! Straight down the slope away from where they had camped. Why? No matter why. He was doing it. *She* left behind *her* own place of safety and took off down the slope. *She* would not—*she would* not!—lose them again.

And that was where *she* abandoned *her* own safety. *She* knew the hyænas were behind, but *she* didn't care. *She* knew it was foolhardy to run downhill right toward that unmanageable fire, but *she* did so anyway. *She* would be the one the hyænas went for first, too, with *her* female-bleed.

Her mind played again the panic which suddenly gripped *her* as the hyænas behind them abandoned silence and came charging, crashing, yipping at full speed. There *she* went, slipping and staggering out across the boggy bottomland. Coming to this riffly stream and finding this pool. Immersing *herself* as the flames leaped the stream and danced all around and past *her.* Fighting against *her* all-powerful instinct to avoid water.

And then it dawned. Aha! Of course! Now *she* knew the reason for the fire, for the hyænas, for everything. The spirits of this place desperately wanted *her* to find *her* Gar! There was no other reason. *She* was destined for him and he for *her.* The orange woman with powerful magic was trying to keep them separated, but the spirits were against that one and behind *her* all the way, helping *her*. Desperate? Absolutely. They were forced to devise a very dangerous ruse, the wildfire, to reveal *her* Gar to *her* and funnel all four of them into close proximity.

So the orange woman was responsible for all this after all, albeit indirectly.

She gagged on the gorge rising in *her* throat, fought down the nausea and sucked in another painful breath. It ripped *her* lungs out.

The spirits might be on *her* side, but they just might kill *her* yet.

24

He Relishes Being a Protector

Gar considered it a poor day indeed when he didn't learn something. For example, he never before knew that he floated so persistently. Even when he didn't want to. Each time he drew in a deep, tortured breath, his body lifted to the surface of this shallow pool. He had to keep turning—back, side, front, other side—to cool the parts of his body that would not go under.

Mouse, he knew, floated even worse, but she had wedged her hips and bound leg under a tree root, giving her a point of leverage to force herself beneath the water. How Hare was coping, he had no idea. Gar could neither see nor hear in this hell.

The air, what there was of it, was virtually unbreathable. It seemed as if the fire took what it wanted from the air and poisoned whatever was left. Gar felt faint and disoriented with each breath. His lungs burned, his head pounded. He vomited.

The heat abated. Eventually, the air became less oppressive. With extreme caution, for he deeply feared both fire and water, Gar rose a bit and looked about. Spot fires flared here and there in the dense blackness. Trees, fallen logs, berry clumps each crackled as an island of flame. An overwhelming stale stink replaced the comparatively clean smell of fire. Between earth and sky hung a most oppressive pall.

The air did not sweeten exactly, but it became breathable as fresh wind chased the wall of flame up the hill to the north—the hill where Gar and Mouse and Hare had meant to spend the night. He stood up and nearly dropped over again, intensely dizzy and sick-feeling. His breath tasted ugly.

Head reeled. Not the least of the horrors forced upon him was irony. Water, this medium he detested so thoroughly, had just now saved their lives.

Mouse came sloshing over to him and wrapped around his middle. "Water is lower now, eh."

Considerably lower, he noticed, once she called his attention to it. The creek had been running shallow to start with, as streams did in late summer, but now it was much shallower than before the fire. No wonder he no longer fit beneath the surface.

He held her close as much to steady himself as to comfort her.

Hare. Gar recalled that as he and Mouse scrambled through the water trying to find a pool deep enough to cover them, the child had run off upstream.

Heart confided, *I fear for the safety of the ugly child.*

And Head marvelled, *I can't believe it! You really are worried about the lad. You who once abhorred him.*

Worry is justified, though. Great peril.

Who would have imagined it?

How did this fire get started? Could the Hyæna woman have somehow worked around ahead of them and now had decided to destroy them? He had lost track of her and assumed she had lost track of them. Might careless hunters on the far side of this mountain have let a fire get away from them? That seemed the easiest explanation in the absence of sky-to-earth lightning.

But what hunters? The three travellers had journeyed far, far beyond any Real People's territory that Gar ever knew about. The whole complexion of game availability had changed perceptibly. He had not seen red deer sign for days. Mammoths had not come in yet, though they had likely drifted south into Scarp Country by now. Probably Newt was putting together a mammoth-hunting party right now.

Come to think of it, no reindeer sign, not even sign a couple years old, such as wads of shed hair on brambles. He noted either bison, wisent, or aurochs—maybe all three; he couldn't distinguish the various cattle droppings. Rhinos and horses aplenty. Ibex all over. Cloven tracks and unusual droppings Gar wasn't sure about. Fewer bears and lions. Strange smells in the caves and overhangs.

The country itself had become more rugged. Gar and his sorry party did, so to speak, much more upping and downing than flat-acrossing. The land seemed more scarred, rockier than the familiar terrain of home.

Splashing sounds drew his attention upstream. Turning, Mouse loosened her embrace and pushed away. She sloshed toward her son.

Hare stepped out onto a gravel bar where, a few

hours ago, water had riffled. He stumbled in the stones, dropped to one knee, lurched to his feet and waded into the water toward them. His elbows lifted high in that way of his, he swished to his mother. And he was still carrying all three spears!

She wrapped around him as only a mother could. He sobbed. Gar had never seen the ugly child come close to tears before. It touched him. Even in this flickering half-light he could make out a broad burnt patch on the lad's right shoulder. And part of that scraggly hair had been singed off behind his right ear.

The lad separated from his mother, doubled over with a spate of dry heaves, and wrapped around her again, trembling violently.

Gar waded over and took the spears, giving the lad both arms to snuggle with. He stepped tentatively out onto the bog to the south of the stream. The ground felt warm all over and dangerously hot in spots. Charred grass and heathers, silky ash, squooshed flat beneath his step. Most of the water puddles he associated with bogs had dried up.

He could not see travelling out across this desolation until the whole area had cooled. Especially not at night. And yet, they could not spend the rest of the night in this chilly water. He still felt very ill, he knew Mouse was shaking, and the lad was exceedingly sick.

A stoat crawled out of a hollow, burning log, its fur smouldering. It staggered down to the stream, slipped on the ash-coated bank, and fell in. Half-heartedly keeping its nose above water, it drifted downstream, more dead than alive.

Head complained, *We're not functioning here. Time to start thinking.*

Not with this monstrous headache. Why was Heart complaining about a headache?

Head pressed on. *There are no predators to guard against. We don't have to worry about that.*

Surely Head was right. No predators, no nothing. Fire had purged all living. And yet, Gar could not bring himself to relax his guard. He simply could not. He skidded down the ashy bank back into the water and waded over to Mouse and Hare.

Mouse was hugging Hare and weeping softly. On sudden impulse, Gar wrapped his arms around the two of them and drew them close. Mouse melted tight against him. It was a gesture of surrender. She had given up; he could feel it in her every fibre.

By tradition, males made themselves the first line of women's and children's defence, even though everyone knew that women were perfectly capable of protecting themselves. But Gar realised just now that there was far more to protecting than merely standing guard against predators. Protection included providing guidance and hope for them who were protected, and finding a way out when there was no way out. Protection included comforting and cosseting as needed.

As sick as he himself felt, he felt a surge of elation. How he relished comforting these two outcasts! How he hungered to protect these two. Yes, even the ugly child, this haggard, burnt, retching lad.

"We'll die now anyway," Mouse murmured. "Everything is gone. No magic can stand against fire. Fire is its own magic."

"We're alive." Gar rubbed her shoulder, her back between her shoulder blades. "We're alive and we'll find the cave, get the magic, and save you. You and Hare. It will be. Tomorrow the land will be cool, and we'll travel again."

"We're too sick. Hare, he can't travel. I can't. Headache, weak. I feel bad. No. It's no good."

"Then we'll wait here a couple days and travel later when everyone feels better."

Good idea to wait, Head offered. *As sick as you are.*

She drew in a long, rasping breath. "Go home, Gar. Go back to your Scarp Country. This is too much. Don't suffer so for us."

Was she tired of him? He was too afraid of the possible answer to ask that. Instead he said, "No. Where you go, I'll stay with you. All the way, everywhere."

Her hug tightened, her head pressed against his breast. He could feel her warm tears on his skin. Presently she loosened her grip a bit and shuddered. "We can't carry fire with us anymore. The bag and pad are all burnt up."

"We don't need fire. We don't want fire now. Fire just shows the Water People where we are."

Hare's voice sounded tiny and hoarse. "Had enough fire, eh."

Gar smiled. "Eh."

He released them then, and made a relatively flat bed for them by levelling bog mounds beside the stream. He yearned for just one of the stack of thickly-haired bear hides that lay unused at the back of Larch Cave. Just one. It was all they needed to keep dirt and ashes off of the lad's sticky burns.

Mouse lay down and laid her son across her to keep him clear of the blackened ground. Gar pretended to keep watch, but as the brown and sulking moon was slipping past zenith toward the west, he fell asleep.

25

These Pictures Are Obscene

Mouse stood on the very top of the hill, staring out across haze. Her topknot had come undone at some time during their ordeal, the loon wingbone which should have been holding it long gone. She was smudged all over with black soot and ash as grey as death. They hadn't eaten for nearly three days, and starvation was beginning to show in her sturdy frame, which had not been too plump to start with.

And she was beautiful!

Gar stood a bit short of the crest of the hill and simply admired the woman as a fresh breeze brushed the tips of her hair across her shoulders. What a lovely view to savour.

The ugly lad was, if anything, uglier. Water People tended to be quite lank anyway, and he looked absolutely gaunt. Just now, he lay on his side on a large, smooth boulder, knees tucked up and arms tucked in.

Mouse shifted a bit, looking off to the southwest, to the southeast. "Hare?"

He uncurled and climbed to his feet. Listlessly, the haggard Hare slogged to the top of the hill and tipped over against her.

She pointed southeast. "Eagles."

Eagles? Gar moved in at her other side to see, but she was indicating mountains, not birds.

"Eh." Hare waved a finger toward the horizon. "And Horse Peak there."

"Eh!" She bobbed her head. She glanced up at Gar. "Those are the Eagle Mountains over there, right across from us. Horse Peak on the other side is where we'll find the cave."

He saw nothing remotely familiar.

Her voice dropped to a gentle purr. "Strange, eh. I wanted to go a different way, but the fire chased us in this direction instead. This is the way we had to go to find the cave. I would have been wrong, going that other way. We'd be too far west to see Horse Peak. Lost. We'd never find the right way. The fire knew best. What great power in fire. A strong spirit. It guided us."

She led the way forward down the burnt hill toward a narrow little valley, propping herself on spears as she walked, for her support sticks had burned. It appeared that the fire had begun beyond the stream in the valley, for this downslope lay charred and the upslope on the far side of a creek appeared green, untouched.

Gone were the usual heathers and other brush common to hillsides; only tortured, blackened skeletons remained. Berry tangles had dissolved into white ash and a few stubs. The bare ground stank. Gar had never seen the effects of a wildfire before, though his father and Cloud both had described them. He remembered now, Rat once saying that sometimes, when the reindeer and saiga failed to return in autumn, northern clans of Hairies would deliberately set fire to the land itself. When new grass came up, the open-country herds returned. It agreed pretty much with what Hare had said. Gar could not imagine that being the case here. These were southern Hairies, and Hare was surely wrong about them setting fires.

Mouse struggled along gamely. Gar disregarded his own persistent nausea and headache and hitched her onto his back. She had already suffered more than enough. One would think that their illness would have abated after two days of rest. He wondered when they would recover—if at all.

They crossed the stream by wading it and passed from horror into peace. Green grass and tree clumps. So cool. So welcome.

Mouse squirmed down off his back and sat down on the streambank. "Gar, we need red dirt, and certain kinds of roots and bark. I don't know where to find it here."

"Why?"

"For the colours."

Gar settled into cool grass beside her. "I thought a long time about that. I don't want to do Hairy magic. I will speak with their spirits, but I won't try their magic."

She grunted. "Also we need fire, see inside the cave. It's deep, far back in there. But we didn't bring our fire. I wasn't thinking. We should have."

"Rest." He watched a moment as Hare immediately curled up on the green sward and closed his eyes.

To carry fire, one soaked three skin bags and packed them with water-logged lichen. Fresh embers were tucked into one of the bags. When they dried the lichens and scorched them, turning the lichens into embers as well, one transferred the fire to the next bag. Feed the embers as needed during the day and keep them from eating through the skin. Bring them to life that evening, gather them again come morning, resoaking the bags and lichens, begin the process anew. How could Gar do that with neither lichens nor bags?

In preparation for fire they did not have, Gar laid firewood, tinder in the middle, small sticks around it, larger sticks on top. Then he strolled down to the streamside.

He scooped together moss and grass into a round, deep nest and wetted it thoroughly before he carried it back across the water into the burnt land. Curls of smoke here and there told him where fallen logs still smouldered. He dug around underneath three different logs before he found dull red living embers. With a stick he tipped them into his grass nest and carried them back across the stream. It didn't take long to bring the laid firewood up to a full blaze. They'd need it, too, with hungry animals of various sorts lurking on this unburnt mountainside.

Gar did the foraging, for neither Hare nor Mouse was up to it. That evening, they ate, a welcome return to near normalcy.

Overhangs abounded, another sign of normalcy. Gar had no trouble finding a good place to spend the night. As his two protectees struggled up to the shelter, he moved the fire to their retreat.

While Mouse and Hare slept, he fashioned three

torches, heavy sticks with grass and moss wound tightly around one end. He made nests for carrying embers such as he had used this midday and soaked them in a seep.

The next morning they crossed what Hare had identified as Horse Peak and angled down the other side, digging roots as they went. About the time Gar decided they were thoroughly lost again, Hare announced simply, "There," and pointed to the hillside.

Mouse nodded.

Gar tried to assay her mood and could not. Her demeanour puzzled him, being part apprehension and part relief, part happiness and part dread.

Gar would not have noticed the cave entrance at all, so deeply was it tucked among heathers. He had anticipated a magnificent cavern, perhaps even decorated with the gleaming, wet sheets and columns and ribbons of rock that one occasionally found. Something which would attract powerful spirits, not this narrow, insignificant black spot. How strangely anti-climactic.

He asked, "Time to build a fire?"

"Eh." Mouse sat down wearily and stretched her bound leg out across damp grass.

Hare seemed to recover some of his usual ebullience as he helped Gar build up a fire. With it they ignited one of the torches. Gar handed it to Mouse. Hers was the magic that had brought them here. Let her lead.

As soon as her torch burned well, Mouse crawled to the cave entrance. "In here." Her voice dropped to a near whisper. Dragging her bound leg out behind, she squeezed through the brush and crept three-legged into the teeny, tiny slot in the Mother Earth.

Gar shuddered. When he vowed to stay with Mouse, he certainly did not have this in mind.

Shoving his unlit brand ahead of him, he ducked low and stretched out. He could not imagine a whole clan of Hairies entering through this narrow aperture. The sides pressed low; his topknot scraped the ceiling; its loon wingbone came loose.

The cave entrance widened almost immediately, once they got inside. Hare could stand up. Two man-lengths farther and so could Gar. Mouse lighted his torch from hers. He waited for his eyes to adjust to the gloom.

And then he saw the magic.

Gawking, he sucked in air. He stared, stunned. Directly above his head, the likeness of a bison bucketed across the ceiling. Behind it thundered the rest of the herd. Gar thrust his torch high, the better to see. Over here, a horse. Two horses! And here, an elk in its antlered splendour. Exact bison, from horns to cloven feet. Exact horses with stiff manes and flowing tails. Exact elk, the shoulder humps just so, the dark and light of their coats finely etched.

They were not real animals, of course. They were nothing more than marks made on the cold walls and ceiling of a cavern. And yet, when Gar looked at that dank rock with its cold, lifeless marks, live animals cavorted in his mind's eye. These animals were someone's inner thoughts and memories, perhaps even dreams, should the creator of them be a hunter. A person's deepest, most private thoughts, displayed for anyone to see. How obscene!

What immense power! Incredible power! These mere lines and marks smeared upon a wall dictated to the viewer's own mind. To tell the Head what to think, to tell the Heart what to feel, to govern what to picture in the memory's eye—unimaginable magic, to play such a trick upon the mind.

Mouse brought her torch up beside his, doubling the light. Browns and ochres glowed.

"How did they do this?" Gar could not stop gaping.

"Rub colour onto the rock with tufts of hide, fur-out. In some places, they used long-hair hide like rhinos'. In other places, short thick hair like otter, beaver. See. They think for a long time, then pick exactly the places to make their art. Here the bison, there the rhino. Make the animal just right on the wall, over a bulge where the shoulder is, see? Dip where the flank is. All that they think about a long time first, then call up many spirits."

"Hoo."

So this was what the Hairies had named *art.*

Over on this wall, about head high, here were nearly a dozen human hands—hand shapes outlined in red and yellow.

Hare ran to the wall, stretched high, and laid his hand against one of the hand shapes. "Look." He spoke with the hushed voice this cavern required. "I'm almost big enough." His hand did not quite fit. But close.

Mouse whispered, "His father made that one. You put colour in your mouth, press your hand to the wall, and then blow the colour on and around it. The colour is not where the hand is. This is great magic."

Hare mimed the process and watched Gar.

Mouse studied Gar closely.

He shook his head. "I'm surprised how powerful this is, but it's Hairy magic. I will listen to the spirits, but I won't take on Hairy magic." He gazed some more upon the splendid animals trooping up the walls and across the undulant ceiling.

Unthinkable! Unimaginable. And yet, here it all was.

The voices of men and animals, myriad voices, clamoured silently in the silence. They overwhelmed him with their raucous silence.

He sat down in this cavernous room cross-legged and raised both arms toward those amazing, magical animals, not quite knowing what to expect.

The whispers came upon him gently at first, as from a distance, then louder and more intimate. Like soft winter furs, they wrapped around him. They sang to him with a beautiful melody he could neither remember nor repeat.

Time and the cave withdrew.

They were here. Powerful, intense spirits. He was almost too awed, even say frightened, to address them.

Without speaking aloud, Gar asked of them, Are you my spirits or those of the Hairies?

Yours. We've been with you all along. You were so eager to come to this place, though, you didn't listen to us there.

I listened. I fasted. I waited.

Not like you're doing now. Not nearly as open as you are now.

Tell me what I must know, I beg you.

You already know. You just don't know that you know.

You tease me.

Reach inside yourself. You'll find it.

I hear you clearly as you tell me this, so I will believe it. Also, I beg you to give us protection on the journey home. If we don't return, there is no use to any of this.

Two of you we will protect. Which two shall it be?

The question startled Gar; he wasn't expecting that. He didn't have to think about the answer, though. Mouse and Hare.

Well thought. What else?

One thing else. Why all this? Why art?

Art is the soul of a people.

What about dance? And storytelling? There is our soul. And our genealogies...?

The spirits fell silent. They must have fled, for Gar could not sense them in any way. Why did they leave so abruptly? How might he call them back? He still had questions.

Ah. Now he understood. He had slipped too deeply into his conversation, for he had ceased listening to his own senses, especially to smell and vision.

He smelled Hairies. When he opened his eyes, he looked into a face, a distorted, bearded face with long, stringy brown hair tied behind. Pale eyes, yellow teeth.

And a wicked, wicked grin.

26

You Have No Private Life

He was the loneliest, the alone-est Person in the whole, wide world. Moments ago, Gar had been forcibly plopped down to sitting in the midst of a multitude of Hairies who looked grotesque, spoke a totally unintelligible tongue, laughed at odd times—usually at Gar, it would seem—and persisted in squirming about incessantly and chatting amongst themselves whether their leader was speaking at the moment or not. In short, they were the ugliest and most ill-mannered, uncivil people Gar had ever dreamt of. Repulsive by any measure, in superlatives.

Curiously, he was not afraid. No use for fear. He was dead. He knew that fact as surely as he knew the sun was setting out there beyond the trees, as surely as he knew the modest fire beside him was hot. Hairies held no compunctions about killing a Real Person under any circumstance and Gar had trespassed on sacred ground. It was no longer a question of whether but of when. His only desire now was to show these self-important, unprincipled boors what death with honour and dignity looks like.

He wondered what they had done with Mouse and Hare. Both of them stood a fair chance of surviving, Hare in particular, and for that Gar was grateful. Ah, Mouse, with her golden sunset skin, her pure speech and quiet, gentle ways, so at odds with these undesirables. He yearned for her, to at least say goodbye.

Better, though, that she not be associated with him. Let her alterable fate unfold without being damaged by his inalterable one. He felt comfortably resigned. And so he sat quietly, at repose, as pale, lanky, hairy brutes with distorted faces and thick beards churned all around him.

He had been conducted into a temporary camp of some sort, it would appear. Within a ring limned by a dozen small fires, men and women scraped and pounded hides, sliced thin strips off what was probably ibex hindquarters, and hastened about lashing together frames on which to dry either stripped meat or fish. Children and adults both seemed exceedingly noisy and active, constantly yakking and moving about.

Typical of Water People, the women were covered neck to knee by chewed reindeer hide, the men waist to knee by lion or horse hides. Water People had to move a lot of fur out of the way to handle basic functions.

It occurred to him that any number of children—most of the moiety's children in fact (or was this a whole clan?)—stared at him and tittered. More exactly, they stared at his most private parts, so to speak. He had always assumed that Hairy males possessed the normal equipment of the usual size, and the females breasts, but come to think of it, he'd never actually seen confirmation. Perhaps there was something unusual about the Hairies that made him seem strange to these children.

Three callow young men guarded Gar—at least, he assumed they were guards or captors of some sort. Scrawny and pallid, they looked too weak to be of much use. At random intervals, one or the other of them would sit beside him, get up, move about, sit behind him, get up, go do something, return, sit beside him. It was as if they were periodically attacked by invisible ants to the point of being unable to sit. Their beards, like the manes of young lions, were scraggly and ill-developed.

One of the two wore a full bear's-worth of bear claws, braided elaborately into a long plait and draped around his neck. The other had drilled holes through the roots of the upper canines of several bears and strung them on a thong around his neck. If the third fellow was also somehow adopting attributes of a bear, he wasn't displaying them.

Why bears? Bears were huge, certainly, but unless cornered, injured, or fiercely threatened, they didn't cause much trouble. And anyone who cornered, injured, or threatened a bear was a fool who deserved whatever came. But lions. Hyænas. Wolves. They roamed forth to seize a man, fool or no. Why did these people seem so enamoured of bears? Perhaps it was a secret society or some such. Come to think of it, many of the Water People wandering about had adorned themselves with shells, amulets, or animal parts of some sort. If they all represented secret societies, there was not much secret around here.

She's here! Heart seized his thoughts and directed them behind him.

He twisted around to look. Flanked by several women, Mouse approached, climbing the long slope to where Gar and these others sat. She was doing well with her bound leg and two new walking sticks, but one of the young men here seemed impatient, as if she should hurry. He barked at her impatiently. Head down, she kept doggedly to the task and arrived neither sooner nor later than had he not shouted at her.

She dropped to sitting midway between Gar and these three and stretched out her leg. Heart sang in spite of his concern for her safety. She offered no indication that the two of them had ever been intimate, so Gar carefully masked his own feelings and more or less pounded Heart into shutting up and hiding.

One of the three young men reached out and jabbed Mouse. Whatever he said seemed to disgust Mouse and delight the other two. Then, in a fractured sort of Real People's language, barely understandable, he said as he pointed to Gar, "You hear story too. Like the story, eh. Laugh."

Mouse glared at the lad. Gar began rapidly calculating just how to protect her and from whom. He could see the necessity of it looming on their immediate horizon.

The young man leered. "Man and woman kissing, eh."

Kissing. A Hairy word. Gar had no idea what it meant.

Mouse looked just plain angry as the young man continued, "Man says, 'Can I stick my finger in your belly button?' And the woman says, 'If you want.' Minute later, she says 'Wait! That's not my belly button!' Man says, 'That's not my finger.'"

Everyone stared expectantly at Gar. He waited patiently for the conclusion of the story.

A few moments later, Mouse grimaced. "Is a joke."

Joke. Another word not in Gar's vocabulary.

She explained, "Something, a story or something to make you laugh. Most times, joke is about men and women in union, or something. Hard to explain."

The young man who spoke the Real Language, however crudely, laughed and chattered to his friends. They seemed to find the whole thing most amusing.

"The chief and his clan chiefs—not these three—say I am to be the..." She thought a moment and combined *long thong* with *together.* "Connector. When you speak, I will tell them what you say, but I'm not to change anything. And I'm to tell you what they are saying without changing anything."

"Good. Good." He nodded. "You know our culture and language, and theirs also. Is Hare all right?"

"No."

Gar frowned. "Story."

"First he said he was happy to be here. This is home to him, you know. At Larch Cave, the other lads teased him. They'd poke him, hurt him, call him ugly. But now the lads here already tease him, poke him and hurt him, the same as Larch Cave. Worse than Larch Cave. They torment him." She waved a hand, as if trying to gather in thoughts which defied expression. "This hurts him more, much more, because these lads used to be his friends. They're the lads he grew up with. Enemies don't hurt much; friends hurt terribly."

"So they turned on him. By and by, maybe they'll

all be friends again."

She wagged her head *no*. "He is so angry. It's a bad time, now, for Hare."

The sun had pretty much disappeared for the day, leaving behind the ephemeral blue of pre-dark. How beautiful Mouse looked in the wavering firelight.

The ceaseless activity around him didn't stop exactly, but it slowed and changed somewhat. Two women spread several layers of stiff, unchewed bear skins out in front of Gar, fur up. Three men approached and sat down upon the bear robes, facing Gar. Most of the rest of the adults gathered about. The three young captors, if that was what they were, moved back, giving way to the older men. If Gar was reading all this correctly, they would talk and toy with him before killing him. He was ready.

From their lofty bearing, Gar assumed these men held high positions in the tribal structure. Just what that structure was, he wasn't sure.

The centre fellow, presumably therefore the highest in rank, must have adorned himself just for this occasion of meeting with Gar, for he wore so many ornaments that would hinder or even prevent efficient hunting or other work. As if he didn't already have enough grizzled hair, he had framed his face with a loosely fitting wolverine skin. Incongruously, cuckoo tailfeathers stuck up from the back of it. If he turned his head quickly, it would surely fall off. Amulets cascaded down his chest below the beard, suspended from his neck, and around his waist he sported an elaborately braided band of bird skins.

The fellow to this warlord's right wore a figure carved from mammoth tusk on a thong looped around his neck. It appeared to be a woman with fat breasts and a bulgy stomach. It was attractive in a Real-People way, but almost none of these Hairy women was so fat and round.

The man to the warlord's left had adorned himself in a lion skin, its back on his back, its front legs—claws still attached—draped over his shoulders and dangling down the front, its head covering most of the back of his head. The tawny lion with the bearded face of a Hairy looked ludicrous—not a bad idea, come to think of it. This fellow need only wear his get-up on the hunt to keep his compatriots safe; real lions would laugh themselves into falling-down weakness.

Mouse spoke briefly to the three in that guttural language which required no simultaneous hand signs or gestures. The words were apparently a greeting or obeisance of some sort, but she did not present her back to them. Apparently that was strictly a Real People custom.

She turned to Gar. "Already I have told them your name and clan, and that you are a shaman with great power. I told them why we're here, and told them what we know about Kelp." She pointed to the fellow to Gar's left, the one with the carved female figure. "Goro, medicine man. A shaman, sort of." She pointed to the middle one with the wolverine head cover. "Shinnan, the chief of chiefs, like a warlord," and to the third in the lion skin, "Bard. Chief hunter. He organises hunting parties."

Gar nodded and performed a perfunctory obeisance to them. With his death looming vividly before him, he was in no mood to kowtow. "What animals are Shinnan, Bard, and Goro?"

"No animals."

"What things?"

"No things. Just words."

"Then what totems do these three men have?"

"Baboon."

"Baboon is their clan. Each person, what is his totem?"

"They don't have totems for each person. They all take the clan totem only. They're all Baboons."

"Hoo."

Shinnan spoke, and almost as soon as he began, Mouse commenced a translation. Indeed, she was an excellent go-between, being so fluent in both languages and both cultures. It was only polite to look straight into a person's eyes when speaking, and Gar was determined to remain the soul of politeness to the very end. He instantly realised, however, that he could look right at the Hairies only when speaking to them, for as Mouse was translating their speech, he was going to have to watch her. He had to see her gestures as well as hear her words, for gesture was an essential part of Real speech. He would have preferred, though, to stare down these prideful Hairies, particularly since they seemed uncomfortable with direct eye contact.

Posing still another problem, the smelly crowd which clustered in so close about chattered constantly in undertone, including those young men. Gar was not used to this continual background noisy-ness. Real People were polite enough to allow a speaker the honour of being heard without distraction. He had to concentrate carefully on Mouse, on any speaker here, in order to hear clearly with both ears.

Shinnan had just said, in effect, "Your mission amuses us. It's different. Mouse says that you have never talked to our kind before. So tell us. What do you think of us?"

The question surprised Gar. He needed a few moments to consider his answer. "I feel great pity for you." He doubled the *pity* gesture for emphasis. "And very much sadness." As an afterthought, he doubled that one also.

The noise level dropped precipitately.

Shinnan opened his mouth and closed it again.

The tone of voice of the one called Goro dripped with disdain. Mouse translated his as "Tell why" rather than "story." *Provide the underlying reasons, not the surface observation.*

Gar found himself relishing this wonderful freedom. With death a given, candour or lack of it no longer mattered. He could speak truth as he knew it without bothering to soften his words or protect someone's feelings. There was one hitch, though. How could he describe this adequately?

"Naturally, I am curious about you. So I've been looking around. I see people wearing shells, teeth, bones that belonged to animals. These bits and pieces are not the people. They are part of something else." He thought a moment. "I see that it is not enough to be just you. You have to add to yourself, add value to yourself, because you are not enough without that extra. You seem afraid to be just plain you.

"I listen, too. I hear people talking all the time, chatter, chatter, chatter. Some of your people are talking now, while I am talking. They don't listen with both ears. They miss the depth of what people say.

"I see busy, busy, busy. Everyone is hurrying about. No one is resting, no one is sitting and thinking. It takes time and quiet to think thoroughly. You seem to be running away from yourself, afraid of silence."

He paused for Mouse to catch up. Some of this was obviously difficult for her to phrase. He continued, "Most of all, I have seen your art."

Shinnan, dark as a thundercloud, muttered. "You don't like our art? You think you can do better?"

"Like it? What does it matter to you whether I like it or don't like it? It amazes me greatly. I would never dare to try to accomplish such a thing myself. I wouldn't want to. Your art is beautiful. Very beautiful. It's also very frightening, the way you make the wall of a cave tell a stranger's mind what to think."

Shinnan smirked.

"But it's obscene."

Goro roared, "Your kind runs around naked and you call our art obscene?"

It delighted Gar to have produced such an outburst. He kept his own voice soft. "The mind and heart are like a pool of water, with some shallow parts and some deep parts. Words and dance express the shallow parts just fine. Weather, how you feel, where to find game. But the deeps lie far beyond words. The deeps are a flower too beautiful to describe. Try to bring them out as words and all the petals fall off. They are supposed to stay deep, unseen."

"You ramble."

"No." Gar rephrased. "What is the most private thing a Person has? Not the penis or the breast. Those are outside. Everyone knows everyone else has them, and what they look like. So those are not private. They are the surface.

"Dreams. Thoughts. They arise from deep inside and they stay deep inside. All hidden. They are unknown and unguessed, even by one's closest friends. They are real only to the Person who has them."

Mouse paused in her translation and suggested to Gar the word, "Intimate."

"Intimate. Eh! The best of them cannot be expressed to the outside at all. They are the deepest, closest thing within us. Our most private parts. You! You give your deep thoughts and dreams a face, a form. You spread them out and expose them across the walls and ceiling of your cave for all the world to look upon. You have spread what should be very private across the outside, across the surface. That is obscene.

"I pity you that you throw away your precious privacy so easily. That you expose your souls and give them away to everyone. Don't you see? It's gone then. Not private anymore. Your sorry state makes me sad."

Shinnan did not take nearly as long to digest all this as he ought, in Gar's opinion. He should spend some time pondering ramifications. Instead, he came back almost immediately with, "You say, 'sorry state.' We don't think we are so sorry."

"I am content. With peace." Gar looked from face to face. "Are you?"

27

You Can't Trust Hairies Worth Spit

Despite philosophers' claims, some things in life were simple black and white. Gar sat cross-legged with his elbows on his knees, bowed forward toward the bright fire. Total light. Beyond the fire circle lay total blackness, for the first of the autumnal rains had blotted out the night sky.

Fresh rainwater poured off the upper lip of this cave and spattered on the man's-length of floor extending out beyond the overhang. Rather than choosing a more rainproof shelter to start with, these Water People had erected an elaborate buffer of brush and hides to keep the splashes from reaching them inside the cave. Ridiculous. A people who think nothing of immersing themselves and swimming around in large bodies of water go to extreme lengths to avoid a few drops splashing on them.

If Gar would picture cultures any particular hue,

the Water People's would have to be black.

For two days now, he had sat patiently in this place or that as the Hairies churned all around him. He still could not recognise any of the words and phrases they yammered so incessantly. He almost would guess that they sometimes used more than one word for a thing.

Was he a prisoner? Always, several young men with slim lances hovered near him. Either the Hairies were teasing him with hopes of life just before torturing and killing him, or they wanted him to try to escape. Perhaps they thought he would become interesting or entertaining as prey for them to hunt. Hardly could he imagine that they planned to let him go.

Where was Mouse? Since that first night when she translated that initial conversation, he had not seen her or Hare.

As Mouse had so carefully explained away back at the beginning of their relationship, these Hairies divided themselves out not as moieties but as blood groups—a woman, her man, and the children they had produced together. It would appear that sometimes grandparents were included also, particularly if they were crippled. *Family*, Mouse called it. What happened to the family when a man decided to take another woman, as Newt had taken Kohl? Even after all this time, Crow's unjust death galled Gar. What would have happened to Crow's child when she was gone, had there been a family instead of a moiety to take over the child's upbringing? Score another white mark for the Real People's way, a black mark for the Hairies'. The Real People's way took care of children, widows, and mate shifts just fine.

And why all the children? Were Water People that much more fertile? A Real woman could expect to give birth to perhaps three children in her lifetime, of which one or two would survive long enough to produce their own offspring. These Hairies seemed to pop out a child at least once a winter. Children of varying ages clattered and chattered all over the place. Much as Gar liked and valued children, these swarming, overactive half-talls were getting on his nerves.

Forced by the circumstance into inactivity, Gar used some of the time to query the spirits around him. It was very difficult; spirits seemed as distracted by these babbling children as was Gar. In fact, the busy-ness of the adults was nearly as hard to ignore. By staring past the constant hubbub to the skyline of the distant hills, Gar could fairly well block out the noise and movement, at least during the less hectic times of day. It didn't do much good.

Now this evening, as the black thickness of rain and night hid the horizon and its hills, he studied the nervous flames, the quivering coals of this central fire.

He addressed whichever spirits might be nearby: You were so clear when I communed with you in the cave. Return, I beg you.

No contact.

He remembered how they fled when the Hairies entered. Perhaps they disliked the busy-ness, or the noise, or maybe even the Water People themselves. Spirits with good taste? It would seem so.

You have agreed to save Mouse and Hare. I am grateful. But the question of who killed Kelp has become more than just a point of curiosity to me. I hunger to solve the puzzle for its own sake. What do you mean, I already know the answer? Please tell me more.

No comment.

I beg you, reassure me.

That we will do. You are not abandoned even now.

He almost smiled, so relieved did he feel.

We make an even greater promise. Before you die, you will learn the most important spiritual secret of all. Saiga knows it now.

It is the key to his power? Gar asked.

One of them.

Only powerful spirits can release Mouse and Hare from their bondage among these people. I cannot. I doubt even Rat could. Will you do it?

No comment.

Their silence was the first thing to alert him to the Hairies' presence. The triumvirate of Goro, Shinnan, and Bard had entered this cave. And here came Mouse tagging after, struggling along on one stick rather than two. She seemed to be using her bound leg a little more, a good sign. Her eyes looked puffy, as though she had been weeping. Gar hoped it was not more trouble with Hare.

As before, two women spread furs for the three to sit upon. Gar turned around, his back to the fire, in order to face the three squarely. Mouse settled into the beaten dirt midway between the Hairies and him.

The three wore their special adornments again—Bard with his lion skin, Goro with his female fetish, Shinnan with his many doodads and the wolverine-and-feather cap. It lent them all an air of extreme silliness Gar was certain they did not intend.

Bard spoke. Gar had not heard him till now. His voice rasped, full of gravel, and Gar noticed for the first time the scars on the side of the man's throat. They were parallel white lines like a lion's deep clawmarks. The lion skin nearly hid them.

Mouse translated. "We admire your restraint. You have asked no questions about your fate."

Restraint. Gar had not heard that word, but he could guess its meaning. He smiled. "I think I will find out in due time."

"Right now, in fact." Bard smiled too. "You are a powerful man among your people and ours, to commune with spirits. Strong medicine. We agreed it would be unwise to harm you unless you force us to." He paused and waited. Mouse ended her translation, so it was not Mouse he waited for.

Gar nodded. "I see. I will determine my own fate by doing the right thing or the wrong thing. Very well. What is the right thing?"

"Go quietly."

"Real People do not come and go noisily. You mean, go without killing anyone as I leave."

Shinnan and Bard chuckled. Goro remained black as the sky out there.

Gar wagged his head in mock doubt, for inside, he was hopelessly confused. He must watch carefully for cues to what was really happening—watch Mouse also for her initial reaction to these men's words. "It will be very difficult for me to leave here without killing a few of you first. You kill Real People for sport. I could make some sport myself, eh." He smiled broadly. "But I will try."

"We are grateful." Shinnan did not dance his thanks. Gar doubted the warlord could move fast enough to dance anything at all, with that wolverine fur perched so precariously up there.

Inside, Gar still questioned his safe passage. He looked from Shinnan to Goro, uncertain whom to address. "If I leave now, it will be without what I came to find. I want to learn who killed Kelp. So I ask a boon."

Shinnan frowned at the translation. Mouse rephrased.

"Ah." Shinnan nodded. "What boon?"

Gar directed his request to Goro, their shaman. "Let me stay three days. No food. Water only at dawn. Then I will sit in the cave of animals—the art—to hear the voices. By and by perhaps I will learn the truth. I will not stay long in the cave. Either they will speak or they will not. They will tell me or they won't."

Shinnan was staring expectantly toward Goro.

The grumpy one rumbled, "No need for you to ask spirits. I killed him, that Kelp. I cut off his head."

The confession startled Gar. "Story."

"We were scouting ahead for game when we came upon him, so we killed him. As you say, for sport."

"Were you alone when you killed him or with others?"

"Alone."

Gar shook his head. "Water People—that is, you people—are far to the north then, hunting reindeer, not south in our Scarp Country."

"We came south early. It's going to be a long winter. The reindeer and mammoth herds are moving south early, so we did as well."

"Mm." Gar leaned forward, elbows on his knees, and tried to assay this shaman's mood and veracity. The mood remained as it always seemed. Surly. The confession fit, more or less.

A fine mess! Head. *Assuming for a moment that Goro be telling the truth...*

Heart: *Not for one moment can you trust these Hairies*

to be truthful!

Head: *I know, I know. But if he's right, the problem takes a whole new turn. The Seashore People want the culprit, not a confession of guilt from afar off. Not unless they hear a confession from the killer's own mouth will they absolve Mouse. We must somehow transport Goro to the Seashores. A wicked twist, this!*

Heart: *Here's worse. We have no idea where Seashore territory lies relative to here.*

Head moaned heavily, *Another wicked twist.*

And then Heart rubbed salt in the wound. *Or home either, for all that.*

"You don't believe me," Goro accused.

"Thinking."

Mouse yammered, apparently explaining the Real People habit of digesting information before acting or speculating upon it.

Gar perceived the three were growing restless, as Water People so quickly become, so he spoke before he was really ready to. "The Seashore People will want more than words. What will I take with me that supports your claim? What can I show them?"

"Nothing." Goro sounded proud, defiant.

"They will not believe it. Kelp had double power. He was a shaman as well as warlord of a strong clan. Killing him would be very difficult. To kill him is a triumph, a thing to boast about to your grandchildren all your life. Seashore People don't know that you did it, so they cannot treat you with awe. They cannot dance of your power. I must take them something to prove your claim." Gar paused. "Or take them you."

Goro smirked, his voice low and rumbling, as he pinched thumb and first finger together, a gesture. "I don't care this much what Uglies think about me."

Gar asked Mouse, "Did you tell Goro about Kelp's death?"

"His head cut off, all of it. Yes."

"Mm." And so he sat silently, assaying Goro's mood. The Hairies did not wait well. They fidgeted. They babbled amongst themselves. They demanded something of Mouse and she shrugged, glancing at Gar. And then Heart smugly announced, *He's lying. Watch his eyes. He is playing you for a simpleton.*

Gar would accept that. He dipped his head. "Then tomorrow morning, first light, you will give me my spear and give Hare his, and we will go."

"No." Shinnan.

Ah hah. So Gar had been right. He never did think they'd let him go. "You changed your mind suddenly."

"No. You go, but you go alone. Mouse and Hare are ours. They will stay here forever."

28

They Really Don't Want Him

Gar's mind swirled, black as the night out there. No! Not after all they had survived already! No wonder Mouse's eyes were puffy. These three must have told her before they met with Gar that they would not allow her to leave. Her voice broke as she translated, her gestures faltered.

He desperately needed time to think, and he had none.

With uncommon vigour, Heart insisted, *Let me take over. I don't need time. You rarely trust me. Trust me now!*

And Gar had no choice. He let Heart guide his words. "I am one and you are many. What can I do? But. You owe me a great debt. I brought the woman and her son back here. They were lost, now they are found. You are boors if you send me away empty-handed, without a gift."

"You may take your spear."

"No gift, that. My spear is of no use to you. Real People use a thick, strong spear to grip tightly and thrust. You carry a puny spear because you like to throw it. My spear is so much bigger than yours, it's too heavy to throw. It's no use to you. Give me something else." He paused for Mouse to catch up. "Give me Hare."

She gasped. She gaped. Shinnan prodded her and she translated.

Gar looked from face to face. "Lads who were once his friends hate him. Ask any of them; they don't want him. He is ugly, strange, no use to you. The others, children and adults, don't want him. They laugh at him and chase him. Torment him. By and by, when you three are old, Hare will be grown up. He could cause problems when the time comes to choose a new shaman or warlord, because he is half Goro's. If I take him away from you, I will take away all the problems."

Goro glared. "Why do you want him?"

"To get home with. He knows the way. I don't."

Beautiful, Head purred. *And true.*

Partly true, Heart replied.

"This is a new thing." Shinnan's brow puckered. All Water People had shaggy eyebrows, but his were particularly thick and ratty, vying with that ludicrous wolverine skin for an observer's attention. The brows crowded together on his face. "We will talk about it, tell you tomorrow at midday what we decide. Then you can go."

Gar nodded. "Quietly, of course."

Bard grinned. "Of course."

Gar stood up, briefly considered performing obeisance, decided against it, and dipped his head. "I await your words." He walked away, quickly and proudly but not too quickly, not too haughtily.

His first night in this cave, he had been directed to that part of the floor nearest the rain buffer. Despite the barrier, the floor there stayed wet and a few drops splashed inside. He didn't care. He realised now that Real People didn't mind cold and damp nearly as much as did Hairies. He was not uncomfortable here and he was the only person sleeping so close to the mouth. He was also the only person not sleeping on furs. No problem there either. Real People sleep on furs in their caves, but they certainly don't bother carrying hides with them when travelling, the way Hairies do.

He stretched out now in his place with his right side toward the night, besprinkled by an occasional cleansing raindrop, and stared at the dark ceiling. He forgot these ill-mannered savages, for he could not cease thinking about Mouse.

Mouse. Poor Mouse. Wonderful Mouse.

To his left, people dispersed, retiring, snuggling into their furs the way Real People do on truly cold nights. Whatever did these people do in midwinter, when it really got cold? The fires cooled down to coals; the air directly above them no longer quivered. At long last, the cave enjoyed some small semblance of peace.

Where was Mouse? She had not left the area, he was sure of that. Several of the covering furs moved rhythmically, men and women joining in union as they seemed to do just about every night. Assuming this was normal behaviour, no wonder so many children cavorted about.

Heart murmured, *You realise, I trust, that one of those is Mouse and her man.*

Head sniffed.

Plain old nausea swept across Gar. Heart was right. And he knew the man. Goro, the "medicine man" with the ivory amulet. All those years ago, Rat had enslaved her to the shaman here. That had to be Goro. He fathered Hare. Now he had his slave back, not to mention his half-breed son. Gar searched his memory for the look on Goro's face when Gar announced that he wanted to take Hare. All three Hairies registered surprise; Gar himself was caught off guard by Heart's request. But he could recall no shock, no disgust, no angry defence or denial in the man. Goro didn't give a poop.

Gar dozed, drifted. Mouse caressed him in that gentle way of hers. He awoke with an acute need to take care of something he had not bothered with since well before he sat down with the three chiefs. He climbed to his feet and carefully made his way through the darkness to a drop-off along the cave's west edge, where the men went to take a pee.

Curious, he thought as he relieved himself, how this people divided up the places where men and women function, as if it were somehow a secret that women peed and men peed and each had to somehow protect that secret from the other. Women went somewhere beyond the east end of the floor, out among boulders. How did they squat successfully with those bulky fur garments? It would be bad enough functioning as a male with that fur skirt the men wore to deliberately cover up the functioning member.

He turned away to start back toward his place. A pallid form loomed directly ahead of him. He stopped. Squinted. The form moved in close enough to see. A woman, as tall as he but much slimmer. Gar wasn't certain—most Hairy women looked pretty much alike—

but he thought this might be one of the two who spread the furs out for the three chiefs to sit upon.

Smiling, she laid her hands on his shoulders, then let one slide down his right arm. She took his hand in hers and led him west, out from under the cavern overhang and uphill through broken boulders. Apparently, Hairies shared with Real People the custom of providing a woman to a visiting male dignitary. Until just now, Gar had assumed they did not.

They stepped out into the rain. Fortunately, it had pretty much subsided to a coarse, penetrating mist. Hard beside a nearly vertical slick clay cliff, stood a young man and a girl embracing. Ardently the lad pressed his mouth against hers. Gar recognised him, despite that another's face was mashed against his—the joke teller who guarded him that first day.

The custom of pressing one's mouth to another's piqued Gar's curiosity, and almost as quickly as the thought crossed his mind, this pallid woman did just that. Gar had been for far too many winters the sophisticate to find himself a beginner again; it felt odd, but that was much the case here. Her mouth was not quite closed, her lips cool and soft. He opened his mouth a bit and copied whatever she did.

She wrapped around him, so he wrapped around her. Her garment, fur out, provided an interesting sensation pressed between them like this. She opened her mouth further and did intriguing things with her tongue which he tried also. The custom delighted and aroused him far more than he would have guessed. He could hardly wait to show Kohl this one!

Here was Gar's chance to learn the particulars of hidden Hairy anatomy, should he so choose. The murky darkness obscured the Hairy woman's grotesque appearance, making intimacy slightly more palatable. After all, a woman was a woman.

This woman, however, seemed to consider him a child. He might not have known about these mouth games, but he was hardly a novice. She was guiding each step as if he'd never seen a woman before. Being patronised like this irritated him greatly.

And then Head intruded. *You know who this is, don't you?* and without waiting for an answer added, *Goro's neglected wife. He's with Mouse and she wants to claim you as a trophy of like kind.*

Heart protested, *Providing a woman is a fine old custom from—*

Head countered with, *Then why was none provided before? And why is this meeting an apparently clandestine one? A properly assigned woman would come to your bed, not drag you out into the rain. You've been here for days, and not as an honoured guest. You sleep in the least honoured place.*

Head was correct, of course. Did Gar want to go along with this? He had no idea what expectations were demanded of a Hairy family situation; he knew only Real People's customs. Somehow, from Mouse's description of it, he doubted that this was preferred Hairy behaviour. Mouse had mentioned how a man and woman in marry, or however she phrased it, joined only with each other. No, this was no polite offer of clan custom.

How could he gracefully end it?

You sure? Heart was profoundly disappointed.

Positive. Head.

Pouting, Heart grumbled, *Oh, all right. Let me lead.*

She was just beginning to guide his hand when he

separated their mouths and lifted back a bit. He gathered both her hands into his, brushed their backs and knuckles with his lips in the same manner that they had been brushing their mouths together, stepped back and walked away. Very easy. Extremely difficult.

The lad and his young woman were still pursuing their mouth games.

When Gar returned to his place, the woman did not follow. He was uncomfortably unsated, but he subsided after a while and drifted fitfully off to sleep, wondering about his fate. Shinnan had said it depended upon whether Gar did right or wrong.

He was not the least certain which was which.

29

The Shaman Hates Everybody

It was too early in autumn for frost, or not late enough in the summer, depending upon one's viewpoint. Still, here it lay, crisp and sparkling despite the gloomy overcast, the holdover from last night's rain. It made Gar's toes ache as he waded through it.

Bad dreams he could not remember had awakened him before dawn. And hunger. He was very hungry, so he went out foraging. By the time the sun made it above the trees, he had found himself a couple frogs, some grubs, and a nice patch of amaranth. He stashed all but the grubs in his travel ditty. The grubs he beheaded and carried in his hand, lest they be accidentally squashed before he could roast them.

The young men assigned to watch him—not, incidentally, the feckless fellow of last night—tagged along behind. In a way, they were attempting a very clumsy ruse. They pretended they were not following him. Probably they were also pretending that he didn't know they were there. Surely they did not actually believe he was unaware of them. They carried light lances, small, slim weapons even for Hairies.

Some of the Hairy women were out and abroad gathering also. The men did not seem to forage to any degree. As Gar started back toward the cave, two grown men came down off the hill up ahead, each carrying a ewe ibex. Ibex was game for children to practice upon, and even children took the ram. These people seemed to deliberately relish ignominy and eschew glory.

Disgusting.

Gar noted as an aside that he was the only person out here in the frost who did not wear covering on his feet.

And then, halfway back to the cave, he corrected that impression. One other went barefoot—Mouse, not a quarter mile up ahead on an open hillside. She knelt with her back to him and her bound leg stretched out, using her walking stick to dig industriously at roots of some sort.

He calculated briefly. Until this moment, the callow young men following him about had meant nothing to him, either as comfort or as irritant. Suddenly they irked him. He began "foraging" again, working a great circle around Mouse. Had the young men seen her? He doubted it. Now he led them away so that they certainly would not. As he moved he tested the air for Mouse's scent. He found it, eventually. Faint. He would use that to keep track of her.

With nose and ears he placed the exact whereabouts of his two spies behind him. Their eyesight seemed adequate and their ears good, but their noses seemed to function hardly at all. He would use that bit of knowledge. He ambled down the bank of a small stream and waded out into it. Sticking the grubs in his bag—they were on their own—he quickly worked his way downstream ten or twelve man-lengths and, as silently as possible, grabbed a twig of an overhanging alder limb, drew the limb down to him, and swung his legs up, hooking his heels around the branch. Unless the bough broke, he would score a tidy little coup here.

His ditty hanging loose beneath him, he crept back the limb to the alder trunk, hauled himself upright in the crotch and climbed out another limb which arched over the streamside trail. Carefully he adjusted his ditty so it would not swing loose. Then he listened, tickled, as the young men tried to piece together where he had just disappeared.

They whispered. Through the branches, he could barely discern them examining the stream bank, one on each shore. They disappeared upstream. They abandoned whispering and yammered. Gar could have followed their movements if he were napping. Here they came back, checking the streamside trail. They began working downstream, pausing almost directly beneath him. Were he to urinate just now, he could get the one lad right in the ear. The youth bent over and studied the trail closely, but he did not look straight up.

As soon as they moved downstream far enough that their chatter was not so clear, he dropped to the trail below, moved to the side of it and brushed out the prints from his landing. Then he hurried back the way he had come, stepping in the melted footmarks in the frost that his own and other feet had already made.

Mouse. He detected her before long and abandoned efforts to cover his trail. She must have dug what she wanted of those roots, for now she ranged out across a shallow, brush-covered slope among straggly heath and scrub-willows. It would be hard to slip up on her undetected out in the open that way, for he would have to stay downwind and that meant approaching her from virtually in front of her. But he didn't want her turning away before they could talk, snubbing and refusing him. He needed the element of surprise to stop her cold.

Every time she bent over to examine something or gather something in, he moved forward, hunkering low when she started to rise again. He groped in his ditty.

Five man-lengths from her, he stood up and extended his hand with the two frogs. "Put these in your bag, eh."

She gasped, gaped, then scowled black. She glanced hastily about. "Where are the lads? They're supposed to keep you away from me."

"I though maybe that was their job." He moved forward until he could have reached out and touched her. Instead, he pulled her ditty close enough that he could drop the frogs in. It was hard to talk with frogs in his hand.

The glare had not softened. "So you will take my son away from me, eh. Goro says maybe you can have him."

"He doesn't want him. I do."

"To get home." She spat.

"To make him a shaman." To turn her heart, he must press his case quickly. "Think, Mouse! A shaman commands respect. It's the only way Hare will ever get respect. A shaman can be ugly, crippled, blind, no matter. He's still the shaman."

"Hare is a good hunter. That will win him a place."

"Lots of men are good hunters. Clansmen don't have to listen to a hunter. They don't have to obey him or respect him. They have to pay attention to a shaman. Hare is smart. Very smart, and clever. He learns fast. He knows his own head. He's brave and strong. And good hunter also, eh. A perfect shaman, eh."

She was softening. The glare had melted to a slightly-less-black frown. "Your clan doesn't want him any more than this one does, shaman or not."

"They don't have any say in who is a shaman or who is not. I do. I pick the people I will teach." He moved in closer and lowered his voice. "I'll take good care of him, like a son. Maybe by and by I can have you too, but maybe not. Hare is of you. Even if I never get to see you again, at least I can have a part of you."

She stared at him eye to eye, frozen in the moment, and he could not assay her mood. Then she melted against him, wrapped around him. He wrapped instantly around her. She sobbed wildly, her shoulders heaving. Breaths came to her in tortured gulps. His own eyes grew wet as he hugged her close.

Poor, star-crossed Mouse. Her life, never easy or happy, kept plunging deeper and deeper into misery. How Gar yearned to provide respite somehow, and he had no idea what to do. He could not shake the terrible feeling that whatever he did, whatever anyone did, would only make her life worse.

She brought herself under control eventually. The shuddering sobs abated but the hug did not. His whole breast was slimy wet from her weeping.

"Gar. Last night. Why didn't you join with Goro's wife?"

Now that was not a question he would have expected. He thought briefly of trying to explain that her own description of the Water People's "marry" pictured it as more binding even than pledging. He tried to frame his ethical reservations, and abandoned that. He answered simply, "She's a Hairy."

"Goro's furious."

"Because I didn't violate his wife?" Maybe he was misreading local customs and mores completely.

"Eh. He'd be mad if you did, but he's even more mad that you didn't."

"Story."

"He saw her get up from her bed and go toward you, out toward rain wall. He knew what she wanted, eh. He told me—"

"You and he were together."

"Eh. He told me he was going to catch you in union with her and kill you both. Kill you two in the very moment. He said if I make a sound, he'd kill me too. And he would. Then he picked up a skinning blade and a flint bone-cutting adze, and followed her.

"I follow him. I couldn't stand not to. For a long time she watched you. Then you got up, headed for the men's side. We saw her meet you over there. Goro waited, giving you time, I suppose. But before he could get close, you came back. You were—you know—your most private parts proved you didn't do anything with her, see. Now he says, you think she isn't good enough for you. And that makes him madder."

Gar smirked. "He's right. She isn't good enough for me. Why didn't he kill me anyway, if he's so mad?"

"He can't. You can kill a man who joins with your wife. That's all right. You're defending your honour. But if you kill a man for no reason, that's very wrong."

"I'm Real People. Nobody cares if he kills me."

"You're powerful. Everyone is afraid of you."

"Mm." Where did they get that idea? He couldn't even make a good connection with his own spirits. "You said he'd kill his own wife?"

"It would be a good excuse to, if she joined with you. He hates her."

Not so unthinkable. Crow's senseless murder by Newt's hand leapt to mind yet again. Should he tell Mouse? He decided not, despite that Crow had been her friend. She carried enough heaviness just now.

The last flies of summer buzzed around his sticky-wet chest. "Seems like Goro hates about everybody."

"Eh." Silence. Then, "Gar? That makes me very happy, that you didn't join with her."

He was going to say something on the order of "Me too," and maybe even initiate a union. But someone was shouting around beyond the curve of the hill.

Mouse tensed. "Hare!"

It sounded more like Hairies to Gar, but what did he know? He wasn't a mother.

She ripped herself away from him and doddered off toward the noise, not even pausing to grab her walking stick.

He had at least that much presence of mind. He scooped up her stick and took off after her.

Downhill to the right, from whence Gar had come, those two young men who were supposed to be guarding him popped out of the forested stream channel. They pointed toward Gar, shouting.

At the same time in the opposite direction, Hare came running for all he was worth. As he appeared from around the hillside, Gar could see that his left arm was bloodied. Hard on Hare's heels, three Hairy men brandishing light spears called to each other. All four were stumbling with weariness; none seemed inclined to slow up. Gar's two young guards came angling up the hill toward them.

Gar ignored those lads, for more pressing concerns caught his attention. He charged right on past Mouse toward Hare. Those Hairies weren't merely teasing and tormenting the ugly child.

They were out to kill him.

30

Bad Odds Aren't Good

It occurred briefly to Gar as he sprinted across this hillside that he was facing odds of five to one. Three Hairies chasing Hare plus two Hairies chasing Gar equalled a considerable handful. Fortunately, they were only Hairies, and not Real People.

He could see Hare's face clearly, and the look on it startled him. Hare had spotted him and was grinning! No terror there; the expression told Gar in no uncertain terms that the lad was confident now that he would be saved. Completely confident. And the implied trust frightened Gar. He might not be up to the task of saving them all.

One of Hare's tormentors, the tallest and broadest of the three, slowed and arched back into spear-throwing position. From behind Gar, Mouse screamed, "Down!" Hare flung himself forward and bellied out across the sparse grass. That spear sailed past his ear and plowed into dirt a man's-length beyond Gar's foot.

Gar continued running, past Hare toward the three. Two man-lengths in front of him, the Hairies skidded to a halt, wary, so he stopped too. They were gasping, totally winded and slathered in sweat. What cowards!—for they gave pause to a solitary fighter armed with nothing but a woman's walking stick.

Or was he? He thought he heard the encouraging whispers of the spirits of this place.

Why did these three not simply throw their remaining two spears and skewer him? They were watching both him and the hillside behind him. Gar kept his eyes on the three and let his nose and ears tell him what was going on behind him. Mouse was galumphing toward them and Hare, breathing noisily, braced back to back with Gar. Hare had scooped up the Hairies' thrown spear; Gar could just see the tip of it, rock steady, behind him. The gouge in his own side, now scarred over, testified to the lad's prowess with a spear.

"Story."

"They say I rape a girl." Hare gulped breath between words.

"What is 'rape'?"

"Union, she don't want to."

"Did you?"

"No." More gulping of air. "She says I did that. I didn't."

Gar's two erstwhile guards were approaching rapidly. They slowed coming up the hill. He heard them move in behind him, beyond Mouse and Hare.

Mouse shouted something apparently in Hare's defence.

The three in front of Gar protested angrily, unmollified in the least. They yammered to the other two.

So it was over, this situation. No going back now. Hare could not remain with the Hairies, so Mouse surely would not either.

Gar straightened, drew himself up tall, and deliberately relaxed. He smiled casually at those three and without taking his eyes away, passed the walking stick behind him. It left his hand. "Mouse. Run north. We will all meet where we hid from the fire."

"I can help here."

"You're slow yet with your leg. Start now. Go. We'll take these ones, Hare and I. Then we'll catch up to you."

The briefest pause, and he heard her thump away rapidly with that stick. He hoped desperately that these Hairies would disregard a fleeing crippled woman not directly involved here.

They did. She brushed right past the two young men and hastened down toward the trees.

The spirits promised him two of three lives saved, and he identified Mouse and Hare. That pretty much sealed his own fate.

He was ready.

Without a care in the world, he sauntered toward the three. He realised now why the two with spears hesitated to throw them. They had already inadvertently armed Hare. They surely didn't want to arm Gar as well. They braced, their spears pointed at Gar's belly. He didn't even bother to pull his ditty bag, slung over his shoulder, around to the front as protection. Their look of defiance had melted to disdain and now it appeared tinged with fear. Gar could see that it might certainly be unsettling, facing down a formidable foe who didn't care about the outcome.

Staring at those two still holding spears, Gar lunged aside suddenly and grabbed the third fellow, the big one, by an arm and a leg. In one fast swing, he hauled the Hairy up over his head and hurled him forward two man-lengths into the other two. He was not nearly as heavy as Aster had been. All three went down in a screaming heap as the two young guards behind him yelled. Glory!

He leapt forward, grabbed a spear from the mess of thrashing arms and legs, and drove it into its owner with all his weight behind it. It snapped. Glory! He stomped on the other spearman's belly, in the notch just below the rib cage; his heel sank deep. He retrieved that weapon also.

Armed now, however flimsily, he spun around to meet his guards. One of them was facing down Hare; they stared at each other, crouched, both loathe to throw. The other was coming at Gar. The fellow skidded to a halt so instantly, his fur-clad feet slipped out from under him in the wet grass. He scrambled back to standing.

Gar's ears told him the third behind him was charging. Without turning, he thrust straight backward with the butt of his lance. He connected, but at an angle. The fellow oofed and collapsed, but Gar didn't do nearly as much damage as he would wish.

Gar stepped in beside his protégé. "When Goro hears this, he'll try to kill your mother. Go, protect her, eh. Get her out of the territory." He spared a glance at Hare.

The lad's face radiated with exhilaration. "I want to kill this one first!"

"Others are coming. I hear them. Go! Her safety is first!"

Hare took off at a run across the hill, and his obedience rather surprised Gar, as caught up in blood lust as the ugly child was.

Gar now faced three, two of them armed and the third to be expected to regain his feet any moment. He had no idea how many more were running toward them. He wheeled, turning his back on the two guards only long enough to spear the fallen third attacker. Glory! Not too slow to learn, he put less weight behind it this time, lest he break another of these slim spears. He yanked the bloodied spear free as one of the guard's spears sailed past him, wavering, and scudded down the hill into a heather. The bad shot suggested a frightened shooter.

Grinning, he turned back to the two youths. "I killed these ones, and now I will kill you." He started toward them.

They didn't know what he had just said; still, they panicked—two of them and the one still armed, and yet they panicked. What children! They ran away, down toward the woods along the stream from whence they had come.

It occurred to Gar that although the spirits did not ensure his safety, neither did they say he was doomed this instant. He just might escape this yet. Once he got out of sight, the Hairies would have to track him painstakingly; their sense of smell was not sharp enough to follow him. And he possibly could outrun them, given the time to do so. No way could a full-blooded Real Person outrun a Hairy. Hairies were too fleet over the short haul. But they seemed to lack stamina. Given enough time and distance, a Real Person would eventually overtake even the fastest Hairy. Gar would depend upon that now.

He toyed with the idea of pausing to find that loose spear in the heather and decided not to when he saw two more Hairies coming around the side of the slope with at least one more following, laggard. Keeping the flimsy one he had, he turned tail and broke into a run, at an angle different from Mouse and Hare's route. He would circle around and head true north later.

This might not have been the wisest idea, for his route took him out across sloping, broken ground and low heather. The pursuers behind him could see him from afar. He altered course somewhat toward northwest and headed for the enclosing woods along the bottomland.

The fleet Hairies were gaining. To be expected. But the trees—and safety—waited just ahead. This was the Hairies' territory and virtually unfamiliar to Gar. Still, once he reached the woodland—

A blow to his back knocked all the wind out of him and sent him sprawling. He skidded across sharp stones, weeds, and pea gravel, all of it gouging marks into him. He slammed into a loose boulder and stopped.

He could not draw breath. The world swirled, but he was not so addled that he could not hear women screaming. His whole torso ached, desperate to breathe.

The Hairies should be here very quickly. Then that would be the end of him.

He was defended! With a cry to curdle nerves, Hare had returned; he slid to a halt hard beside Gar. Glory! The ugly child reared back with that light lance he carried, in throwing position.

Gar wanted to yell, "Don't throw it!" but his lungs were empty—no air yet with which to make a sound.

He twisted up onto one elbow and reached out toward the lad.

Hare's whole body flexed and whipped; Gar could actually hear that spear whistle as it left, could hear the surprised grunt of a Hairy in the near distance.

Heart purred, *I know a death rattle when I hear one; perfect aim the lad has.* Glory!

Immediately Hare darted aside and scooped up the light spear Gar had been carrying. He swung around to meet the enemy and braced with it. He spoke rapidly in staccato, eagerly, his eyes bright and crackling. How he must love this; his whole face glowed! "The one I speared is dead. You: I don't see any blood. Your spear is too heavy—they can't throw it right. They're not strong enough. It tumbled in the air and hit you wrong on your ditty bag, sideways. Bounced right off you, eh. Can you run?"

My spear? Gar lurched to his knees. The butt end of his own thick, hefty spear fell away from across his shoulders. It clunked against the loose boulder Gar himself had just clunked against. He reared erect on his knees and twisted to look behind.

Three armed Hairies faced them; it used to be four, but one now lay sprawled across the slope with Hare's spear in him.

The middle one of the three was Goro. He screamed furiously at Hare, a long, rattling diatribe.

Hare, that remarkable lad, waited politely until Goro paused. In that Water-People gibberish, he spoke a few words. His voice still vibrated with enthusiasm. Goro resumed shouting, no less irate.

A fifth Hairy came around the brow of the hill in the distance, trying to hold a wolverine cap in place as he ran.

Gar managed at last to draw a breath. Before he could draw his second, everything happened.

He heard footfalls coming up from the woods, one of them Mouse with her hobbling gait and her walking stick. But he didn't have time to look, for the fellow to Goro's left hauled back without warning and instantly threw his spear.

Looking startled, Hare whipped just as instantly from a brace into a throwing position; his spear left his hand at almost the same moment the Hairy's did. It lodged in the Hairy's hip right at the joint as the Hairy's spear thudded into Hare's belly. The lad's face blanched white. Rather casually he dropped onto his knees; his hair bobbed with the jolt.

No! In one long movement, Gar heaved to his feet, snatched up that boulder two-handed, wheeled, and hurled it. Wide-eyed, Goro tried to duck aside, but he was nowhere near fast enough. The boulder slammed into his belly and carried him backward a man's-length before he fell. Glory! The rock poised the barest moment on top of him and nonchalantly rolled off.

Even as Gar snatched up his spear, Mouse and a wretched pallid woman arrived. The Hyæna? The woman yanked that light spear out of Hare as Mouse scooped him up and flung him belly-down over her shoulder. Mouse doddered away, her son flopping against her back, leaving behind the strong odour of offal.

The sole remaining Hairy stared only a moment at Gar and the Hyæna. He nearly tripped over himself turning around to flee.

As he braced with his spear at ready, Gar sucked in another breath. A third. His spear tip wavered and he could not fully steady it. The woman beside him crouched poised with that light spear, as formidable as he.

The Hairy ran back across the hill to the approaching Shinnan. They stood out there beyond throwing range arguing, but neither made a move in this direction.

Gar stepped backward a pace and fell to his knees. His belly lurched up into his throat and he vomited. He managed to get up on his feet again and stagger off after Mouse. The Hyæna walked backwards at his side, watching their enemy. They pushed through willow tangles and stepped into dank woodland, beneath alders dying with the dying summer.

The woman turned around and picked up speed, following the wispy scent of Mouse and blood and the stricken Hare. Gar did little more than tag along behind her.

Gar marvelled at the distance Mouse had carried her child when they finally caught up to her. Mouse continued without slowing, leading them up a raggedy slope to a stained limestone overhang. Sweaty, she carefully laid Hare out in the cool, powdery dust.

Good choice for a refuge. Gar stacked a couple of large boulders to close off their only really exposed end. The rest of the overhang was easily defensible. One person or two, experienced with a spear, could hold off a dozen. And from this ærie they could see most of the hills beside and before them.

Hare lay curled on his side, his arms crossing his poor, ripped belly. Blood and gut contents still trickled out, and no one here entertained any fool notion that he might survive. His eyes were open, and he appeared to be aware.

Gar danced his thanks to him, doubling every gesture.

Hare smiled and whispered, "How many?"

Gar counted off on his fingers, "Between us, three and one and one. Five dead. Four others ran away in fear of us."

Glory.

······31············

They Finally Worked in Concert

In the time he'd known her, Gar had seen Mouse furious, cautious, frightened, joyous, and post-coital, but never had he seen her defeated, in such total, abject listlessness. As he carried her pick-a-back, her free leg flopped, her shoulders sagged. Lifeless. Without hope. Stricken. He might as well be carrying a couple of butchered horse forequarters.

Rains had laid down the ashes from that wildfire, but the ground, the charred stumps and logs, the occasional burnt animal still stank. He slogged up the slope they had once gone running down—long ago, it seemed—when they tried to reach that stream before the fire did. The stream lay well behind them now. Where they were going, he didn't exactly know. What they would do he did not know.

He did know now that he could not bear to lose

Mouse. He would die himself before he would give up Mouse.

And the depth of his own grief for the ugly child amazed him.

How close behind were the Hairies? He didn't want to think about it.

The Hyæna woman ranged ahead, jogging a zigzag search pattern across the pillaged slope. She had said almost nothing over the last two days, and did not, so far, bother to explain how she found them or why she so persistently tagged along. She did not seem to mourn the lost child in any way, but then, considering that she had once attacked the lad and he had dumped her in a beaver pond, that was understandable.

Gar really ought to ferret out answers to some of the many questions enshrouding the Hyæna woman, but Mouse distracted him. Mouse was the woman he had to reach. This Hyæna woman meant nothing.

The woman topped out and disappeared down the far side of the hill. So slick with sweat that Mouse kept sliding around on his back, Gar reached the top not long thereafter.

Were he not so preoccupied, he would have liked to think more about the scene before him. Charring indicated that the fire had more or less died down at about this point on the hillcrest. From here to northward, it had burned the ground cover without destroying the trees. It had scorched their trunks and turned their lower leaves a frizzled brown, but it had not consumed them, a most curious phenomenon.

Beyond the next little drainage, a steep slope offered several excellent overhangs in which they might spend the night. Gar picked his way down the hill to the creek, followed it upstream to some riffles, and paused before crossing. How he hated water.

He laid aside his spear and Mouse's walking stick. "Want a drink?" He repeated it.

Mouse muttered something that sounded like a no.

"Ought to have one." Gar let her slide off his back. She slumped to a sorry pile beside the stream and stared at infinity on the far bank. She made no attempt to sip water or even splash it in her mouth. Should he force the issue? Not yet.

On the other hand, though, perhaps he should. He had no idea what to do, how to reach her. She needed to eat. She needed to drink. He didn't know where to start to make her or cajole her into doing either. He drank heavily, then rested a few moments. He pulled her to her feet and hitched her back up onto his hips. He almost fell and dumped her as he staggered across the stream.

He crossed the Hyæna woman's tracks twice as he climbed the hill toward those overhangs. At one place along her trackway, he noted fresh digging beneath a bush. She was foraging. He ought to also. But he was not hungry enough to bother, and with Mouse not eating...

The first overhang he approached reeked of death. A lion cub, a young of the year, had wedged itself back under amongst rocks. Its hideaway protected it from scavengers but not from fire. Its decomposing remains suggested to Gar in no uncertain odour that they spend the night elsewhere. The next was obviously a bear den, though it did not seem to have been inhabited since the fire. The third one they came to smelled safe and offered decent protection, but he could not see out across the valley whence they had come. He eventually chose a fourth near the crest of the next hill.

He stepped inside, ducking a bit, and let Mouse down off his back. She curled up on her side in the cool powder dust, her unbound knee against her belly, and closed her eyes.

Again.

They had no fire, but that was probably good. Fire would only alert the Water People to their location. Gar shored up the vulnerable places in this overhang with boulders.

The Hyæna came in by and by as Gar hunkered close to Mouse. She carried the season's first ripe beech-nuts, a handful of grubs, and the singed, stinking carcase of a young-of-the-year horse colt, long dead.

Gar waved a hand. "Eat that downwind, eh."

"You want it? Here." Hyæna's spoken communications tended strongly to falter and pause, as if she were greatly unused to talking to anyone.

Gar shook his head. "Where did you get the nuts?"

"Long ways, over hill. You think they pretty?" That was another thing about her that irritated Gar greatly. She never seemed to know what to say, so she said inane things. Pretty nuts? Of course beechnuts are pretty. She gestured. "You take them, I eat the colt."

He didn't argue. She offered him again a haunch of the colt and he declined with wrinkled nose.

She stacked the nuts and a few of the beheaded grubs in a pile beside his knee. "You act like Kelp and Bison, don't like old meat. Some men think is good, eh. I think is good."

He was gaping. Kelp...? And her...?

Kelp and the Hyæna! He tried to keep his voice sounding disinterested. "Kelp. You mean Seashore People,

Elk Clan, that Kelp."

"Eh." She stiffened.

"You and Kelp, you were friends, eh."

She asked guardedly, "You know him?"

"Medium brown, soft hands, curly pubic hair."

Instantly, she became quite nervous. "I go eat, eh, all that." She stood up as straight as the overhang would let her, gathered up her stinking colt, and hastened off into the dusk.

Kelp and the Hyæna.

Gar poked Mouse. "Good stuff here. Eat, eh."

No response.

He cracked the beechnuts and carefully separated out the meats, hoping that hearing the shells pop would stir some sort of eating response in her. It didn't.

At length he said, "Tomorrow we won't travel. I will go talk to spirits. Try to. Too much of what is in my head I don't understand. You can rest here."

Still no response.

He spent quite a while more trying to entice Mouse to eat a few nuts or at least a couple grubs, but she refused. He left some close beside her in case she changed her mind.

Reeking from her meal, the Hyæna returned eventually and curled up uncomfortably close to Gar. He prayed a quick arrival for the dawn, but it came at the same old time, which was to say later than the previous dawn, for the days were shortening rapidly. That was probably what he detested most about winter, the swift, truncated days.

The Hyæna woman and Kelp!

The next morning very early, he went out to seek answers.

A north wind was dragging in a pearlescent haze, not quite thick enough to be called clouds, to dim the blue sky. It would rain tonight. He followed a stream he had never seen before up into hills he had never trod before. At the top of a small, brushy hill, he found himself standing before a mountain.

This mountain, high in its own right, ended in a craggy outcrop at the very top, a rough rock finger pointing to forever. Gar crossed the saddle and began to climb. It took him halfway through the morning to reach the very top, using his spear as a walking staff.

He leapt up on a shoulder-high boulder. Now, nothing out there appeared to be higher than he. He wove a route across the outcrop to its very nether end. On crisp, cold stone, he sat down with his spear by his leg, his feet dangling over the side. The land dropped away precipitously on three sides. Uncut distance spread before him and beside him and behind him. He sat as close to the sky as a land-bound creature can get, with nothing but the chill breeze pressing against his feet.

He relaxed and let the vastness and beauty of the scene before him seep into him, calm him, stir his heart. After the harried flight, repose. After Hare's tragedy, peace. After this horrendous climb, rest. It occurred to him that he could not help Mouse find peace and repose until he himself possessed it.

The spirits back in that Hairies' cave had told him that the answer to his dilemma lay within him—that he already knew it. How could one know something and not know that he knew? Besides, that was before the death of Hare.

Did Hare's loss change things? If Hare had been Kelp's killer, how would they deliver him to the Seashore People? They had already buried him. Gar probably should have thought of that before interring the lad. On the other hand, the last thing Mouse needed was to travel many miles in the company of her son's decaying corpse. No. Come what may, burying the child was the right thing to do.

He stretched upward, raised his arms high, drew in breath. And he listened to the silence and the faint whisper of the wind. Would they come to him? Ought he summon them? Did spirits still attend him?

They hovered near. Gar could tell. But they made no overture to communicate with him. It seemed that they were watching, waiting for him to act somehow on his own. This new attitude toward spirits, and they toward him, unsettled him. What was the purpose of communing with them if they expected you to tell them what they should be telling you? It was all topsy-turvy. This whole summer was.

He waited.

Heart lost patience. *You promised safety for two of the three of us and Mouse and Hare were supposed to be spared. You promised! Now Hare is gone!*

He felt fury towards the spirits well up inside him. How could he commune with them with this wall of anger? Was a promise worth nothing?

We did not promise.

The words came as clearly to his ears as if they had been spoken aloud. They were here, and they were speaking to him regardless of his anger.

You did!

Did not. We asked your opinion. You gave it, and it was an honourable one. We did not promise we'd follow your opinion, your advice. Our question was a test of your own heart, and you passed the test. We had no intention of acting on your request.

Do you always pose tests like that?

Now and then.

How can I trust your word if you pose tests?

Either you trust or you don't. But yes. We guarantee you can trust us.

These revelations required a great deal of thoughtful meditation. Gar would have all the time in the world to ponder them during travels. For now he put them aside.

I trusted you to help us. You did not.

We helped, every step of the way.

Eh, but...

Would you have found your Mouse without the eclipse?

But Hare...

We guided Mouse. When she persisted in going astray, we sent the fire to set her on the right path. Many such instances.

How did the fire begin?

Set by Water People.

You guide and instruct Water People?

Why not? They are people. Do you see them pursuing you?

No, and that puzzles me. They should have caught us by now, we are so slow.

We planted a spirit of fear in them. Easy to do. You are a formidable foe. Your glory and prowess provide powerful threats. We work together well—you and spirits.

Together? Now that was a whole new thing to think about. Gar had never considered actually entering into partnership or relationship with spirits. Perhaps that was the secret Saiga used to such excellent advantage. This was something else to ponder later, at leisure.

You say I know who killed Kelp. But I am not clairvoyant. Can you help me?

You don't need help.

Silence, but for the soft wind.

Head grumbled, *If I'm supposed to know something, we have a real problem, because I don't.*

Mused Heart, *It could be I who knows. I'm just as smart, you realise.*

Head snorted, so to speak. *And it's amazing that you are, considering that you pay no real attention to facts.*

I see beyond them. And then, Heart hit the key. *We must come together on this. In concert.*

Without words or any other discernible communication, the invisible cloud of spiritual presence around Gar registered approval. A most curious phenomenon.

How could Gar sit back and yet let Heart and Head work on this? He tried deliberately to allow them to float untrammelled. He sat forward, legs crossed and elbows on his knees. He thought about nothing; he thought about everything. He let things flit in and out of his awareness. Kohl. Rat. Newt. Mouse and Hare. Eel and Saiga. The Hyæna woman. Even the poor, lost Crow. He let his memory replay every word he had heard in whatever way it wished, knowing full well that his memory was not recalling absolutely every nuance, worried about the prospect of omissions.

The sun coasted west, started its precipitate slide down the pearl blue sky.

And suddenly, when he had about given up and really expected nothing, it came. The memories reassembled themselves into a pointing finger.

He couldn't say for certain, but he was pretty sure

he knew who killed Kelp.

32

She Doesn't Deserve to Live

She was supposed to be out foraging, but that didn't interest *her* now. Why did they not continue on their journey? *Her* Gar had left before dawn, alone, climbing over the hill to northward. And there lay the odious orange woman in her usual position, curled up beneath the overhang.

She knew better than to think that *her* Gar had abandoned them. On the other hand, though, why didn't he tell *her* about the change of plans? If he was going to spend the morning foraging or hunting instead of travelling, he should have said so. *She* thought about the times *she* tried to initiate a nice, pleasant conversation about some trifle—nothing deep—and how he let *her* attempts die aborning. *She* fully expected him to be much friendlier toward *her,* tender and caring, particularly since *she* had saved his life. Instead, he acted consistently annoyed.

Men. Bah!

Oh, but wait. Sometimes a lad was so smitten by some woman that he became tongue-tied in her presence. *She* knew well that in the very instance where you want to speak eloquently, you speak inanely. The person you love thinks you are a dolt and cannot see the true you. Could that be the case here? The notion tickled *her*.

Soon after *she* went out this morning, *she* had happened upon this ledge overlooking most of the curving hillside. From here *she* could see the overhang, the route where Gar had gone, the valley beyond—everything. So here *she* stayed, watching and waiting, as hyænas do so much.

The orange woman got up to go pee, then sat down, her legs straight out and her back against the rear wall of the overhead. She gazed off at the distant hills.

The sun climbed its faceless track toward midday. *She* grew terribly hungry. *She* should go out and find something. On the other hand, those grubs must still be lying there beside the orange woman, somewhat shrivelled now, and the beechnuts from yesterday. *Her* Gar had left them for the orange woman, and the orange woman had not touched them. They really ought to be eaten soon, the grubs especially. *She* could simply eat those *herself* since the orange woman had not and see what Gar brought back. He should be returning any time now.

She picked up *her* spear, climbed down off the ledge, and strolled casually back to the overhang.

She knew *she* needed to be careful. *She* approached the overhang and the orange woman with extreme caution, ready to leap back at any hint of aggression. The woman remained sitting, staring at nothing, and did not so much as look at *her.*

Just as *she* feared, the grubs had collapsed and shrivelled so badly that they were no longer edible. What a waste. They had been such plump morsels, a choice gift to *her* Gar. And he had given them to this ingrate. The fool.

On the other hand, he had shelled all the nuts. Carefully, carefully, *she* reached out toward the little pile of nutmeats. *She* snatched a pinch and pulled *her* hand back.

The orange woman did not react.

Bolder now, *she* grabbed another morsel. No response. *She* moved in closer and ate the rest of the nutmeats.

The orange woman said neither yea nor nay.

She tucked *her* spear close beside, handy, and hunkered down near the woman. "You. You better off dead, eh." *She* waited. Nothing. So *she* elaborated. "Everything you walk past rots. You, you are like the white hand of winter, destroy whatever you touch."

No response, but the woman's face lost its far-away look.

She pressed the point. "You do nobody good. Nobody should be near you."

The woman turned her head slowly and looked at *her.* Her voice sounded flat, lustreless, but menace lurked in it. "Then go, don't be near me. You stink."

"Stink on outside, no big thing. Stink inside, bad. You stink all over, in, out. You don't deserve to be alive. No good."

The orange woman did not take nearly as much umbrage as she ought. What was the matter with her, anyway? Besides being a gutless weakling, of course. Her face gaunt with sadness, she wagged her head. "So much sadness. You just don't know."

"I know! You have a baby, the baby is hideous. Ugly child inside and out! Then you send that ugly thing try to kill me, throw me in beaver pond. You send hyænas to tear me up. You send fire try to burn me up. Burn us all up. Everywhere I go, your hatred pursues me. Kelp and I, we would be beautiful together, but you come, destroy the beauty."

"You never knew Kelp."

She laughed, a hyæna's laugh with much power and no mirth. "Everything about Kelp I know. How big he is, how he grabs your shoulders when he comes, everything. How he thinks too much of himself, goes hunting for trouble."

The woman's eyes opened wider.

She wanted to make certain this orange woman, *her* enemy, knew why *she* was the enemy. "That dark woman—"

"Kohl?"

"Kelp's woman, eh, that one as bad as you! Turn Kelp against *me*. Then you come, you turn him against *me* too."

"You killed him!"

"No, *you* kill him like you kill everyone comes near you. Don't know how *my* Gar manages to stay alive this long."

"*Your* Gar—" The orange woman gaped, fully alert now, wagging her head as if she had suspected none of this.

"Everywhere *my* Gar goes, you spoil his way. Snub his gifts. Look at those grubs, eh! Lure him to his death, eh, like a spider."

The orange woman looked so shocked and confused right now that she'd no doubt do anything anyone suggested.

A hyæna seized any opportunity. *She* seized *hers* now. "Go ahead, kill yourself like you kill everything else. Like you killed your son. Help everybody out by going to Beyond. Give yourself to the hyænas, if they want you. Maybe they don't want you either. Is what you deserve, make up for all the misery you bring, eh!"

"Who are you, crazy woman?"

"*Me* crazy? You make bad things happen to people. You not brave enough kill yourself, *I* help you, eh. Save *my* Gar from you!"

The orange woman stared at *her* and stared at *her*. *She* smiled to *herself*. Certainly this orange woman was thinking about killing herself. That would, of course, be the best solution. Then *her* Gar would not be angry with *her* for disposing of this hideous female, this rival. He seemed to hold the orange woman in some affection; he would be cross with *her* if *she* did the woman in *herself*. But what could he say if the orange woman recognised the folly of fighting any longer and took her own life by her own hand?

She reminded the orange woman, "So easy. Jump off a cliff. Sit out for the lions tonight. Jump in a lake and drown. No big thing. World is better. Then you don't bring misery any more to people you like. Kill your own son."

The woman kept staring at *her*. No, this weak woman had nowhere near enough courage to kill herself. She needed help to complete the deed.

And *she* would help. *She* leaped to *her* feet, swiftly, like a hyæna, and crossed to the far end of the overhang.

Her Gar had stacked boulders there, jamming them in, for protection should Hairies or animals attack. *She* chose one of them, a rock so big it taxed *her* limits to pick it up. In fact, as *she* thought about it, *she* could perhaps make it look like an accident. *She* was simply re-stacking these rocks, wedging them in a little tighter, when this big one got away from *her* and hit the orange woman on the head. What a splendid plan! That was it!

She turned, smiling, and walked quietly toward the orange woman.

The orange woman leaped to her feet, remarkably agile for someone with a bound leg. She did not look frightened, and that was a minor drawback. Hyænas loved to terrify their intended prey; then the victim panicked, did something foolish, and became an easy target instead of a difficult one. It would be so much better if the orange woman were frightened.

She laughed, loud and long. Surely that would strike fear in this woman's heart! Instead, it seemed to strike anger, or revulsion.

The orange woman dipped forward, took a hopping little step and snatched up her spear! The spear whipped through the air a swift half-turn and tucked under the woman's elbow—so quick!

Now *she* could not just heave this rock against the woman's head. Maybe *she* should simply knock the woman down and drag her out onto the hillside. Let *her* sisters the hyænas have her.

She went back to the makeshift defensive wall, dropped this very heavy rock, and chose instead a smaller one. *She* turned back toward the orange woman and found *herself* facing intense, raw fury. *She* lifted *her* boulder high as much in defence as in attack.

"Murderer!" The orange woman stabbed forward with that spear. "Because of you, Gar cannot go home, I cannot go home, I lost my son... You ruined my life, you hyæna bitch!" Tears slathered her face. But she did not run recklessly forward, exposing herself to attack. Rather, she advanced slowly, a step at a time, her whole body tight with power.

With that spear point menacing *her, she* could not hit the orange woman with *her* rock without throwing it. And that woman was going to be close enough in just a moment to spear *her. She* backed up until the rocked-up wall stopped *her. She* dropped *her* rock and ran out onto the hillside.

She could not kill this woman unaided. *She* needed the pack. It was late enough in the day that *she* should be able to draw the local pack up to here. Watching over *her* shoulder lest that madwoman be coming after *her, she* clambered out onto an open hillock.

She stretched *her* neck, tilted *her* chin up, and yodelled, *prey*! *Her* voice ululated off the opposite hill. *She* called again to *her* hyæna sisters. Again.

The longest time passed.

She had about despaired when from somewhere among the overhangs downslope came the deep, husky voice of a queen. The local pack had heard *her! She* shifted the tenor of *her* call but not its volume. *Up here!* Again. Again.

What would the orange woman do when she suddenly found herself surrounded by a pack of eager hyænas? Delicious to think about! With that defensive wall torn down, at least one of the animals would be able to gain entrance to the overhang whilst the woman was fighting off the others.

The place was perfectly suited to a flanking attack, so *she* sent out the call for a spreading manoeuvre. Would the queen accept *her* instruction? Probably. The lead hyæna almost always followed scouts' advice.

But *she herself* was not of their pack. They would as eagerly savage *her* as the orange woman. *She* angled up the hill a short distance to a clump of firs and shinned up the largest of them. The branches were close, the bark harsh and prickly. *She* hated climbing firs, but this was the only safe spot around. *She* wormed *her* way out a limb to where *she* could more or less see the orange woman's overhang, though not the woman herself.

She listened and sniffed and watched. *She* detected no one, but then, if the hyænas were indeed coming up from below, they would be approaching silently, fanning out across the hillside, reading the signs. Soon they would smell the orange woman.

From *her* redoubt *she* called again. Three voices downslope chorused an answer. Here they came! Hah!

And *she* perched safely in a perfect spot from which to watch them tear that orange woman apart.

33

She Wants to Live After All

Gar simply was not created to be a traveller—not if he wanted to go somewhere and return to the place where he had started. How Rat could do it, he would never understand. Gar knew exactly how he had climbed this mountain. And yet, now as he headed back downhill, nothing looked the same. Nothing resembled what he had passed on the upward trek.

He should be able to cross a grassy swale, head up an incline and over the top of a small hill, and descend directly to the overhang where Mouse waited. Nothing of the sort presented itself. Stumbling and picking his route, using his spear occasionally for support, he worked his way down the steep slope. No saddle. No lesser hill.

He stopped. Enough of this wild wandering. When he sat up there next to the sky's elbow, the spirits had attended him. Here on a ragged slope, he called upon them again. He did not really expect the same reassuring intensity of the experience. Any little word from them would suffice. *Lead me back to Mouse.*

Nothing happened.

He thought about that new concept of working together in a relationship with the spiritual realm. Hand in hand. After all, very little of communication was words. He did not know where to go now. He would yield control to the spirits. Let them lead. On impulse, he commenced a downhill traverse approximately to the southwest. He would move and let others guide him with no input on his own part.

It was an exceedingly difficult thing to do, this yielding of control to another, especially to one unseen and unknown.

His new and impromptu route took him around the broad curve of the mountain. He watched for any landmark, any sign, and saw none. He crossed a scree slope he had not noticed on the way up. Although plenty of daylight remained, he thought he heard hyænas. Was this another of those cute little tests in which the spirits seemed to delight?

He stopped and sniffed. The sun did not quite touch the horizon yet; still, hyænas already prowled out and about. Why so early? A pack had moved up this slope, and very recently. Within moments. Perhaps it was just that Hyæna woman. No, more than one worked the hillside just beyond.

Somewhere beyond the curve of the hill, a lead female laughed and two others yodelled a response. They were deploying themselves into a coordinated hunting pattern, closing on something. A cold shiver trilled down his breastbone and he didn't know why. Holding his spear high, he broke into a jog across the hillside to westward.

He came suddenly upon an overhang—the one with the stinking lion cub remains. Instantly, he knew exactly where he was—quite a way downhill of the place where he had left Mouse. And he knew exactly where those hyænas were headed! The prevailing breeze was still moving upslope. How could the hyænas, bedded downslope of Mouse's cave, know where she was before the breeze shifted enough to bring her scent down to them?

How they found her was immaterial. They had! The lead female cackled, very close to Mouse's overhang. Gar lurched into a ponderous run. Would that he were swifter, more nimble! Would that Hare were here to help!

You are afraid, you scurrilous bitch! Riddled with fear! Gar's spirit shrieked at the queen, the lead female. *You do not dare attack! You do not!*

His mind's eye pictured Mouse curled up on her side or slumped flaccid against the rocks, unaware of the approaching danger, unarmed. She had not eaten or drunk lately; she was so weak. In her present state she did not seem to care whether she lived or died. Perhaps she would not bother to fight at all.

Frantic, he upped the pace.

Fall back! His spirit roared at the hyæna's. *Do you hear me? We People are far too dangerous to oppose!*

He was overtaking the pack; he became aware of a yearling male to his right. With a howl, he feinted toward the hyæna; the yearling yipped a warning call as he broke away from the hunt pattern. From uphill to the left, two others relayed the warning.

Still at an uphill run, Gar ducked aside after a sub-adult female he could not see clearly. He screamed at her and waved his spear. She cut out across the hill to westward. Her wild-eyed huntmate also bucketed off across the slope at a lurching, ungainly gallop.

Those three would circle and close in behind him; he knew that; but he would deal with them later. He must reach Mouse before the lead female.

He heard Mouse scream, but it was not a cry of terror. Hers was a howl of defiance, a shrieking dare! She was still alive, and she was fighting!

Just ahead up there! Their overhang!

For some unknown reason, the protective rock wall along the exposed side of the overhang had been partially dismantled. Mouse stood braced, her back bent and her good leg flexed, as far back under the ceiling as she could get. Wielding the Hyæna woman's lightweight spear from its nether end, she seemed to be defending herself quite capably.

Hah and yea! Gar's Heart sang.

Despite that Mouse's flank was partially exposed, the lead female appeared reluctant to move in too close. Gar repeated beyond spoken words, *Fall back! You are no match for us!*

The queen seemed to be waiting for one of her younger, foolhardier minions to dash in and occupy the attention of that menacing spear.

Mouse thrust forward with all her weight behind her spear. She caught the throat of the pack's lead male with its tip and ripped it out. He fell, thrashing, voiceless, spewing blood.

Flee, you ragged, toothless beast! So close was he to this lead female—two man-lengths or less—Gar's spirit virtually vibrated her. *Flee!*

The hyæna laughed raucously, her eyes glittering in that pale sphere of a face. Then she turned tail, ran downslope four man-lengths, and spun back around to challenge Gar. He knew what was happening; she was decoying him. He took one feinting step toward her and wheeled to meet the two hyænas charging in behind him. He speared one deeply enough that with his spear he lifted it off its feet and heaved it against the other. Both beasts, one dead and one alive, tumbled downslope.

He ran up to the overhang. Back to back, he and Mouse could fend off a full pride of lions.

And the hyænas knew it. They made a few half-hearted passes, lunging toward the overhang and pulling up short, then slunk off to the cover of rocks and brush, leaving their two dead behind.

Mouse was sobbing, but the mood Gar assayed in her was fury. By slow degrees, she relaxed a bit. Just a bit. "The lead female, the queen. She was right beside me, and her male was coming at me; I was doomed. But she didn't attack, didn't kill me. And I don't know why."

Inside, Gar permitted himself a happy smile. His protective magic always delighted him when it worked—which was not always. On the outside, he kept his demeanour of stern surveillance. He watched the darkening slope, listened to the silence. "Where is the Hyæna woman?"

"Run off. By and by maybe these ones find her, eh! Good riddance."

Gar was going to say, "You rest. I'll watch," but Head interrupted. *Build up the walls.*

Of course. He put down his spear and stacked boulders to protect both flanks. It took him a while. The moment he picked his spear up again, Mouse flopped down to sitting.

Her hands trembled. Her voice sounded as weak as a newborn wolf cub. "I wanted to die. Then that woman said out loud all the things I was already thinking inside myself. She said it was my fault that so many have suffered and died. She said I'm bad, no good. I should not live. Just what I was saying to my heart inside."

"It's not true!" It burst out of him.

"Then I thought to myself, this woman cannot speak the truth. She's a hyæna. A deceiver. If she said those things, they must be wrong. That means I was wrong and they weren't true. Then she told me to kill myself, and I got angry. How I hate this woman! I would never do what she tells me just because she was the one saying it, I hate her so much. That time then, that was when I knew I want to live. So then she tried to kill me herself."

She struggled to her feet with difficulty, not just because that bound leg posed such a problem but because she was so utterly weak and weary. She wrapped her arms around his waist, laid her head on his shoulder and whispered, "Hare."

"Eh, Hare." With his free arm, he pulled her in tight against him.

"Hairies know a lot about fighting with each other. They do it a lot. One of their biggest rules is: If you know you are going to die, you take the enemy with you. You don't die with your spear still in your hand, unused. Hare, he didn't die with a spear in his hand. He took his killer with him."

"A true hero, that one. Great, great glory."

"You'll tell his story, eh."

"Eh! And it's certain that the Hairies will tell his story too. He's a hero to both his Peoples."

She clung awhile, sniffling, and changed subjects. "What do we do now?"

"It's too dangerous to travel now. We're both too tired and you're too weak. Then there's the hyænas. Tomorrow, we'll go."

"Go where? And maybe that Hyæna woman will follow us."

"I want her to. We need her to be with us."

Mouse loosened and pushed back to stare at him. "No!"

"Eh. We can't make her come, so we hope she follows us. We'll find Eel and Saiga and bring them back to Scarp Country, to my Mammoths."

"Gar..."

"My Mammoth clan needs to know the truth if you and I are ever going to live in peace with them later. So we have to bring the Seashore People and the Scarp Country tribes together somehow. There we will give them the person who killed Kelp."

34

Now He Has to Cooperate with Eel

Mouse had this charming habit of squirming in ecstasy at the conclusion of a successful encounter, and Gar took a certain selfish pride in bringing her to that point. As happened this midday, for instance. Now Gar lay asprawl on the open hillside, as Mouse's sleek softness curled up against him. With her beside him and the noon sun of the waning summer warming him through, he felt splendidly content.

It was taking him longer and longer each morning to work off the chill from the night before. With nights so rapidly stretching out and getting colder, they were going to need furs soon.

A lone hunter, or even two hunters, cannot bring down the large animals, bears, reindeer, and horses, that provide warm winter covers. They needed the clan. Very soon they would need the clan desperately. This business of producing Kelp's murderer must be completed quickly, or Gar and Mouse might freeze to death.

She stirred and murmured, "You didn't notice yet."

"What?"

"No female bleed for a long time now."

He rootched his head around to look at her.

"Not Goro." She tilted her own head back to see him eye to eye. "Even before we went to the Baboon clan, I had no bleed."

"Kelp."

"I don't think so. He joined mostly with Kohl and only used me for the magic." She snuggled in again. "Crow says you never pledged."

"Eh." The most delightful happiness washed across him. "I'll pledge to you, though. Baby or no baby, it won't make any difference. I'll pledge to you anyway."

Her voice sounded tentative, uncertain. "Gar? There's another way, besides a pledge."

"What?"

"Marry."

The feeling of happiness ebbed. "Like Hairies." He felt like spitting but restrained himself.

"Eh. I don't know how to explain uh—" She pondered a moment, then gestured *stick together*.

"So is a pledge, if you do it right." He thought about this a moment. "Marry is no good. If only two people raise the child up, one of them is bound to die soon, before the child is grown. When you pledge, the whole clan raises the child up. The child belongs to the whole clan, and the clan takes responsibility. And that way the child learns everything a Person must know."

"Learns what?"

"Oh, the snake biting the moon. All that. Our ancestors back across the generations."

"Shamans, they keep all the ancestors in memory."

"Eh, but the whole clan knows about them."

She lay silent a bit. "Maybe both, eh. Marry *and* pledge. Then we can both feel right about it."

He smiled. She was so eager to please, but her desire to please, to make him happy, was a thoughtful one. Not just rote behaviour, something one did. She did not sacrifice her own pleasures and happiness to his as some women did, nor did she expect him to cede happiness. She worked to ensure that everyone enjoyed life, so much as she was able.

Her sex was that way too, and he found himself comparing her to Kohl. Always, Kohl carefully honed her technique; it was a cold, calculating attitude, now that he thought about it. Mouse simply let loose with happy enthusiasm. Kohl made certain he knew how fortunate he was to be receiving her favours. Mouse seemed to consider herself fortunate to be his partner.

Ah, Mouse!

He wagged his head. "I don't see the difference between pledge, marry. If you want to marry, we'll do that. Just because the Hairies do it, I suppose, doesn't mean it's bad. They eat and sleep, too."

"A pledge is good until someone better comes along. Then you break that pledge and make your promises to the new one. But marrying is for all time. No other, even if you feel like it."

Was Gar willing to make that kind of all-out commitment? He should have thought about it longer than he did. "We'll marry."

Grinning outrageously, Mouse straightened and rolled away. "We have to go on now, eh."

"Eh. The sun doesn't stay up as long anymore." Gar felt a twinge of guilt, spending daylight hours this way. But at night, one or the other of them had to keep watch. At night one did not relax one's guard. Not just lions, hyænas, and wolves prowled the darkness. There was also the Hyæna woman out there somewhere—if her companions of the night hadn't eaten her. If they had, Gar was going to have to come up with an alternative plan. Lately, he had not experienced that odd feeling of being watched. He had no idea if that little datum meant anything at all.

He sat up and scanned the gentle hillside. "How close are we to the Seashore People?"

"Tomorrow we'll enter their territory, I think. I don't know where they are in it, though. I didn't stay with them very long, so I don't know their seasons."

"Do they wait for the reindeer?"

She thought about it a moment. "I don't remember many reindeer hides or antlers. They use elk antlers. And horse hides."

"Horses and elk like open country. Where is the open country in their territory?"

"Ah." She nodded. "I know where to look first." She flipped around onto one knee, her bound leg cocked aside, and studied Gar face to face. "Are you sure we must do it this way? I'm afraid to go there. I don't trust Eel. And what if Saiga hears the wrong spirits? You go and I'll hide until you return."

"It's a big chance we have to take, but I don't know any other way." He scooped up his spear and climbed to his feet. "You have to stay with me. You defend yourself well, but you can't climb trees. We have to watch all night, and that takes two people. Especially with that Hyæna woman. One person alone can't run well, especially with a bound leg. It's too dangerous to leave you behind." He laid a hand flat on her shoulder. "It will come right."

"Eh. Still. I fear." Mouse lurched to standing and doddered off, using her spear as a walking staff. Gar fell in behind.

They spent that night in a shallow overhang shrouded by berry bushes—bushes with a goodly number of berries still clinging to them. It was a welcome change from their normal diet of grasshoppers, grass seed, roots, and bog leaves.

The first quarter moon peered in upon them as it rose. Mouse spent their brief moonlight time drawing lines in the powdery dirt of the floor, showing Gar the lay of the land. He took first watch as she slept then, and second as well, for he could not sleep.

She was right. Eel would probably try to snatch her, and Gar didn't know how to stop him.

But what occupied him most was the baby. She had a baby in her. His baby. He could not cease thinking about it. Heart sang as Head smugly considered the ramifications.

Wait! The baby. Of course. There was the answer! With a smile, he jabbed Mouse awake for a stint on watch and drifted off to sleep.

Light arrived late next morning, for a heavy overcast had settled in during the predawn hours, masking the sun. By noon, when they saw in the distance the curl of smoke marking the Seashore People's main group, soft, misting rain was making travel chilly.

An hour before dark, they arrived at the Elk clan's cave, a great, open cavern six man-lengths high at the mouth and sloping nearly ten man-lengths to its back.

Though considerably larger, it looked a lot like Larch Cave, Gar's favourite in his own territory. Over a dozen people moved about in it, and some of the children already wore winter furs.

A partnership with spirits. Gar felt a little nervous about relating to spirits in a new and different way when he needed them now so desperately. How tempting it was to fall back into the old methods. He draped his arm protectively across Mouse's shoulders and led her into the midst of the people who would condemn her for murder.

Saiga was not here. Eel was. Obviously, lookouts had sent word ahead, for a half-dozen men stood about watching, as if waiting for the newcomers. None made an overtly hostile move.

Smiling, Eel approached to within an arm's length. He performed no obeisance due a shaman older than he. "Saiga said you would bring her." He reached out to seize Mouse's arm.

Gar stepped between them and deflected that huge haunch-sized hand.

I suppose you think you're going to throw this giant out of the cave, Head pouted.

Mouse quailed, pressing against Gar. "I told you you can't trust this one."

Gar smiled also. "She is mine. She stays with me."

The hulking warlord's smile melted into a scowl. "This business about Rat trading a Real Person is wrong. She's not yours just because you got her from Rat."

"She carries a baby. Not Kelp's. Mine. Not Seashore People. Scarp Country. Not Elks. Mammoths. She cannot find her Horse clan or even her tribe. Her clan can't take the baby, so I have the right to bring it into my clan.

I claim that right. The baby stays with me, so she must stay with me until it comes. Then if you want her, you may have her. But not the baby. It is Mammoth."

Eel opened and closed his mouth a couple times, rather like a fish considering the seine which just dragged it out onto shore. But no one dared oppose the inalterable laws of life and clanship. Gar's clan claim held precedence even over vengeance, at least until three elders declared otherwise. Eel knew that.

Good time to let me take over. And Heart did so.

Gar found himself saying, "Eel, Real People need each other. You and Saiga need the person who killed Kelp. It has to be the exact one. You asked me to help and I will. Saiga and I can find what you need."

"Saiga says he doesn't know."

"I think I do. Send for Saiga, bring him here."

"He's already sent for."

Head purred, *Figured as much.*

And then Eel added a comment that struck Gar dumb. "We need Saiga to pull Mouse's spirit out of her and give it to someone else."

35

They Are All One Together

This cave looked something like Gar's favourite back home, but it was not nearly so comfortable. With its ceiling yawning so high up there, it let too much hard wind whistle through. In fact, Gar had spent most of last night ruing the chill north wind that swept through so relentlessly.

Now he sat with his back propped against a smooth, cold boulder at the rear of this cave. He twisted his right leg around until he could catch his right heel in the crook of his flexed left arm. It was the only way he could bend enough to see the bottom of his foot.

Sniggering, Eel flopped to sitting beside him and made some sort of remark about how ludicrous he looked in that position. Gar did not bother to dignify it with a reply.

He had stepped on something sharp yesterday, and

he had no idea what. Whatever it was had carved a triangular gouge in his instep. Now the gouge had turned red around the edges. Gar's skin colour was so light, these marks seemed to show up more on him than on other People. He wondered about the fair-skinned Water People. While in their midst, he had seen far fewer marks and scars than he expected. Either such things showed much less frequently than one would predict, or those people injured themselves far less often.

At his other side, Mouse twisted around to hands and one knee, her bound leg cocked aside, to see also. "Stand in the creek awhile, eh."

"It's not that bad." Gar did not want to leave the safety of this particular little nook he and Mouse had settled in. He had spent last night with Mouse tucked down behind him, her back against the rock wall, her front shielded by his body. He had come too far and accomplished too much to see the woman he loved summarily speared by some avenging relative of Kelp.

Eel muttered something and wandered off.

Gar flagged down three children bearing bags of mussels. He usurped two of the three bags, roasted them himself, and shared them with Mouse.

All about them, Elk women were spitting aged horse quarters and putting them on to roast, gathering more skin bags full of mussels, bringing in nuts, beating grass heads, shaving roots.

Look at these women scurry! crowed Head. *Obviously, not just Saiga but the whole other moiety is coming. You'll have a full audience tonight. All the Elk clan.*

Heart added, *And all paying attention. What boors those restless, chattering Hairies were!*

Gar couldn't agree more.

What did Eel mean when he said they were going to strip Mouse's spirit out of her? Surely they couldn't do that. But Saiga possessed awesome powers. What if they could?

Saiga and the other moiety, a score of People, descended upon the vast cave some time after midday. Gar yearned to pull the sage aside and ask about this business of robbing a Person of her spirit, but formalities prevailed. Women presenting their backs, the young men doing obeisance and the older men exchanging gifts, the thank-you dances and the flirting, all proceeded as they had since People began remembering.

For the feast itself, Gar accepted a seat of honour to Saiga's left. Eel did not yield to Saiga's age, as Newt was wont to do with Cloud, and give the shaman the centre seat.

Makes you appreciate Newt more, doesn't it, Heart sniggered.

Gar made certain Mouse sat beside him, a mild little breach of etiquette, but necessary if he was to protect her adequately. The feast unfolded without incident. These Elks expressed the same open cheerfulness that Mammoths enjoyed. The dour air of suspicion among the Dark Mountain People, not to mention the dearth of true feasting, flitted past Gar's memory, and he pitied them.

That night, as the quarter moon sailed high and hyænas called somewhere in the milky-grey distance, Gar danced the incredible story of their exploits amongst the Hairies. He told about all those innermost thoughts and dreams spread out across a cavern for the world to see, and the Elks wagged their heads in pity and disbelief. Gar heavily emphasised Hare's role in their escape and accorded the child the status of an elevated hero. His tale elicited more than one *hoo.* A couple of times, he glanced surreptitiously toward Mouse. The tears in her eyes and on her cheeks caught little twinkles of orange firelight. It reminded him again how much she had lost.

Even though one customarily declared one's pledges only to one's own clan, Gar declared his pledge to Mouse here, since he had the floor anyway. He identified the pledge as the Hairy concept of marry, a union forever. She had been an Elk, at least for a brief while, and he wanted them to know.

Next a woman brought her boy-baby forward and named the father. The scrawny child hung listless on her arm. Her milk sustained him now, but he would surely die as soon as winter bit down hard. Saiga recited his ancestry back ten generations. The Elephants crossed Gar's mind, a people without a shaman and without their past. How sad.

He found himself expecting his own baby—a boy, of course—to be born robust and to thrive. But what if it were sickly, like this child? He put those thoughts aside.

Eventually, formalities and festivities trickled to a close. With Mouse still hard at his elbow, Gar settled down cross-legged beside Saiga and Eel.

Eel stared right at Mouse although he addressed Gar. "You didn't dance anything about Kelp. I was thinking that today you brought us his killer, and you'd tell us about it."

"Maybe the wrong person is watching."

Eel's eyes narrowed. "You say the killer is here, in the Elk People? Or do you mean her? This Mouse."

Gar shrugged. "Others are watching also, maybe. Where is the pallid Hyæna woman? Have you heard from any foragers that maybe she is around here?"

Eel frowned, a perplexed *huh?* expression.

"No one has seen her lately." Saiga was following Gar, even if Eel was not. "I feel your spirit. It's very excited and very cautious. If your spirits told you the truth in this matter, why the caution?"

"They didn't tell me. They're sitting back to watch my head and heart work it out. Maybe I'm right. But I don't know. I have to be careful."

Saiga nodded. Then, "Why are you here?"

That should have been Eel's first question. Newt may not be brilliant, but he outshines Eel like sun over moon. Head sounded contemptuous.

"To ask a boon. I need you, Eel, and two other Elks to come with me and Mouse to Scarp Country. I need Rat too. Then we'll gather with the Mammoths, find the killer, and you can have that one."

"No." Eel shook his giant head. "Already we have the killer. Your Mouse here. If she goes with you, maybe by and by she'll escape again. Maybe even you'll let her. You can go, but she stays here."

"We need—"

"She stays here."

"I'm getting old, Eel. This is my first baby. It goes with me and it's inside her. That's the end of it. How do we—"

"See, Saiga! It's as I said. She has a baby. That proves it." Eel roared, triumphant.

Triumphant over what, Gar had no idea. "So? A baby is a thing many women do." He turned to Saiga, hoping to change the subject. "Eel said something about pulling the spirit out of a Person, and giving it to someone else. How can that be?"

For a moment, Saiga studied the fire before them. "No, not many women do that any more—have babies, I mean. I know every Person born into our Elk clan. You know every Mammoth. So you know as I know, long ago, there used to be more People than now. Lots more."

Gar tried to think of lines that had died out completely. Only two came to mind. "Some more. Not lots more."

"We need more babies. More People. Eel is certain that Mouse killed Kelp. When we found his body, we smelled her."

"But what does that—"

"Fecund." Fortunately, Saiga defined his own word, for Gar had forgotten he had heard it. "Fertile. A woman who has lots of babies easily is fecund. Mouse is fecund enough to make a child with a Hairy, something that does not happen. For years, she took a part in the Hairies' magic. Add it together, that magic and being fecund, and you have very powerful magic. Any tribe needs that power. Eel wants to bring it to us, to Elks."

"Eh, but..." And Gar saw. Every Person gives something to the clan. "You think that is Mouse's gift, to bring babies to the clan."

"Hers and others', through her magic. Eh."

Eel interrupted. "Magic doesn't begin, doesn't end. If it dies in one place, it comes alive in another. Kelp had good power and good magic. Lots of it. The person who kills him, maybe his magic goes to that person. Jumps to that person."

And Gar saw the light. "You are sure that Mouse killed him, and now she has his magic."

And magic is part of a Person's spirit. Strip it out of her, spread it to many women. Head saw too.

So. Gar's head and heart understood together now. No wonder not just any clan member would do for revenge. The Elks had to have the real murderer, for only that Person now carried Kelp's considerable power.

Power and fecundity. As sterility seemed to spread among Real People, so ought fecundity. In a sense, Mouse could be the saviour of whole tribes, should Eel and Saiga's theories be true.

But...

"But what if Mouse didn't kill Kelp? What then?"

"She's still fecund, so maybe she has some power. She knows the paint."

Mouse pressed closer to Gar. "I used to think like you do, that the magic was in that paint. But maybe not. Maybe the paint doesn't hold the magic at all. Gar, when we went there, you and I and Hare, I looked a long time at the ceiling of the cave, and I think maybe it's more than that."

Gar needed to give his Head some time to consider all this and come up with a response, a working plan, so he shifted topics. "We need Rat. How can we find Rat? He doesn't seem to be following his usual routes."

The change of subject seemed to throw Eel off his line of thought. He faltered, frowning. "Rat. Don't like Rat." He spat.

"Everyone spits. He's important this once."

Saiga was watching Gar's face intently. Not just meeting him eye to eye. Watching his whole outside. "Call him."

"I've seen Cloud do that once or twice. I watched the Elephant shaman, named Beaver, do that. But I—"

"How many spirits are there?"

It was Gar's turn to be thrown off the trail. He pondered the question a long while. "Too many. You can't count them. They're everywhere, some following you, probably some staying with a place. Each Real Person has a spirit. I don't know whether Water People each have one. Water People don't have a personal totem. Maybe no spirit either." He studied the sage's face. "You have a reason to ask such a question. I beg you, tell me the reason and also the answer."

Saiga's obsidian eyes crackled. His face virtually glowed with happiness. "The reason: It gives you great strength and power to know about that world."

"And the answer of the question."

Saiga smiled. "Mist. Snow. Ice. Rain. Frost. River. Bog."

Gar sat silent, jolted to the core. He must mull this, but the ramifications would take a lifetime to sort. So amazingly simple, so amazingly profound! He nodded as revelation washed across him, delicious, invigourating, wildly exciting!

Many forms, none identical, but all one. Water.

Many forms, none identical, but all one. Spirit.

They were not many. They were but one. One great one, yet at the same time, many parts. One in many, many in one. He and Saiga tapped into the same spirit. When he sent his protective spirits off with Rat, they remained with him as well, for they were one. The spirits he invoked on that mountain, as he perched out so near the sky, was the spirit that hovered near him this moment. All-knowing, all-powered, all-encompassing, and yet, accessible in whatever form he needed. Of course.

Head and Heart sang together.

Of course!

He watched the fire—flames dancing on the big

limbs, blue light flittering nervously about on the glowing red coals, the little yellow licks that jumped out of the ends of the branches unbidden. Never the same from moment to moment. All fire.

Mouse, ever different, now pregnant, always Mouse. Cautious, defiant, jubilant, grief-stricken, Mouse.

The nut moon was growing now, and the three starvation moons would follow predictably, and yet this autumn was not quite like any others Gar had known. Within the memory of all Real People who came before him, collected in the shaman's lore, the great waters to the south once lapped very near here and People lived where vast mountains of ice now barred movement. Everything, absolutely everything, constantly differed in a pattern of one-ness.

Even Gar differed moment to moment. He learned things. He picked up an occasional new scar—he fingered the scar across his ribs which marked Hare's attempt to spear him.

Hare.

In the Beyond, did things change or remain the same? Now that Gar saw the ubiquitous nature of change and sameness, he could not imagine a Beyond without change.

"Gar!" Mouse poked his thigh. "What now?"

He must ponder these things later. "Saiga, I pose a special challenge. You and I must call Rat not to here but to the Mammoths. To Larch Cave. We must call in the Hyæna woman to there too, eh."

"That Hyæna woman!" Eel scowled. "We can't trust her."

"No. We can't trust her. But we can read her, like you read a pack of hyænas crossing a hillside. You know what they are going to do when maybe they don't know themselves yet. Saiga. Can we do that? Call them to the Mammoths' Larch Cave?"

"We can do that." And the wise old man rubbed his hands with glee.

36

His Spirit Calls to Her

Hard frost this morning. Its grey-white sparkle, such chilly beauty, coated the meadows all around this solitary oak. Aloft in its branches, *she* rearranged *her* legs and stretched *her* shoulders. The oak leaves had sheltered *her* from the night somewhat, but their crisp whispers reminded *her* that *she* must not depend upon them much longer. True, oaks held their leaves longer into winter than did other trees, but they didn't stop the wind.

She felt incredibly stiff and cold. Somehow *she* must either join with a hyæna pack that would accept *her* or enter human habitation for the winter. Where was *her* Gar? If only *she* could find him again, along with that orange woman he called Mouse. Get rid of Mouse—he paid no attention to *her* when that Mouse was near—and *she* would be set for the winter. As a shaman, he need only sit there and call game in, not to mention cast a protective spirit upon the hunter, and *she* would go kill the meat for him. They would both do well and love each other. Perfect!

Again, as in so many times before, *she* imagined *herself* and *her* Gar hunting together, their spears at ready, their hearts melded into unity. *Her* nose was better than his, his eyes and ears better than *hers,* especially in daylight. And of course, there were his shaman's powers. Together, they would be invincible!

She had great difficulty climbing down, for *her* cold hands could not close and grip branches adequately. *She* paused on a lower limb to study the frozen grass below. No large animals had passed near, and certainly no Real People. On the east brow of the hill, a small band of something had disturbed the frost, breaking a ragged brown line across the white. *She* dropped to the ground and crossed the hillside to investigate.

Saiga. Half a dozen of the comical little antelope had passed through here in the very early morning. *She* could still smell them, albeit very faintly, and here were their cloven tracks, the streaks where they had dragged their feet across the rime. If the saiga were migrating this far south already, winter could not be far behind. *She* must act quickly to find a survivable situation.

That was another problem. Sniff as *she* would, *she* could not smell well in cold weather. That greatly hampered *her* hunting ability. Already, nut moon was rising. What would *she* do when the first starvation moon rose? *She* very nearly died last winter. This year wasn't going to be any easier, and it showed every sign of lasting longer.

She took two steps towards following the saiga down the hill southbound and stopped, for a sudden, urgent thought struck *her*. *She* must go north, not south. To *her*

Gar's home territory. Why?

Of course! It was so simple. That Mouse and *her* Gar had been talking about travelling to the Seashore People, but the orange woman had seemed reluctant. *Her* Gar was much too gentle a Person to drag the odious woman somewhere against her will. If not to the Seashores, he would naturally take her home, right? And home to him was that gloriously expansive cave where once *she* had watched him at a feast...the time he picked a man up bodily and threw the fellow across the room.

Could *she* find that cave again? *She* was pretty sure *she* could. It lay to the east beyond a mountain upon which lived a pride of lions and a pack of hyænas. *She* knew the hyænas, if only casually. *She* could find it.

She hoped it would cloud over, warm up, and rain. Warm rain promoted excellent smelling. Once in his vicinity, *she* could follow *her* nose to *her* Gar. Perhaps his spirit would call *her*. Wouldn't that be grand!

She dismissed the saiga to their fate and jogged off toward the north. Probably by full moon *she* could get there, if carnivores did not delay *her* travel.

Another thought slammed into *her* so abruptly *she* nearly stopped. What if the black woman, that Kohl, still lived with *her* Gar's clan? That one would pose an even greater problem than the orange woman because the dark one was greedy. She always wanted the best, the most, the nicest. She always wanted to put down other women, to supplant them.

To be safe, to guarantee that *her* Gar would live only for *her, she* must eliminate that dark woman also.

But then, thoughts of *her* Gar crowded into *her* head, forcing everything else out, and painted their pictures vividly in *her* mind's eye. *She* fancied his attentions lavished upon *her* as he had lavished them upon that undeserving orange woman.

Forget Kelp! What a rough, sadistic boor he had been, and to think *she* had once cared for him. Forget the callow youths *she* from time to time led astray. *She* was about to meet *her* heart's intended, *her* Gar! His spirit called. *She* was on *her* way.

37

Here Is Kelp's Killer

Home!

Home! Heart sang for joy.

I never appreciated how much home means until now. Head didn't appreciate a lot of life, but Gar certainly agreed with this latest observation.

The warm and drizzling rain that had commenced last night failed to dampen his spirits. This thick cloud cover did not darken his happiness. His senses functioned more sharply. The world seemed more intense, more intriguing, more satisfying.

As he crossed the crest of Ibex Mountain into his Mammoths' territory, he could feel his strength grow. Mouse, on his back with her bound leg extended, seemed to get lighter and lighter as he descended a scree slope stiff-legged. He remembered how weary, dispirited, and sluggish he had been when last he traversed Ibex Mountain, having just left the lion he had speared through the throat.

On that occasion, Rat had pointed the way before continuing north, Gar's protective spirits ostensibly shielding the trader from all harm. Were Gar and Saiga's gifts sufficient to bring Rat to Larch Cave now? Saiga seemed to think so.

That shaman rock-hopped downhill at Gar's right side, surprisingly agile for an aged one who did not routinely take part in high-country hunts. At Gar's left, Eel proceeded cautiously, balancing, precarious, spear and arms extended, trying to avoid tumbling down the mountain. There were disadvantages to being very large.

An Elk party ten strong came lumbering down the hillside behind them. When Eel first announced how many Elks would accompany them, Gar had protested aloud that far fewer would suffice. Privately, he welcomed the safety of travelling with so many accomplished hunters. Let the lions and hyænas of Ibex Mountain attack now!

Like water, the bevy of travellers poured down the slope, trickling through the clusters of fir trees and between the ragged little outcrops, dropping down over rocks and boulders.

"Stop!" Gar skidded to a halt. He listened and watched and sniffed. It wasn't eyes, ears, or nose telling him that People were hiding along the stream below. It was spiritual, this message, yet neither clamouring nor coy. Interesting. It seemed as if the spirits regarded Gar in a new way, a more deferential and respectful way, as he regarded them anew. "Stay here."

Behind him, the Elks stumbled and clattered to rest.

Eel braced his spear at ready. "How many? I feel many out there."

Gar shrugged. "Ten, maybe. About. Newt almost

never fields more than that." He sensed both Mammoth moieties. Why were so many afoot? He let Mouse slide to the ground so that he could handle his spear. "You follow me, stay close. The rest of you, wait here."

He worked his way down to an outcrop of creamy rock a dozen man-lengths from where the valley became boggy. He stepped out onto it. Although it placed him on a good vantage point, reeds, brush, and berry tangles made visual contact with the lurking Mammoths impossible. He raised his voice. "Newt! Dor! It's safe."

The white head bobbed, vaguely detectable, up by a willow thicket.

From out in the alders by the creek, a flock of crows lifted and swirled, cawing raucously. They told Gar where most of the Mammoths were moving. In full view of everyone at this end of the valley, he stood out on his rock and relaxed, waiting. He cocked one knee and rested a hand on his hip. He let the point of his spear drop until it touched the ground.

This concept that the spirits were one and worked best with him as a team still seemed foreign to him. But look! Here were the Elks he needed and the Mammoths, all in one place. Unheard of. He and the spirits that were one did indeed seem to work well together.

The drizzle ended, and not a moment too soon. In fact, it would seem that the hide-thick overcast was thinning.

By and by, Dor emerged from a willow clump on the far side of the stream. *Come*, Gar beckoned to the lad's spirit.

Rat is here. The message rang clearly in Gar's mind, yet not in the form of a voice. The trader was approaching from downstream. Again, Gar somehow received this information through no channel he could identify, for Rat had not yet come into view.

Saiga was right! Head crowed. *You brought him.*

Gar twisted to the south. "Rat! Come! We need you here!"

Wide-eyed, Dor looked south, searching, but the lad was much too low on the stream shore to see anything.

Rat stood in the partial shadow of a fir clump, his travel bag laden to bulging and a Hairy lad at his heels carrying a smaller bag. The Hairy lad looked at Gar, looked at the Elks arrayed across the hillside, and looked at Dor. In one smooth, quick movement, he dropped his burden, wheeled, and raced away down the streamshore.

Agile and swift, these Hairies, mused Heart.

Rat yelled to his departing former protégé, shaking a fist. Then, wrapped in a thick, dark cloud of disgust, the trader came slogging along the stream bank, still carrying his own load and dragging the second bag behind him.

Gar permitted himself a smug little smile, for he distinctly felt himself being watched. It was that old feeling, the one that had once made the back of his neck prickle. He welcomed it now. The Hyæna woman. She was here too. Soon he might need her in order to complete this business.

Turning in a slow circle, he signed *friend* three times for maximum emphasis, danced a welcome to all, then sat down cross-legged on this jutting outcrop and laid his spear aside. And waited.

Slightly behind him, Mouse sat down and stretched her bound leg out. "So many People. I'm afraid. Gar..."

Her voice trailed off. She scooted in to press against him.

"Soon it will be over."

Dor crossed the creek. Cautiously, spears at ready, Newt and his men appeared up and down the stream. Kohl, as dark and fat and sleek as ever, followed closely behind Newt. One by one, they crossed the stream and approached Gar. Gar was surprised and delighted to see that one of them was the ancient Cloud. The sage seemed to be getting along well enough despite his crippling.

Good! Great. Head sounded happy. *I always rather wanted Cloud to be able to meet Saiga.*

The Elks moved forward downhill and arrayed themselves behind Gar's outcrop. Saiga and Eel stepped in beside him.

A man-length from the outcrop, Rat dropped his travel bag and sat down on it.

Not bothering to stand up to dance again, Gar greeted him with hand signs. "Why are you here, Rat? You always go south this time of year. Remember how you keep telling us that you don't like to sit in a cave and starve when there is food elsewhere for the traveller?"

"It's going to be a long winter. I hear that there will be lots of food at Larch Cave this year, but not much in the south."

Gar glanced at Saiga, and Saiga smiled knowingly at Gar. Gar nodded.

"Food?" Newt, now close enough to listen in, frowned at Gar. "I never heard about any food."

"There will be by and by, eh. See how many of you are out hunting."

Newt spoke to Gar, but he stared at Mouse. "The reindeer and saiga are coming in from the north already. Early. The women were all saying, 'Go out! Bring us in lots to strip and jerk.'" Newt dipped his head toward the others. "So here we went for reindeer and saiga, maybe a rhino. And look. What do we see? Elk People all over the mountain, coming. So we watch and hide to see what happens by and by and here you are, perched on a rock like a crow on a snag. Why are you here?"

"To settle this matter of ours. Sit. Be comfortable." Gar waved an arm to include everyone in his invitation. He looked from face to face at the sea of perplexed expressions. "I will tell you a story, and you all will understand why we are here."

The Elks waited for the Mammoths to sit down and the Mammoths waited for the Elks to sit down. Eventually, the impasse yielded to some sort of compromise, as Saiga sat down. So did Cloud. The others followed. Kohl sat down beside Newt and drew her knees up close against her belly.

Good! Good! Head crowed.

Why good? Women sit like that during their female bleed, because their bellies feel full, maybe hurt. Then Heart caught on. *Ah! Of course. Further proof.*

Now how to proceed?

Let me lead, Heart asked, and Gar let him.

But I get to help. I know things, Head reminded.

Gar hopped off his rock in front of Rat. Suddenly he grabbed Rat by an arm and a leg and hauled the trader up high over his head. He held the screaming, kicking man aloft. "Rat! No one trusts you to tell the truth. Today, now, you will tell the truth—exactly the truth—or I will rip you apart." Gar looked at the others. "I promise this before everyone here."

A score of heads nodded, acknowledging the vow.

Gar raised his voice. "Rat. Do you understand?"

"Let me down, I beg you." That did not bring the desired release, so Rat tried again. "I understand! I'll tell the truth!"

Gar swung him to the ground, and gratefully, because his arms had been getting tired. Trembling, Rat started to back up, but Eel blocked his way. Distrusting the world, Rat carefully sat down on his travel bag again. He had broken into a sweat.

Gar settled himself back on his perch. "Some years ago, Rat traded a young Real girl of the Cold Lakes tribe—Mouse here—to Hairies in the south, the Baboon people. The Baboon shaman, Goro, took her. Goro used her for sex, but more important to the story, she also helped him prepare the things he needed for his magic and his art."

Gar used the Hairy word, *art,* although he assumed that Newt and the Mammoths did not know it. "She made the paint Goro uses. The colours. She finished growing up there. By and by she had a baby, half Hairy. Hare. But Goro now had a Hairy wife and was getting Hairy sons. He hated Hare; quite probably, he was afraid of him. At any rate, he treated Mouse and Hare badly."

Mouse seemed as rapt as everyone else. She no longer pressed against him. Instead, she moved back far enough to watch his face and hands.

Gar continued. "Early this spring, Mouse took Hare and ran away north, looking for her old Horse clan. She found Rat, or Rat found her. Rat promised her that if she stayed with him, they would find her Horse clan by and by. Instead, he traded her to Kelp in the Elk clan." Gar stared at Rat. "Is that true?"

Rat muttered, "It's true."

"Tell everyone why Kelp would want her."

Rat raised his voice slightly. "Kelp hungered for power—power as warlord and power as shaman. He said maybe—"

"Tell why he sought power." Saiga interrupted.

Rat grunted. "Eh. He saw that Real People don't have many babies. That we lose more People than our babies can replace. The clans shrink. He was afraid for us all, that by and by we might disappear out of the world. I agreed with him. The clans I used to trade with aren't any bigger than they were when my grandfather travelled, but the Hairies keep becoming more and more. Kelp wanted the power to turn that around, to make Real People many again."

Gar gaped at the revelation. It had never occurred to him to ask exactly why Kelp might burn so with ambition.

Rat went on. "Kelp thought maybe he could become strong enough to take on Hairy magic and Real People's spirits all at once. Hairy magic would give him the secret for having many babies because Hairies have lots of babies."

Rat glanced guiltily from face to face. "When I talked to Mouse, I heard about the paint and the magic that she knows. I knew Kelp would give much for a Person who knows such powerful magic." He shrugged. "No Horses are left around close and she needed a clan. Kelp was powerful, the Elks strong. I did her a big favour, placing her in so fine a clan."

Eel and Saiga were nodding.

Rat seemed finished, so Gar picked it up again. "So Rat found Mouse, heard her story, and took her to Kelp. I don't doubt that Kelp traded many, many things to get Mouse." Now at last, Gar could see some of the depths in this story. "You see, Mouse is cun—fun—" He couldn't think of the word.

"Fecund." Saiga helped him out.

"Eh. When Real People and Hairies join, no baby results. And yet, here is Hare, so Mouse must carry much magic for making babies. It was another sign that she was just what Kelp was looking for.

"Now another story that will join to this one: While Mouse was with the Hairies, Kohl here left our Mammoth clan and went seeking a bigger, more powerful tribe to be pledged in. The Seashores are the strongest of Real People. Kohl hungers for power just like Kelp did, but not for the same reasons. She just likes power. She's selfish." Gar glanced at her.

Kohl glowered at him. As always since childhood, she obviously did not like being cast in a less-than-flattering light.

"Kelp pledged to her, and she was happy for a time." Knowing her, Gar added, "Maybe.

"But then, here came Mouse, taking a part of Kohl's place. Mouse ran away once, escaping from the Hairies. Kelp was afraid she might do it again. So he threatened to harm Hare if Mouse did not stay and do whatever he wanted. She taught him about the paint, but not details about the Hairy magic. He could make and use paint; I saw that paint in his fingernails that day I found his body and head. But why did he come here to Mammoth territory?

"Everyone knows spirits live in a place. Each has a territory. Kelp decided that by taking power over more territory, he would have more spirits to deal with—that is, more power in the spirit realm as well. So he came to our Mammoth territory thinking he might somehow take it over as Elk territory. His People, especially Saiga, told him, 'Don't do it,' but he did anyway." Gar asked Saiga, "Is all this true?"

Saiga and Eel were both nodding.

Saiga added, "We did not know about the threats to Kelp's paint-maker here. We knew Mouse ran away and seemed to come this way, toward you Mammoths. That was the biggest reason Kelp came here, to find Mouse and catch her again."

Eh. It figures. It all falls into place. Head seemed satisfied.

Gar sensed the Hyæna woman strongly now. She lurked perhaps halfway upslope or even closer.

Cloud straightened his back and stared uphill, toward the crest of Ibex Mountain. Frowning, he looked at Gar.

Gar nodded. "I know. Let her be."

He looked not at Kohl but at Newt. "On his travel, Kelp took the woman he pledged, Kohl, because she gave him good sex. It's why Newt brings Kohl along with him now."

Newt smirked.

Gar stared right at the white-haired warlord. "Newt, you worried that Kelp might take over your position. Rat, you worried that Kelp might join the two clans together, and then you couldn't trade anymore between us. Maybe, Eel, you followed him to kill him here, so you can be warlord and take all that power for yourself."

"No!" Eel might not be the brightest of leaders, but he was quick on the defence. He looked worried, though, as if afraid he might not be believed. "It was Mouse!"

Gar went on. "You, Saiga, Elks all were sure it was Mouse. You smelled her odour, knew she had been by the body. So she must be the killer."

Saiga smiled. "We smelled you there too. You canted him into the Beyond?"

"Eh."

"We didn't know then that the Mammoth we smelled was a shaman. So I canted him too."

Gar smiled. "Maybe he's there twice, eh. Both parts of him. You told us you wanted the killer. Not just any Mammoth. Only the true killer. Really, what you wanted was Mouse, but you didn't say that. You would threaten us into finding her for you, or helping us find her. You wanted her not because she killed Kelp but because she carried magic. You should have simply said you wanted her back."

Saiga shrugged.

Gar continued. "When I picked up Kelp's dead hand, it was stiff. He had been dead awhile before I found him, to be getting stiff like that. Also, his blood had turned black. That takes a while. So there was Mouse standing over him with tools, but she don't kill him—at least, not just then."

Newt chimed in, "She killed him earlier."

"Then why would she come back there?

"Kohl returned with me to Larch Cave, but Newt was not there. His moiety stays at Alder Cave. He and his moiety came to Larch Cave. We feasted and then he brought Kohl back into the clan. Kohl danced her story, telling how the man who pledged her had died, with his head cut off." Gar shifted his gaze to Kohl. "How did you know that, Kohl? Newt hadn't talked to you yet, so he didn't tell you. I didn't tell you or take you back to the body."

"Mouse told me!"

"No. Mouse wouldn't tell you anything. She hates you and you hate her. Besides, Toad didn't bring Mouse into Larch Cave until after you danced your story. No one had told you anything yet, but you knew. How did you know?"

The only answer she could have made would be, *I found him that way, already dead, probably just before Mouse did.* That simple statement would have weakened or destroyed his case, but she didn't offer it. She apparently didn't think of it in time, for she merely repeated, "It's Mouse!"

So far, so good. Head and Heart as one.

Gar went on. "Later, you told me that Mouse killed Kelp out of jealousy. That is when you gave me that good sex, the kind we used to enjoy, so that I wouldn't think anything bad about you. I'd only remember good. You got me to remember the old days to distract me from thinking about this new day."

"It's not true!" Kohl leaped to her feet.

Newt hopped to his feet too, glaring at Kohl. "You gave him sex after you said you'd pledge to me?"

Gar didn't want this moment to dissolve into a lovers' fight. He pressed on. "Why did you tell me Mouse was jealous? She was trying to escape Kelp by running away. That's not jealousy. A jealous Person wouldn't try so desperately to get away. The only jealous person is you, Kohl. You worried that Kelp might abandon you, like you later enticed Newt to abandon Crow. When Kelp left his territory he left behind his strength, and you saw a good chance. You decided to get rid of him before he abandoned you. Then you would still have his status among the Elks, and maybe do even better among the Mammoths."

"No! You're saying all this to protect Mouse. She did it!" Kohl surged forward in fury, waving an arm and pointing her finger at Mouse.

Gar expected Mouse to cringe and hide behind him. Instead, she snatched up his spear to defend herself. She sprang up and braced beside him, balanced on her good leg. He could feel the fury in her.

Cloud nodded. "But you haven't mentioned the Hyæna woman. Tell about her."

"I don't know how to explain her. You feel her spirit. It's dark. Very troubled. Jealous. Outsider, no clan, no tribe. Maybe she was kicked out of her clan, maybe abandoned. I don't know. She feels a kinship with hyænas, but they are her enemies, just as they are ours. She tried to kill Hare, and she tried to kill Mouse."

"Perhaps she killed Kelp." Saiga scowled. "Kelp knew her. I think he joined her once, twice, but no pledge."

"I think so too. But she couldn't kill Hare, a half-grown lad, and she didn't kill Mouse, a woman weakened by hunger and that leg. Two easy victims. Still, she is very dangerous. But strong enough to kill a powerful man? Maybe not. Also, he would be wary of her, but not of Kohl."

Gar had no idea where to go from here. Rat had corroborated parts of his story, Eel and Saiga other parts. That corroboration had been Rat's sole purpose in being brought here. For to be satisfied, Eel and Saiga had to hear the full story from others' lips as well as Gar's. But now, the only corroboration could come from Kohl herself unless someone else witnessed her deed, and he greatly doubted that.

Then he thought of something else. "Eel, you think Kelp's magic passed to his killer. I don't think so. Here is

Kohl with no baby in all these years, so she obviously has no magic of her own. No baby now." He smiled at Newt. "And Newt gives her every chance, eh."

Newt smirked. "Eh."

Just a tiny twinge of envy tweaked Heart. It passed quickly. Gar nodded toward Kohl. "She's in her female bleed now. If she has the magic to make Real People fecund, she would surely have a baby in her now."

Lunging, Kohl grabbed for the spear in Mouse's hands. She seized the point end and twisted it; Kohl was strong enough to fling Mouse sideways off the rock, but she was not strong enough to wrest the weapon out of her hands.

Kohl broke and ran, shoving past the slow and startled Eel, the seated Rat. Unarmed, she raced away, bounding, up the hillside.

Eel looked at Saiga; Newt looked at Cloud; Cloud and Saiga looked at each other. Then they all stared at Gar.

Two shamans, both greater than he, were looking to him now. Didn't they realise he was not their elder? And yet, he saw much.

He paused a few moments to frame his thoughts. "Saiga showed me a great truth. All the spirits are one. Kelp could not add to his power by adding to himself spirits from other territories. All those are the same one. Saiga knew that and counselled him to stay home. Kelp could not add to his power by adding Mouse to himself. Neither can anyone else. All is one."

Saiga was nodding.

No one said anything, so Gar went on. "Eel and Saiga were very wise to demand the one who killed Kelp and no other. The only reason to kill a killer is to keep that Person from killing again. If a Person is not the killer but is only a—uh,..."

From his voluminous vocabulary, Rat offered, "Innocent. Did not do anything bad."

"Eh! Innocent! If a Person is innocent, it is very wrong to kill him. Or her. You have to know the Person is guilty, or you are nothing but a killer of innocents yourself. Today, just now, I told you why I think Kohl is the killer you look for, but no one knows for sure, because no one saw her do it. I say, let the one spirit who is all spirits see to her now. That spirit knows for sure. We do not. Let the spirits condemn her or save her."

Still seated, Cloud stared at the ground in front of Gar's jagged little outcrop. "I see Kohl. She's up beyond the willows at that seep below Goat Rock. Still running uphill, but getting tired. I don't understand why, but she is in danger from hyænas." He looked at Saiga and used Rat's word. "Can you feel her, feel if she is guilty or innocent?"

Saiga was staring at nothing also, intent on things that cannot be seen. "No. Her spirit is troubled and angry, but it is silent to me. What Gar says satisfies me."

Newt snorted. "Danger from hyænas? No hyænas out this time of day." He glared at Gar. "If you are wrong—"

Cloud sucked in air, then closed his eyes. He looked incredibly sad.

Somewhere far up on the slope of Ibex Mountain, Kohl screamed.

The shock of the sound stabbed at Gar's breastbone, jolted the back of his neck. Kohl. Friend from infancy, his first true love. Kohl. Selfish and wicked, but ever Kohl.

He looked at Newt and his whole body and mind cried out to the warlord, *I'm sorry. I'm so sorry.*

Newt knew now. You could see the grief in his face, the loss. His Kohl was gone, his Crow gone. All gone.

The losses wrenched Gar nearly as much. Kohl. His Kohl.

They heard a second scream.

Quiet. The overcast broke, revealing a patch of blue.

And then, in the distance, a lone hyæna cackled glee-fully.

About the Author

When Sandy Dengler wangled a job as part-time assistant to paleontologists, she fulfilled a lifelong dream. She has turned that recondite sideline into a new field of writing interest. She grew up in Ohio, earned degrees in Ohio and Arizona, and resides in Oklahoma near one of her two daughters (the other lives in the mists of Washington state). Her husband, now retired, worked for thirty-three years in the National Park Service with tours of duty in the areas of the Grand Canyon, Saguaro, Death Valley, Joshua Tree, Acadia, Yosemite, and Mount Rainier.

Would you like additional copies of *Hyænas*?

They are available from your local bookseller, or you may order directly from the publisher using the form at right.

Or go to www.skpub.com/stkitts/ for special prices.

St Kitts Press
PO Box 8173
Wichita KS 67208
1-888-705-4887 (toll-free)
685-3201 (local)
316-685-6650 (fax)
stkitts@skpub.com
www.skpub.com/stkitts/

Order Form

___ copy(ies) *Hyænas*, Sandy Dengler ($24.99, KS residents add 5.9% sales tax)

__ Check enclosed in the amount of $ ______________

__ Charge to credit card # ______________

Expiration date ______________

____
Name

____
Shipping Address

____
City, State, Zip

St Kitts Press
PO Box 8173
Wichita KS 67208
1-888-705-4887 (toll-free)
685-3201 (local)
316-685-6650 (fax)
stkitts@skpub.com
www.skpub.com/stkitts/